BRIAN J. ROBB

STEAMPUNK

An Illustrated History of Fantastical Fiction, Fanciful Film and Other Victorian Visions

FOREWORD BY
JAMES P. BLAYLOCK

Voyageur Press

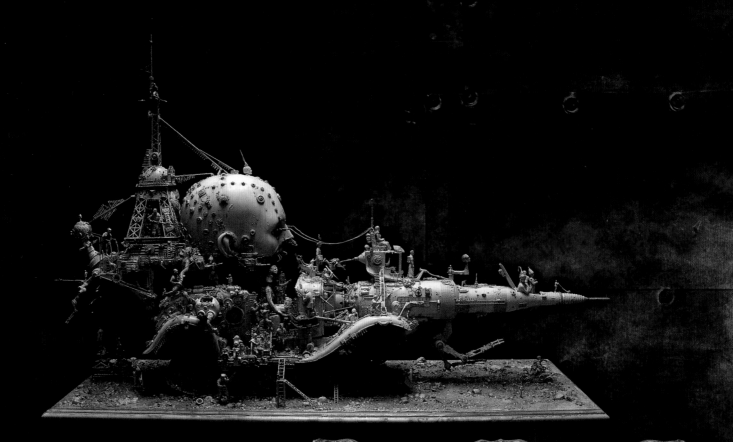

ISBN-13: 978-0-7603-4376-0

Front cover images: © 2010–2012 RichMorgan (top); © Stardog, Lord Cockswain from WetaNZ/Darkhorse
(bottom, right); © April 'Kethaera' Burgess (bottom, left).

Back cover images: courtesy of the Perseus Books Group from Steampunk Poe by Zdenko Basic and Manuel
Sumberac (top); INSECT LAB (Mike Libby), www.insectlabstudio.com (bottom, right).

Commissioning editor: Sam Harrison
Picture research: Melissa Smith
Designed by: Estuary English Ltd
Printed in Thailand

10 9 8 7 6 5 4 3 2 1

CONTENTS

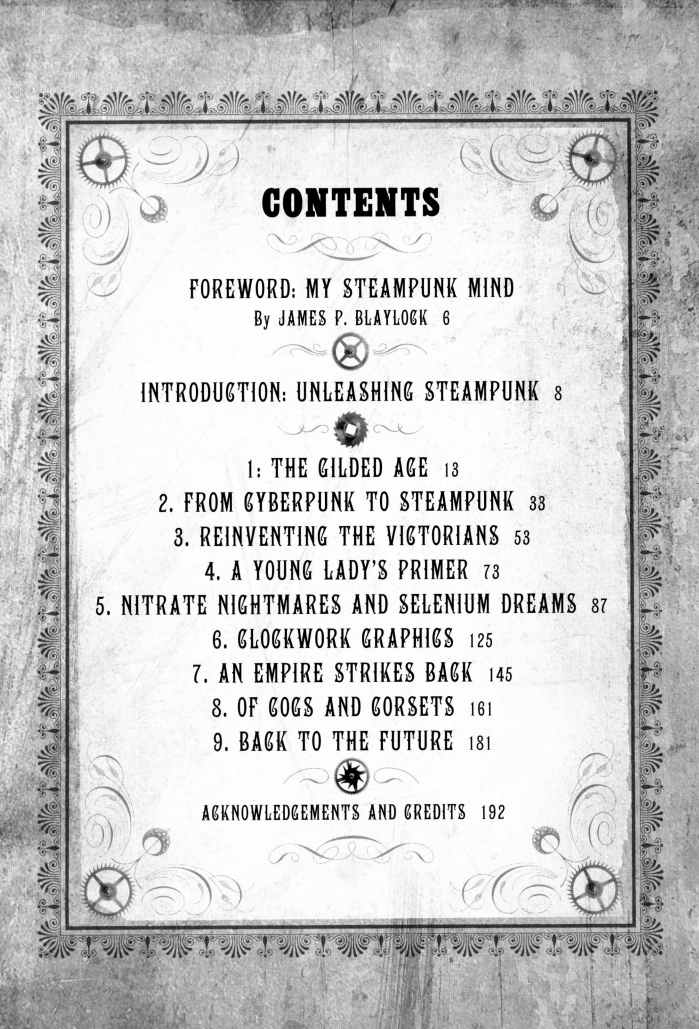

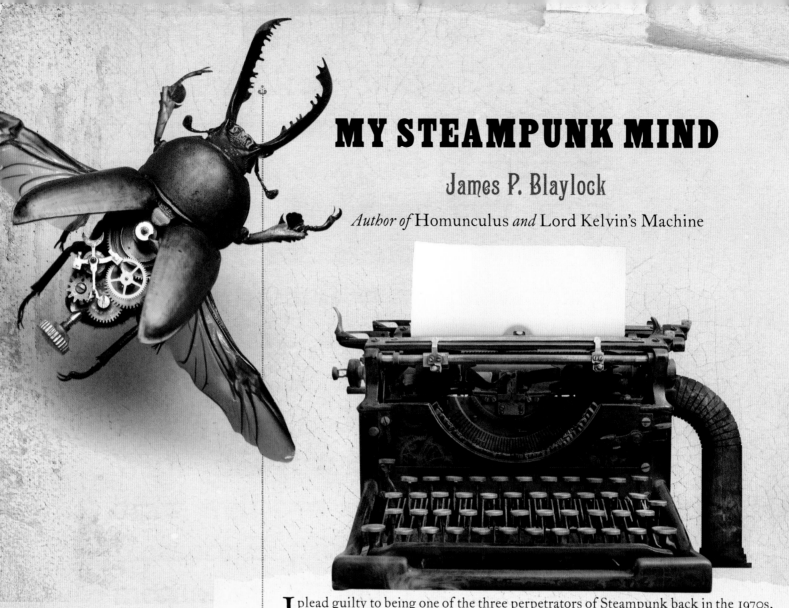

MY STEAMPUNK MIND

James P. Blaylock

Author of Homunculus *and* Lord Kelvin's Machine

I plead guilty to being one of the three perpetrators of Steampunk back in the 1970s, years before the word was coined. At that time Tim Powers, K.W. Jeter and I were all writing our early fantasy and science fiction stories. We'd attended the same university, read the same Victorian novels, essays and poetry, and shared the same fascination with the language and the trappings of the Victorian era. We lived within a couple of miles of each other, which gave us the opportunity to hang around together doing 'research' at O'Hara's Pub in downtown Orange, among other places. It was during one of those long afternoons that K.W. told Tim and I about Henry Mayhew's London books, which I mined when I wrote my novel *Homunculus*. K.W. was a fount of information and Tim and I were happy to borrow it from him.

During one fairly typical conversation the subject of black holes came up, probably in regard to time travel or some other useful science fiction idea. K.W. pointed out (quite rightly) that if Blaylock were to write a story about a black hole the characters would try to plug the hole with a 'Fitzall-sizes' cork. Stunned by the idea, I asked him whether I could have it. 'Knock yourself out,' he said. I started writing the story that very afternoon (one of my very few space alien stories), titled it 'The Hole in Space', and mailed it off to *Starwind* magazine, which bought it for forty dollars and then immediately went broke.

That would have been my second Steampunk story to make it into print, the first being 'The Ape-Box Affair', published by *Unearth* in 1978. K.W. was writing *Morlock Night* at the time and Tim was writing *The Drawing of the Dark*, both of which were published in 1979. I wouldn't publish a Steampunk novel until *Homunculus* came out in 1985. Two years later K.W. would coin the term Steampunk in a letter to *Locus* magazine. That was the first time I had any idea that those stories and novels might add up to something like a subgenre of science fiction – that they were anything more than three friends caught up in literary horsing around.

My own Steampunk tendencies were instilled in me at an early age. One of the first books I borrowed from my mother's library at home was *The Return of Sherlock Holmes*. I was perhaps 10 or 11 at the time and I was instantaneously caught up in the foggy, gothic, gaslight quality of the setting and the language. That was the gateway book, so to speak. My mother saw that I might be a reader, so on Tuesday afternoons we drove down to the local library where she suggested H.G. Wells and Jules Verne to me – *The First Men in the Moon* and *Twenty Thousand Leagues Under the Sea*. I moved on to Edgar Rice Burroughs and pirate and seafaring novels. At that same time I happened upon two astonishing films by the Czech director Karel Zeman: *The Fabulous World of Jules Verne* and *The Fabulous Baron Munchhausen*, which are pure, unadulterated Steampunk. My goose was cooked by then. I had unwittingly developed a Steampunk mind, and the world conspired to promote my habit at every turn.

Steampunk is something that happened to me and that's still happening, apparently. Even today I much prefer the faux science of that age, when an intrepid explorer might build a spaceship in the backyard and blast off to Mars with the idea of fishing in the canals. There were lost cities and prehistoric monsters in the jungles back then, and a person didn't need much more than a Ruhmkorff lamp and a coil of rope to descend into the land at the centre of the Hollow Earth. Occasionally I'm asked whether I'm surprised that Steampunk has 'caught on'. But of course I'm not; it caught on with me fifty years ago and never left.

UNLEASHING STEAMPUNK

What is Steampunk, and why has it now reached a popular critical mass beyond the realms of science fiction and fantasy fandom? How has a literary subgenre become, for some, an all-pervasive way of life? And can this 'retro-futuristic' cultural movement be sustained beyond its breakthrough into the mainstream?

Steampunk is a subgenre of science fiction and fantasy literature, primarily concerned with alternative history, especially an imaginary 'Victorian era' when steam power and mechanical clockwork dominated technology. The initial literary works of Steampunk chronicled a future that never happened, one in which the industrial revolution took a different direction. It featured the technology (and often attitudes) of today filtered through the past, hence the 'punk' appellation. Out of these literary beginnings has grown an entire aesthetic, encompassing film and television, graphic novels and computer games, music and fashion.

However, it all started with the word. Steampunk was given its label by writer K.W. Jeter. He wrote to *Locus* magazine in April 1987, responding to a growing debate about which author had been first to write in the field of pseudo-historical, often Victorian-set science fiction that would become known as Steampunk. Riffing on the definition of the cutting edge 1980s cyberspace-set science fiction dubbed Cyberpunk (coined by writer Bruce Bethke), Jeter gave the new genre a name that stuck. His *Locus* letter read:

> Enclosed is a copy of my 1979 novel *Morlock Night*; I'd appreciate your being so good as to route it to [critic] Faren Miller, as it's a prime piece of evidence in the great debate as to who in 'the Powers/Blaylock/Jeter fantasy triumvirate' was writing in the "gonzo-historical manner" first. Though, of course, I did find her review in the March *Locus* to be quite flattering. Personally, I think Victorian fantasies are going to be the next big thing, as long as we can come up with a fitting collective term for Powers, Blaylock and myself. Something based on the appropriate technology of the era; like 'Steampunks', perhaps ...

Jeter was correct: Victorian fantasies were the next big thing, with his late-1980s works and those of James P. Blaylock and Tim Powers laying the groundwork for a huge explosion of the genre across all media twenty years later. Collectively, these three authors were drawing on classic science fiction from the genre's earliest days – primarily the works of Jules Verne, H.G. Wells, Edgar Rice Burroughs and Arthur Conan Doyle – as well as their own immediate predecessors in the 1970s, such as Michael Moorcock and Harry Harrison, who'd tentatively begun to explore an alternative Victorian era.

There is no one definition of Steampunk that encompasses everything given that label, but most know it when they see it. From the adventures of mad scientists travelling the world in airships, to steam-driven metal robots and pseudo-Victorian (or even Edwardian) settings, Steampunk is often in the eye of the beholder. It can take the reader

to worlds of land leviathans and cannon-shots to the moon, to lost civilizations in a Hollow Earth, and in the wake of intrepid aeronauts. It provides alternative histories in which the British Empire never fell or the atom was never split.

The current mainstream incarnation of Steampunk was anticipated by the work of various science fiction authors in the 1970s, who, instead of looking towards the future, turned their sensibilities to the past. Fuelled by a cultural and social nostalgia for the Victorian age, an ironic or critical approach to its ideals and an insubordinate outlook on the modern world, these authors took their cues from the 'scientific romances' of Wells and Verne. Writers such as Moorcock, Stephen Baxter and Christopher Priest reworked (and in doing so, critiqued) the ideas expressed in those ur-texts. Priest made Wells a character in *The Space Machine* (1976), while Baxter riffed on Wells's creations with *The Time Ships* (1995). However, Moorcock's Oswald Bastable books, which began in 1971 with *The Warlord of the Air*, were not content to simply function as a nostalgic recreation of such Victorian fantasies, but also served as a critique of the Victorian and Edwardian periods' technological optimism, which was to result in the carnage of the Great War of 1914–18. For later Steampunk author Mark Hodder, such political engagement was key to the genre: 'Empire can offer individuals a sense of belonging and "place" by assigning them to a "class". Steampunk explores the manners and mores of such social systems, and the propaganda and attitudes that maintain them. However, it does so with full awareness of the iniquities of Empire, where a vast majority is kept subjugated so that a small minority can enjoy a privileged lifestyle.'

Jeter himself played with Wells's toys in *Morlock Night* (1979), the first of the 'modern' Steampunk novels. His story saw the monstrous Morlocks from Wells's *The Time Machine* travel back in time from their future to the sewers of Victorian London in an attempt to change the past. Powers and Blaylock contributed their own efforts in *The Anubis Gates* (1983) and *Homunculus* (1986) respectively, thereby giving the impression of a minor literary movement. Each author explored his own territory, with successive books moving slightly further away from the

9

Authors define Steampunk

Those writing in the field have a variety of definitions of Steampunk. Stephen Hunt, author of the Jackelian series, has a personal take, while harking back to the founding fathers of Victorian science fiction:

> Personally, for my work it's always been the hard fusion between fantasy and the society of the Victorians. With my six Jackelian novels, I set out to do for Victoriana what Don Lawrence and Mike Butterworth did for ancient Greece/Rome with their Trigan Empire series. This was a conceit made disgustingly easy by the fact that H.G. Wells and Jules Verne gave us the first science fiction and most of the elements of the aesthetic that Steampunk draws upon ... airships, steam-men, clockwork time machines, tripods and ray beams.

Editor Lou Anders has a simpler definition that emphasizes the Victorian setting as a major factor: 'Steampunk is anachronistic science fiction, chiefly but not exclusively concerned with the nineteenth century. There are those who believe that in order to be true Steampunk a work must be set and centered around Victorian England.'

Mark Hodder, creator of the Burton & Swinburne series, isn't too concerned about the setting, but firmly believes revolutionary political content is central:

> The definition of Steampunk is rather a flexible one, due – in part – to the word 'punk' having a more politicized significance in British English than it does in America. As a Brit, I see the genre as a commentary on the advantages and disadvantages of Empire. It is thus extremely pertinent to current politics, where old empires are being challenged and reshaped – the Arab Spring and the economic chaos in Europe ...

> Part of this political approach includes the steam-driven technology central to the genre. 'Steampunk mischievously takes once hidden motives and makes them overt,' noted

core notion of a 'gonzo-historical' recreation of the past. Jeter's *Infernal Devices: A Mad Victorian Fantasy* (1987), Blaylock's *Lord Kelvin's Machine* (1992) and Powers's more sophisticated *On Stranger Tides* (1987) and *The Stress of Her Regard* (1989) together set out a direction for other writers to adopt or rebel against when crafting their own stories.

Much of the debate about what Steampunk actually is relates more to the 'punk' element than the 'steam'. Originally Jeter simply repurposed the word Cyberpunk to define what he, Blaylock and Powers were up to. He wasn't thinking through the implications in coining an essentially throwaway phrase. Cyberpunk was a more political and dystopic genre, preoccupied with the rise (and often misuse) of technology, and foretelling the collapse of society or governments (sometimes in favour of big corporations). The meaning of 'punk' within Steampunk is far more ambiguous. Much Steampunk literature and storytelling is counter-factual, occasionally counter-cultural, and often displays a resistance to the imperialism of the Victorian age. However, there is just as much that celebrates the 'aristocracy' of the time, with some of the 'cosplay' (essentially dressing up) of Steampunk embracing elitist clothing styles, rather than those of the 'workers' who built and operated the steam-driven machines.

Beyond the literature, Steampunk has split into a head-spinning variety of styles and expressions, all connected to its first formulation through degrees of adoption or execution: there is no such thing as 'Steampunk', only each individual interpretation of

Hodder. 'That's why steam technology has become its icon – its workings are obvious and understandable, in contrast to the esoteric nature of current tech, which is all internal and motionless. The contrast perfectly symbolizes the socio-political struggles that we see in the world.'

That doesn't exclude the playfulness that pervades so much of Steampunk's alt-history. 'It involves an often wry, playful, and postmodern appropriation of the signifiers of Empire,' said Hodder.

We have square-jawed heroes (but often flawed), damsels in distress (but often butt-kicking and rebellious), and, of course, the steam-powered machinery of imperialist expansion. Perhaps the best way to sum it up is to say that Steampunk knowingly – and in many cases unknowingly – draws inspiration from the current zeitgeist, wherein the old order, which was based on a privileged few keeping the truth veiled for their own advantage while feeding deceptive propaganda to the masses, is being challenged. It's also damned good fun.

For *The Great Game*'s Lavie Tidhar, the definition itself is no longer that important: 'I have to confess I don't have a definition as such. I know what it used to mean, sort of ...' Steampunk, it seems, is forever in the eye of the beholder.

it. Arguably Steampunk culture is distinct from its literature, some claiming that the movement's fashions and 'retrotronics' (the outfitting of modern appliances with a Steampunk aesthetic) owe more to craft and DIY traditions, thus offering an alternative interpretation of the 'punk' element. This argument unconsciously posits Steampunk culture as second-hand, as the visual media (in film, television, and graphic novels) was itself directly influenced by the original literature. In turn, the expanding subculture has itself inspired a new generation of Steampunk writers who draw on these wider cultural elements that simply didn't exist when Jeter, Blaylock and Powers were pioneers.

There are various competing phrases that come under the wider Steampunk umbrella. Dieselpunk, applied to the interbellum (roughly 1920–39, between the wars) includes petrol-driven technology (rather than steam) and Art Deco design. Gaslamp fantasy emphasizes the genre's roots in Gothic literature. Clockpunk plays up the cogs and gears of clockwork devices, both small- and large-scale. These are all degrees of Steampunk and no one example will ever encompass all the aspects of the whole. It's a Frankenstein genre, stitched together from an innovative mix of reality and fantasy.

The French translate Steampunk as *futur à vapeur*, dispensing with the 'punk' phrase altogether. This focus on 'vapour' offers a different angle on defining Steampunk, disassociated from any overtly political overtones. The notion of Steampunk aesthetics as 'vapour' is apposite; this literary genre, cultural movement or lifestyle subculture can be hard to pin down. As Michael Moorcock notes, Steampunk is a toolbox, with a range of tools adaptable to a range of needs. In many ways, it's also a 'dressing-up box' from which participants (whether writers, film directors, or cosplayers) can take what they need, and in true 'punk' style, adapt it to serve themselves.

11

1

THE GILDED AGE

*From the extraordinary voyages of Jules Verne and H.G. Wells,
through the youthful inventors of the Edisonades, to explorations of a
fantasy Venus and the political Victoriana of Michael Moorcock,
Steampunk has some serious ancestry.*

A Victorian Science Fiction Primer

Modern Steampunk literature is usually science fiction and fantasy set in and around the Victorian era. But in a pleasing circularity, it was that very era that gave rise to 'science fiction' in the first place.

Ancient literature is rife with tales of the fantastic, often used by developing cultures as a way of exploring and explaining the wider world they were beginning to discover. The ancient Sumerian work *The Epic of Gilgamesh* (generally dated to 2000BC), one of the earliest known works of fantastical literature, was discovered by Assyrian-born Victorian British diplomat Hormuzd Rassam in 1853, while Lucian's *True History* (circa AD100) features a fantastical voyage to the moon.

The Victorian era – covering the reign of Britain's Queen Victoria (1837–1901), but often expanded either side – was a period of great exploration and discovery, not

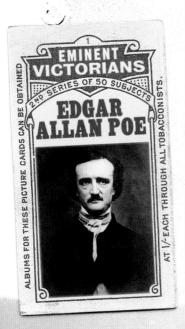

just geographically but technologically. Known as the beginning of the belle époque ('beautiful era') in Europe, the period from the middle of the nineteenth century until the advent of the First World War is popularly regarded as something of a 'golden age' in history. In America, Mark Twain and Charles Dudley Warner dubbed the period after the American Civil War through to the start of the twentieth century as the Gilded Age. Defined by advancements in technology and medicine, this was an optimistic period where the future seemed bright, only for it to be brought to a shocking end by the mechanized carnage of the Western Front.

Modern science fiction can generally be dated to this period, beginning with the early nineteenth-century Gothic of Mary Shelley's *Frankenstein; or, The Modern Prometheus* (1818), through to the speculative novels of Jules Verne, such as *From the Earth to the Moon* (1865). Edgar Allan Poe tackled emergent technology in the Gothic style through works such as *The Balloon-Hoax* (1844), while a series of end-of-the-century novels by H.G. Wells developed many of the basic tropes of modern science fiction, primarily in *The Time Machine* (1895), *The Invisible Man* (1897) and *The War of the Worlds* (1898). Today's Steampunk literature looks back to and re-imagines the work of these writers.

It can be argued that science fiction was the ultimate result of the evolution of Gothic

Edgar Allan Poe (1809-1849)

Poe's work has some pre-echoes of what would become Steampunk. As well as the works of mystery and the macabre that made his name, Poe was also something of a trickster whose mischievous hoaxes pre-figured some of the later fantastic voyages of Jules Verne. His first and most successful came in an 1831 newspaper story in the *New York Sun*. Promoted as the factual journal of a balloonist, the story saw the pilot swept off course only to land in Paris, thereby inadvertently completing the first transatlantic flight. Poe wrote the piece in a dry 'just the facts' style, and followed it up with the story 'Mellonta Tauta' (1849, a Latin title that translates as 'things of the future'), an account of a future period – 2848, to be exact – when ordinary people could spend their leisure time cruising the skies in airships. Several hundred passengers could be carried by each huge airship, although the real thing did not come about for another three years. Poe, however, is the link between the Gothic work of Mary Shelley and the more scientific-based fantasies of Verne and Wells.

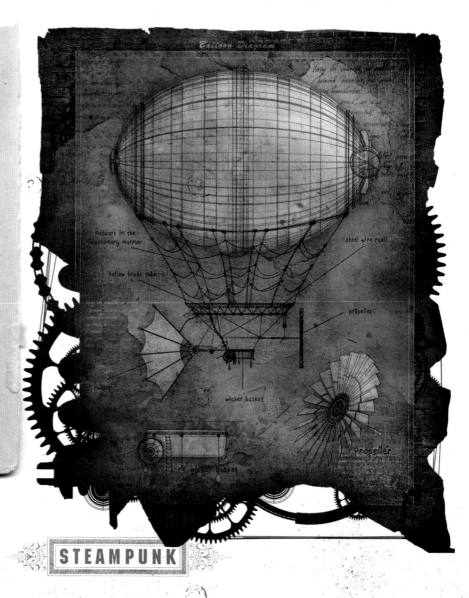

literature through the Industrial Revolution (the period in British history that bridged the eighteenth to the nineteenth century, and was marked by rapid technological development and change). In the face of industrialization that saw the growth of large manufacturing towns and a mass movement of population from the countryside to serve the new industrial machines, Gothic fiction was (to begin with) backward-looking, offering a nostalgia for the pre-industrial age, while also critiquing the new society that gave rise to the sometimes frightening figures of the scientist and the engineer.

Gothic escapism was the shadow twin of the social realist novel, dealing in subjects that were beyond the scope of the dominant form of nineteenth-century literature. From *Frankenstein*, at the century's beginning, to Bram Stoker's *Dracula* (1897), at its end, this shadow literature charted the seemingly unstoppable move from the 'natural world' of the past to the apparent inferno of the machine-made future. These tales were often constructed as quest narratives, with a protagonist in search of enlightenment through the uncovering of a hidden secret, an unknown identity or an obscured relationship. Often these journeys would literally be 'underground' (to the centre of the Earth) or outward-bound to the unknown (in a race to the moon) or even into the future (as in *The Time Machine*). The questing protagonist, through the works of Edgar Allan Poe and Arthur Conan Doyle, would evolve to become the modern detective, or the driven scientist and explorer, out to breach the barriers of knowledge.

The replacement of superstition with science during this period saw the Gothic evolve into the 'scientific romances' of the nineteenth century. It was the theory of evolution itself – as controversially popularized by Charles Darwin in *On The Origin of the Species* (1859) – that drained the theological content from debates about the natural world and shifted thinking towards scientific endeavour, inadvertently giving rise to science fiction. This was a new literature, reflecting the alienation of the new factory workers from both the natural world they'd left behind and the steam-driven machines they built and operated.

Science fiction author and critic Brian Aldiss has made the case for *Frankenstein* marking the beginning of science fiction, arguing that the genre needed the rise of the discipline of science itself before it could be properly formulated. Shelley's tale of a scientist who uses his power of creation, while oblivious to the unforeseen consequences of his hubris, set the template for literary explorations of man's misuse of the new scientific power that would be threaded through the century of science

Left: The gas dirigible *Victoria* from Edgar Allen Poe's 'The Balloon-Hoax', as imagined by Zdenko Basic and Manuel Sumberac in *Steampunk Poe* (2011). Above: Jules Verne's novel *From the Earth to the Moon* describes three lunar explorers being launched into space by cannon-shot.

15

Jules Verne (1828-1905)

French author of fantastic tales, Verne is recognized as a pioneer of science fiction. His trilogy of 'extraordinary voyage' novels – *A Journey to the Centre of the Earth* (1864), *Twenty Thousand Leagues Under the Sea* (1870), and *Around the World in Eighty Days* (1873) – are all regarded as classics. Verne wrote about the technology of transport before anything practical was invented, including air travel, submarines and space travel. Several of his works formed the basis of the first Steampunk movies and he is a constant touchstone in the genre. The Steampunk band Vernian Process take their name from him.

fiction to come. Shelley and Poe paved the way for the more overt 'scientism' of the works of Jules Verne and H.G. Wells that followed.

The work of Verne, born in 1828 in Nantes, France, was centrally concerned with voyages. He was born into an age of exploration, with travel becoming ever easier thanks to the development of the steam locomotive and ocean-going steamships. Rather than looking outward (at least initially), Verne turned inward with 1864's *A Journey to the Centre of the Earth*. The novel's protagonists use the shaft of an extinct Icelandic volcano as their route into the planet, discovering a hollow space at the Earth's core. The concept of a hollow earth was not new, with astronomer Edmond Halley having proposed the idea of the Earth consisting of a series of hollow spheres as long ago as 1692.

Verne used these ideas as the basis for a vibrant adventure narrative, postulating vast subterranean caverns containing primordial oceans and living dinosaurs, those ancient creatures whose bones had only recently been discovered. Verne's underground world was the dungeon of Gothic fiction writ large, but it was his later works that introduced new technologies to his wanderlust. *Twenty Thousand Leagues Under the Sea* (1870) introduced the Nautilus, a magnificent futuristic submarine driven by electricity (then widely regarded as a mysterious, quasi-magical force with unknown potential).

Mistaken for a sea monster by those who do not recognize it, the Nautilus is outfitted in luxurious style including a copious library, works of art, collections of jewellery and valuable oceanic specimens. This fusion of technology with culture (in terms of knowledge and design aesthetic) would go on to become one of the core elements of Steampunk.

Verne developed his remarkable vehicles from then-contemporary scientific principles in order to get his protagonists to interesting and exciting places. Even his 'space ship', the capsule that takes men *From the Earth to the Moon* (1865) is launched from a giant cannon, a propulsion system Verne could understand. It was a realistic solution to a problem, and Verne disdained H.G. Wells's more outlandish version in *The First Men in the Moon* (1901), which required the creation of a gravity-repelling chemical to make the journey feasible.

'I make use of physics. He invents,' said Verne of his rival. 'I go to the moon in a cannon-ball discharged from a cannon. Here there is no invention. He goes to Mars in an airship, which he constructs of a material which does away with the laws of gravitation... Show me this metal. Let him produce it.' So incensed was Verne, apparently, that he got many of the details of Wells's story wrong.

While expressing his desire to explore scientific and technological possibility (rather than the fanciful extrapolations he accused Wells of engaging in), Verne nevertheless could push the boundaries. *The Steam House* (1880) postulates a steam-powered mechanical elephant that allows a group of British colonists to travel across the Raj in wheeled houses pulled by the pneumatic pachyderm. While outlandish in concept, this was simply another vehicle for Verne, a way of moving his adventurers across the landscape so they could encounter new cultures.

Where Verne dealt with exploration by means that seemed almost practical and

H.G. Wells (1866-1946)

The 'Father of Science Fiction', H. G. Wells laid down many of the lasting foundations of the genre, including time travel in *The Time Machine* (1895), alien invasion in *The War of the Worlds* (1898), space travel in *The First Men in the Moon* (1901) and future history in *The Shape of Things to Come* (1933). His short story 'The New Accelerator' (1901) has been widely adapted, notably as the basis of the Star Trek episode 'Wink of an Eye' (1969) and in an episode of the TV series *The Infinite Worlds of H.G. Wells* (2001). The technology of Wells's tales forms the basis of much modern Steampunk, and both Christopher Priest and Stephen Baxter have written sequels to his work.

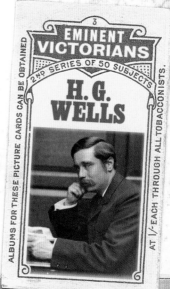

EMINENT VICTORIANS
2ND SERIES OF 50 SUBJECTS
H. G. WELLS

ALBUMS FOR THESE PICTURE CARDS CAN BE OBTAINED AT 1/- EACH THROUGH ALL TOBACCONISTS.

WHAT WILL THE NEXT HUNDRED YEARS BRING TO MANKIND?

H.G. WELLS' "THINGS TO COME"

An ALEXANDER KORDA *production*

with RAYMOND MASSEY · RALPH RICHARDSON
SIR CEDRIC HARDWICKE · PEARL ARGYLE
MARGARETTA SCOTT *and a cast of* 20,000
Directed by WILLIAM CAMERON MENZIES
A London Film · *Released thru* United Artists

17

possible, H.G. Wells was concerned with politics (both national and personal). From his scientific spin on Shelley's *Frankenstein* in *The Island of Dr Moreau* (1896), Wells would move on to more ambitious encounters with the unknown. Wells took the impact of British imperialism (alluded to by Verne in *The Steam House*) as the basis for his novel *The War of the Worlds*: how would things look if Britain were the invaded rather than the invader? His conceit sees Martians arrive in England, unleashing their war machines on the sleepy suburbs of Surrey. His *fin de siècle* terror foreshadowed social and political changes that would eventually see the end of Empire.

Wells has been described by critic Patrick Parrinder as 'the pivotal figure in the evolution of scientific romance into science fiction. His example has done as much to shape SF as any other single literary influence.' The major themes of science fiction's future would be established by Wells (beyond the simple exploration trope of Verne): space travel, time travel, aliens and alien invasion, science gone wrong, biological mutation, dystopia, and the domination of the new city. *The War of the Worlds* brings the unknown to the doorstep of the ordinary, introducing more Victorian (albeit alien) technology in the form of space-traversing cylinders and the Martians' tripod war machines. The alien inhabitants of the deadly devices that stride across the suburban countryside are imperialists dominating the human landscape thanks to their superior technology. There is little – certainly not the steam-driven warship Thunderchild, representing the height of Victorian weapons of mass destruction – that can stand against their onslaught.

Wells used the scientific romance to anticipate the coming twentieth century. Concerned with imperialist excess, racism, class difference (seen in the Morlocks and the Eloi in *The Time Machine*) and warfare, Wells foresaw the fall of Empire and the exhaustion of the new frontiers (geographical and intellectual). While Shelley, Poe, Verne and Wells all contributed to the source literature that would inspire Steampunk, there was one more vital element to come.

Edisonades: Boy Geniuses and Steam-Driven Travel

Taking the works of Verne and Wells one step closer to Steampunk were the Edisonades of the late-Victorian and early-Edwardian age. Coined by critic John Clute, the term covers fantasy tales centring around fictionalized versions of inventor Thomas Alva Edison (or other youthful inventors) and his myriad inventions. Clute defined an Edisonade as 'any story which features a young US male inventor hero who uses his ingenuity to extricate himself from tight spots and who, by so doing, saves himself from foreign oppressors.'

According to Clute's definition, the Edisonade combined Wells's stories of technological invention (time machines, interplanetary war machines) with Verne's inventor heroes and their desire for exploration: 'The Edisonade is not only about saving the country (or planet) through personal spunk and native wit, it is also about lighting out for the Territory. Afterwards, once the hero reaches that virgin strand, he will find yet a further use for his invention: it will serve as a certificate of ownership.'

It was technology pioneer Edison's international fame and pushing of the

Above: Amongst his many other inventions, Thomas Edison created the phonograph, an early means of recording and reproducing sound. The device played from cylinders such as that pictured above.

Thomas Alva Edison (1847-1931)

The American Thomas Edison's life spanned the Victorian and Edwardian periods. He was a prolific inventor who had a hand in developing or popularizing many items of modern technology, including the phonograph, the movie camera and the electric light bulb. He is often erroneously credited as the inventor of cinema, a medium that would do much to popularize the Steampunk aesthetic. He was a pioneer in the field of mass communications and power production and transmission. Based in an extensive research laboratory in Menlo Park, New Jersey, Edison had a team of researchers and innovators who contributed to his over 1,000 patents. Committed to new ideas of mass production and teamwork in research and development, Edison nonetheless became the main model for the 'mad scientist' or lone inventor character that featured in much early science-fiction adventure.

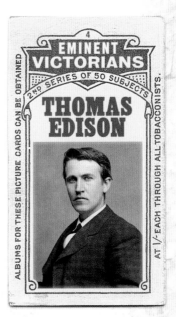

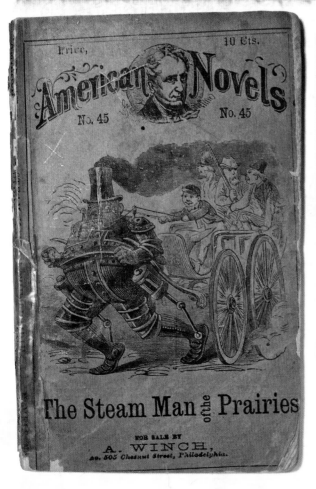

19

technological boundaries that made him (and his ilk) the inspiration for these stories.

The model for such adventures, however, may have been Edward S. Ellis's *The Steam Man of the Prairies, or The Huge Hunter* (1868). A dime novel (cheap serial pulp fiction primarily aimed at young boys), it featured a young inventor (a teenage dwarf named Johnny Brainerd) and combined imminent technology with exploration of the Wild West frontier. The Steam Man of the title was one of the earliest fictional robots (later inspiring the fictional Victorian robot Boilerplate) and was used to pull a carriage containing Brainerd (and his sidekick Baldy Bicknell) westward. Ellis described the invention as:

> ... about ten feet in height, measuring to the top of the 'stove-pipe hat', which was fashioned after the common order of felt coverings, with a broad brim, all painted a shiny black. The face was made of iron, painted a black colour, with a pair of fearful eyes, and a tremendous grinning mouth. A whistle-like contrivance was made to answer for the nose. The steam chest proper and boiler were where the chest in a human being is generally supposed to be, extending also into a large knapsack arrangement over the shoulders and back. A pair of arm-like projections held the shafts, and the broad flat feet were covered with sharp spikes, as though he were the monarch of baseball players. The legs were quite long, and the step was natural, except when running, at which time, the bolt uprightness in the figure differed from a human being.

Ellis's proto-Edisonade gave rise to a host of imitators. The Tom Edison Jr. series (1891–92) by Philip Reade – a house name for authors writing for pulp publisher Street and Smith – introduced the idea of a youthful maverick inventor battling enemies (both personal – his rogue cousin – and of the state, or international), and overcoming them through the use of his marvellous inventions, whether weapons or unusual means of transport. Reade introduced the idea of 'yellow peril' as a racist metaphor for the arrival of Chinese immigrants in the West at the end of the nineteenth century, later giving rise to the great pulp fiction villain Fu Manchu. In Tom Edison Jr.'s *Electric Sea Spider or, The Wizard of the Submarine World* (1892) the antagonist Kiang Ho was a Harvard-educated Chinese or Mongolian – he's interchangeably described as both – pirate. A thread of undigested Oriental exoticism would run through much Victorian (and subsequent Steampunk) fiction as a result.

One identified author of the Philip Reade series was the prolific, and diverse, Henry Livingston Williams (sometimes credited as William Henry Livingston), who wrote Tom Edison Jr.'s *Airship in Australia, or In Search of a Golden Treasure* (1892) which features a Shooting Star airship that is 'flap-winged, propeller driven, ocean liner-like in general appearance'. Another story, Tom Edison Jr.'s *Electric Eagle or, In Search of a Mountain of Gold* (1892), sees Edison becoming a soldier of fortune on yet another new frontier, Africa. These episodic, fast-paced tales featured fantastic flying vehicles, individual flying suits, advanced weaponry and battles in the air and under the sea.

Tom Edison Jr.'s biggest rivals were Frank Reade and his son Frank Reade Jr., featured in another dime novel series (mostly written by Luis Senarens, but created by Harry Enton) which ran between 1892 and 1898. The series kicked off with a familiar-sounding

Electric Bob

The whimsical, tongue-in-cheek Electric Bob satires featured such absurdities as a giant, armed, mechanical ostrich (*Electric Bob's Big Black Ostrich; or, Lost on the Desert*), an enormous, canopy-covered bicycle with storage space for food and equipment (*Electric Bob's Big Bicycle; or, the Nerviest Boy in the World*), and a flying vehicle called the Revenue Hawk (*Electric Bob's Revenue Hawk; or, the Young Inventor Among the Moonshiners*). In an interesting satirical twist, ten-year-old genius Bob's enemies are not Indians or foreigners, but home grown ne'er-do-wells such as Yankee swindlers and West Virginia moonshiners.

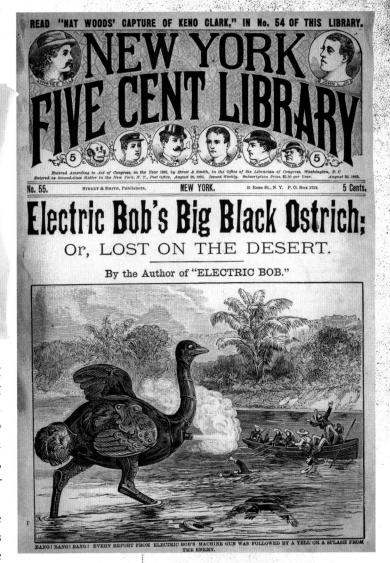

title: *Frank Reade and the Steam Man of the Plains* (emulating Ellis). The Frank Reade series captured a sense of the closing of the American western frontier, while also being packed with incident and plenty of steam-driven transport, from airships to submarines, all inspired by Verne. By 1893, Reade Jr. had followed Edison Jr. to Africa in search of a new frontier in *Frank Reade Jr., Exploring a River of Mystery* (1893), and in *The Island in the Air* (1896) he discovers an exploitable 'lost world'.

While providing plenty of adventure and gadgetry, the Edisonade was a retrograde genre compared to Wells's politically-informed, forward-looking fiction. Indeed, the traditional Edisonade had outlived its usefulness by 1893 when in his address at the Chicago World's Fair, historian Frederick Jackson Turner delivered an essay entitled 'The Significance of the Frontier in American History', declaring an end to the movement west. Moreover, the genre itself was being satirized by the likes of Robert T. Toombs's oddball *Electric Bob* (1893), a series of five witty stories that spoofed the by-now outmoded form. However, the pseudo-Edisonade survived the end of the Old West by striking out in new and ever more inventive directions.

Edison's Conquest of Mars (1898) by Garrett P. Serviss was an unofficial sequel to Wells's *The War of the Worlds* that has 'Edison' striking back against the aggressive Martians. Rounding up the world's 'best' scientists, Edison uses an anti-gravity device to get to Mars, where he then employs a disintegrator ray gun to wipe out the Martians (in the same way that Americans had tackled the Indians in their westward expansion). By the conclusion, Mars has become a colony of Earth, neatly reversing Wells's original intention of critiquing such colonialism. Edison's *Conquest of Mars* also sowed the seeds for the science fiction genre of space opera.

The story broadened the scope for fictional adventures of real-life scientists by including physicist and engineer Lord Kelvin, German physicist Wilhelm Röntgen

21

(discoverer of X-rays), American astronomer E.E. Barnard (who gave his name to Barnard's Star in 1916) and electrical engineer Silvanus P. Thompson (who propagated the fundamentals of calculus). In the story, each of these contributes to the building of Earth's first 'space fleet' and the technology needed to subdue the Martians. Scientists other than Edison were becoming famous worldwide, including Nikola Tesla for his mysterious experiments with generating electricity, and Guglielmo Marconi, who was working on the seemingly equally mysterious concept of radio transmission. Perhaps inevitably, Tesla would appear as a character in a later work, J. Wheldon Cobb's *To Mars With Tesla, or The Hidden Mystery of the World* (1901), aided by Edison's fictional nephew in another encounter with hostile Martians.

Serviss didn't stop at using real-world scientists as characters in *Edison's Conquest of Mars*. He also included several heads of state – inevitably, Queen Victoria, American President William C. McKinley and Kaiser Wilhelm II, depicted as more interested in maintaining their own power than in helping defeat the extra-terrestrial menace, perhaps as a comment on contemporary threats from overseas. The inclusion of such

Nikola Tesla (1856-1943)

A Serbian-born, American-based inventor, Tesla contributed to the development of electricity as a viable power source and developed the theory of electromagnetism. He was as famous in the US as Edison, but he failed to make any progress as a businessman, dying nearly penniless. Among other seemingly 'occult' technologies, he developed a method for wireless transmission of electricity; pioneered an early version of radio-controlled robotics, dubbed Telautomatics; and built giant, and still rather mysterious, 'Tesla coils' at his remote laboratory in Colorado Springs. He also claimed to have developed directed-energy weapons or death rays. And his fictional life has been no less strange. David Bowie played Tesla in Christopher Nolan's film *The Prestige*. The scientist also turns up as a character in Robert Rankin's *The Witches of Chiswick* (2003), Sheh Heri's *The Wonder of the Worlds* (2005), Thomas Pynchon's *Against the Day* (2006) and Scott Westerfeld's *Goliath* (2011). He appears in a variety of comic books and is a major character in the television series *Sanctuary*.

real-life figures would later become a keystone of the Steampunk genre.

By thrusting the Edisonade into space, Serviss inspired a series of similar tales, including *His Wisdom, the Defender* (1900, Simon Newcomb); *A Trip to Mars, or The Spur of Adventure* (1901, J. Wheldon Cobb); and *The Man Who Ended War* (1908, Hollis Godfrey). War – especially the American Civil War of 1861–65 – had been a driver of technology, and so it became a backdrop for further development of Edisonade-style stories into the Edwardian era, prefiguring the Great War that would bring this Gilded Age to an awful end.

The beginning of the 1914-18 war saw writers bring the technology of the earlier Edisonades into the service of defeating European aggressors (just as Frank Reade Jr. defeated the Indians and Edison wiped out the Martians). In *L.P.M.: The End of the Great War* (1915, J.S. Barney), an American inventor called Edestone devises futuristic weaponry that is used to defeat European aggressors and install a 'world government', while *All For His Country* (1915, J.U. Giesy) employs a gravity-defying airplane (invented by a young American, of course) to defeat the Japanese. Another fictional Edison appears in *The Conquest of America: A Romance of Disaster and Victory: USA, 1921 AD* (1916, Cleveland Langston Moffett) as an anti-socialist (just as he was the anti-Wells in *Edison's Conquest of Mars*) using his technology to defeat Germany.

The American individualist Edisonade may have dominated the genre, but Europe produced its own equivalents. *L'Eve Future* (*The Eve of the Future/Tomorrow's Eve*, 1886) by Villiers de L'isle-Adam featured another 'Thomas Alva Edison' as a romantic hero, as well as the builder of an automaton duplicate of a French lord. The Edisonade as a form had, however, finally run its course by the 1920s. Edison's inventions were rapidly becoming commonplace and belief in the mystical properties of electricity and radio was beginning to wear off. Technology was no longer seen as

Left: David Bowie as mysterious Victorian inventor Nikola Tesla in the 2006 Christopher Nolan-directed movie of Christopher Priest's novel *The Prestige*.

magical but merely another tool, one recently used for killing on a mass scale in the Great War.

From the Edisonade's ashes developed what is now recognized as the distinct genre of science fiction. The 'scientific romances' of the late nineteenth century led to the science fiction magazine boom of the early twentieth century, with the genre becoming codified and popularized. Printed on cheap wood-pulp paper (leading to the usually derogative 'pulps' tag), these popular magazines featured fast-paced, Edisonade-style adventure-driven tales and prospered from the mid-1890s (with Frank Munsey's *Argosy Magazine*) through to the mid-1950s, when cheap paperback novels replaced them. Titles such as editor Hugo Gernsback's *Amazing Stories* (from 1926 onwards) and John W. Campbell's *Astounding Science Fiction* (from 1929, later *Analog Magazine*) gave an outlet for the first wave of professional science fiction authors in the 1930s and 1940s. Emerging in this period were writers such as Isaac Asimov, Frederick Pohl, James Blish, E.E. 'Doc' Smith, Robert Heinlein, Arthur C. Clarke and A.E. van Vogt.

The science fiction novel developed in the 1950s and 1960s and brought new, longer-form works to the genre, including epic and influential works by Frank Herbert (*Dune*), Harlan Ellison and Philip K. Dick. With the longer form came a more in-depth exploration of ideas and a better focus on character, along with an improvement in the literary quality of the writing.

The 'heroic engineer' figure of the classic Edisonades and other pulp writing, succeeded by his descendants in contemporary science fiction, follows in a direct evolutionary line from the work of the pioneers, Verne and Wells, and has found a whole new expression in the diverse forms of modern Steampunk.

Top, right: NASA's Mariner 2, the first man-made space probe to visit Venus.

Farewell, Fantastic Venus:
The Death of Victorian Dreams

The Edisonades faded out as the onset of the twentieth century closed the old American frontier and filled in many of the blank spots on the map of the world. It was the Great War (now more commonly referred to as the First World War) that truly marked the demise of the adventurers and explorers of the Victorian and Edwardian ages, confronting them with the prospect of a much darker, forbidding time to come. The word 'steam' had frequently been used to identify escapist stories as parables of the coming machine age. To the Victorian mind, steam power was the future. However, during the Edwardian period oil began to take over, and subsequently, the mid-twentieth century rise of atomic power would define the fiction of a new era.

As the Edisonade mutated into Golden Age science fiction, the new frontier was outer space and other planets. The exoticism of the undiscovered West or the alien and unexplored East could now be transferred 'out there' to an unknown region ripe for challenging a new generation of heroes. Just as the possibilities of genuine 'lost worlds' or underground civilizations on Earth were becoming more remote, the very strangeness of other worlds attracted writers keen to chart the unknowable.

The ever-expanding world of pulp science fiction magazines needed material, quickly and cheaply. A cohort of imaginative authors rose to the challenge, although the speed at which they worked hardly made them great literary stylists. That, however, wasn't the point. Science fiction in the 1920s and 1930s was all about the ideas, and many of those ideas shifted the new frontier off-world, replacing the Indian and Chinese alien with non-humans. Packed with fanciful notions, these voyages to other worlds were escapist in all senses.

The moon, so beloved by Verne and Wells and their heroic travellers, was no longer in vogue (after all, if Poe could send Hans Pfaall to the moon in a hot air balloon, it couldn't be that exotic). Even the 'red planet' Mars of Wells's invaders and the location of the fictional Edison's greatest triumph was old news: it had conquered us and been reconquered in return. The new fascination was for Venus and all the strangeness she could offer. Unlike the rather solid and dull-looking moon and the seemingly dry-as-dust Mars, Venus was a lush world that promised to open herself up to those willing to risk the voyage into fantasy.

Swedish physicist and chemist Svante Arrhenius (he devised the theory of ice ages and pre-figured the greenhouse effect) concluded that the cloud cover on Venus suggested plentiful water, revealing in *The Destinies of Stars* (1918) that, 'A very great part of the surface of Venus is no doubt covered with swamps,' and comparing Venus' humidity to that experienced in the tropical rain forests of the Congo. This opened the door to an entirely imagined planet that writers could populate with all manner of exotic creatures, from unlikely dinosaurs to carnivorous plants, echoing the previous descriptions of the inhabitants of Hollow Earth.

In the 1930s, Liverpool-born Olaf Stapleton's *Last and First Men* (1930) charted the future of humanity across two billion years. Beginning with humanity fleeing a dying Earth and settling on Venus (and following through on the traditional Edisonade occupation of wiping out the local inhabitants), Stapleton's novel has the fifth evolution of mankind make the planet their new home. Continuing to evolve across time, mankind also eventually colonizes Neptune and beyond.

That same decade saw Edgar Rice Burroughs (the creator of Tarzan) instigate a series of 'sword-and-planet'-style science fiction novels set on an imaginary Venus, known by its inhabitants as Amtor. In *Pirates of Venus* (1934), Carson Napier crashes on Venus/ Amtor, discovering a water world consisting of various kingdoms and city-states. Burroughs had ploughed this furrow before, when he disguised Mars as Barsoom in his series of John Carter adventures that started in 1917 and saw two instalments in the 1930s (*A Fighting Man of Mars*, 1931; *Swords of Mars*, 1936). The Venus books featured the same mix of a bold, daring hero, an exotic, alien princess, class warfare, and the overthrow of tyranny.

Between the 1930s heyday of Venusian exoticism and the arrival of space probes at the planet in the 1960s, a host of authors attempted to make their mark on the unspoilt planet. In one of his non-Cthulhu stories, H.P. Lovecraft (with Kenneth Sterling) postulated a Venus inhabited by lizard-like people (*In The Walls of Eryx*, 1939), while Leigh Brackett (later to draft the original screenplay for the *Star Wars* sequel, *The Empire Strikes Back*, 1980) wrote a series of short stories in the 1940s set on an alien-populated, swampy Venus. The days of Venus as a repository of mankind's escapist longings were numbered during the 1940s and 1950s, but that didn't stop Robert Heinlein exploring the planet in his Future History series (1949–62), while C.S. Lewis took a nakedly Christian perspective on this most inscrutable of planets in the second book of his space trilogy, *Perelandra* (1943), establishing this seemingly fecund new world as a second Garden of Eden.

Then, in December 1962, NASA's Mariner 2 space probe arrived at Venus. It found no alien civilizations, no rampant dinosaurs and no intelligent plants. Neither did it happen upon a princess in peril. Instead, it revealed an inhospitably hot world under all that cloud cover, ending any fanciful notions that the planet might harbour life.

Edgar Rice Burroughs (1875-1950)

American author Burroughs is best known for his creation of jungle hero Tarzan, but he was also behind the Martian adventures of John Carter, the Pellucidar series of Hollow Earth stories, and a series of exotic tales of adventure on Venus. Influenced by the Voyages Extraordinaire of Verne and the escapades of the Edisonades, Burroughs's pulp adventures were light-hearted and entertaining. The Carson Napier of Venus series had been initially serialised in *Argosy Magazine* and represented the transplantation of the traditional sword-and-sorcery genre of Conan the Barbarian creator Robert E. Howard to the new 'sword-and-planet' genre, developed by Burroughs.

The Soviet Venera 3 probe went one step further, having a fatal close encounter with the Venusian surface in March 1966 that made it the first man-made object to 'land' on another world. The late 1960s saw more probes (Venera 4, Mariner 5, Venera 5 and 6) further diminish Venus's feminine mystique, unveiling her layer by layer.

With Venus now fully exposed, the planet might have seemed like a dead-end destination for science fiction authors of the 1960s. That proved not to be the case, though, as a series of writers set about updating the ancient Victorian Edisonades as a way of getting around the depressing realities that had now been revealed.

The rehabilitation of Venus would open the doors to a form of science fiction in the 1970s that would look back to the Victorian and Edwardian periods, when the planets were still open to the imposition of human fantasy, before scientific study and hard facts closed them off to such fantastic speculations.

The movement began with the anthology *Farewell Fantastic Venus* (1968), edited by Brian Aldiss and Harry Harrison. The volume collected extracts from works by Stapledon (*Last and First Men*), Burroughs (*Pirates of Venus*), and Lewis (*Perelandra*). These were supplemented by a series of short stories, including two by Poul Anderson (*The Big Rain*, 1954; *Sister Planet*, 1959) and one by Arthur C. Clarke (*Before Eden*, 1961). A group of essays by Aldiss and others explored the role of Venus in science fiction and the new realities that science had laid bare.

Refusing to accept the end of the sense of wonder, writers moved into an alternative reality mode, replacing the 'new Venus' with the traditional model, the planet capable of supporting dinosaur creatures, man-eating plants and entire exotic civilizations. This imaginative retro-fictional response would give rise to the first works that ultimately provided direct inspiration for modern Steampunk.

Roger Zelazny's short story 'Doors of His Face, Lamps of His Mouth' (1965) invoked the traditional Venus of old, relocating Herman Melville's *Moby Dick* to the vast oceans of Venus and featuring monstrous fish-like creatures, in defiance of the scientific reality then apparent. Similarly, his *A Rose for Ecclesiastes* (1963) did the same for Mars, restoring the fantasy of Burroughs's Barsoom in this tale of a human linguist permitted to study Martian documents while falling in love with Braxa, a Martian matriarch.

There was more to this retro-fiction trend than mere imitation. The writers of the 1970s were politicized in much the same way that H.G. Wells had been. While they began to use Victorian or Edwardian settings as ways of escaping the dull scientific realities of modernity, they nonetheless brought the politics of the present to the past. The old theories were about to give birth to whole new punk worlds.

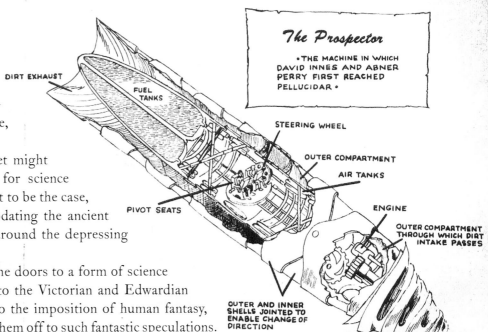

The Prospector

• THE MACHINE IN WHICH DAVID INNES AND ABNER PERRY FIRST REACHED PELLUCIDAR •

DIRT EXHAUST

FUEL TANKS

STEERING WHEEL

OUTER COMPARTMENT

AIR TANKS

PIVOT SEATS

ENGINE

OUTER COMPARTMENT THROUGH WHICH DIRT INTAKE PASSES

OUTER AND INNER SHELLS JOINTED TO ENABLE CHANGE OF DIRECTION

PERELANDRA

"Far superior to other tales of interplanetary adventure"
—Commonweal

AVON 35c T-157

C. S. LEWIS
Complete and Unabridged

27

Steam Goes Punk: Michael Moorcock and Friends

A vibrant early example of proto-Steampunk is Keith Laumer's 1962 *Worlds of the Imperium*. Kidnapped by agents of the Imperium from a parallel world, Brion Bayard finds himself in a reality in which the American Revolution never took place. Inter-world travel is under control of the Imperium world-state, an alternative version of the British Empire. Bayard becomes attached to the aristocrats who run the civilized world from London and is persuaded to replace his alternative-universe double (a dictator from yet another reality). Although not strictly Steampunk as it is now known, Laumer's alternative history does merge Victorian aesthetics with futuristic technology. As the Great War did not erupt and the Royal Houses of Britain, Germany and Sweden pooled their resources instead, this universe never saw an Edison or a Marconi. Rather, it had Maxoni and Cocini, whose marvellous drive apparently allowed inter-world travel, even though it resembled wire wound up Moebius-strip style with an electric current flowing through it. The world of the Imperium is gas-lit Victoriana, complete with polished brass fittings and a sense of Imperial entitlement (as seen in the Edisonades). The historical figures of Hermann Goering and Baron von Richtofen turn up, but they're nice fellas working for the Imperium intelligence service. Choosing to remain in this new world at the first book's conclusion, Bayard featured in two immediate sequels (*The Other Side of Time*, 1965; *Assignment in Nowhere*, 1968) and a belated final volume, *Zone Yellow*, in 1990. Each subsequent book moved

Below: Illustrations from Edgar Rice Burroughs' *Tanar of Pellucidar* (1930), the third in a series of seven novels set in the mysterious interior world.

STEAMPUNK

further away from the retro-Victoriana that would inspire true Steampunk, but Laumer had pointed in the right direction.

If one definition of Steampunk is a re-imagined past (especially Victorian) in which the 'future' has happened sooner, then Ronald W. Clark's *Queen Victoria's Bomb* (1967) surely fits the bill. This tale has the nuclear bomb invented in Victorian times, allowing its use in the Crimean War. But Clark was a biographer who wrote about eminent Victorians Charles Darwin and the Huxleys, as well as a history of the atomic bomb. In *Queen Victoria's Bomb* he cleverly combines both interests in an alternative history that, after a strong narrative start, turns into a moral debate about the use of such weapons. Clark is too reverential towards Victoria and too intent on pastiching the fiction of the era for this to be true Steampunk.

Showing rather less deference, Keith Roberts' *Pavane* (1968) had Queen Elizabeth I assassinated in 1588, thus kicking off a different historical world to the one we know. In his version of 1968 the Roman Catholic Church is supreme, having removed Protestantism entirely. The Pope rules Europe and the 'New World' (America). Feudalism persists and technology has been held back, resulting in a 'present' world in which steam traction engines and mechanical semaphore are still current.

Much more on the mark is Harry Harrison's *A Transatlantic Tunnel, Hurrah!* (1973). It portrays a British Empire in an alternative 1973, which features atomic locomotives, coal-powered flying boats, ornate submarines and cod-Victorian dialogue. Harrison has none of Clark's reserve in portraying Victoria, or Roberts' reverence for religion, but he does explore the implications of a great engineering project – the building of a tunnel between Imperial Britain and the colonies in America (the Revolution having failed to occur once again). Despite putting technology above character (there are airships, space capsules and submarines, as well as the titular tunnel), Harrison's work is just another stepping stone towards true Steampunk.

Laumer's 'multiverse' of the Imperium, Roberts' alternative history, Clark's Victorianism and Harrison's technology would all be taken several steps further towards Steampunk by Michael Moorcock in the mid-1970s. His *A Nomad of the Time Streams* alternative worlds series started in 1971 with *The Warlord of the Air* and continued through two sequels, *The Land Leviathan* (1974) and *The Steel Tsar* (1981).

Centring on British Army Captain Oswald Bastable, *The Warlord of the Air* echoes Laumer in having the central character transported to an alternative world where the Great War was avoided and the British Empire continued to prosper. As happened in history, Britain's colonies nonetheless rise up, only to be subdued by fleets of

Michael Moorcock (b.1939)

Acclaimed author of science fiction and fantasy, Moorcock pioneered the then-unrecognized genre of Steampunk in several 1970s volumes. Influenced by Edgar Rice Burroughs, Moorcock is best known for his 'super cycle' of diverse books concerning the Eternal Champion, a meta-hero incarnated through various figures across time and space. His Nomad of the Time Streams trilogy (1971–81) contains much that is now recognized as Steampunk, with Moorcock following H.G. Wells in dealing with issues of racism, imperialism and socialist politics and the impact of technology in the guise of high adventure fiction.

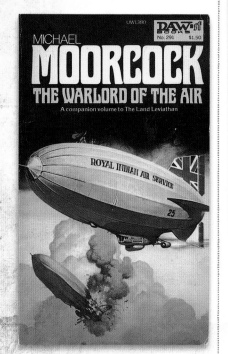

MICHAEL **MOORCOCK**
THE WARLORD OF THE AIR
A companion volume to The Land Leviathan

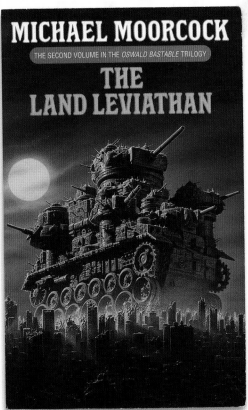

MICHAEL MOORCOCK
THE SECOND VOLUME IN THE *OSWALD BASTABLE* TRILOGY
THE LAND LEVIATHAN

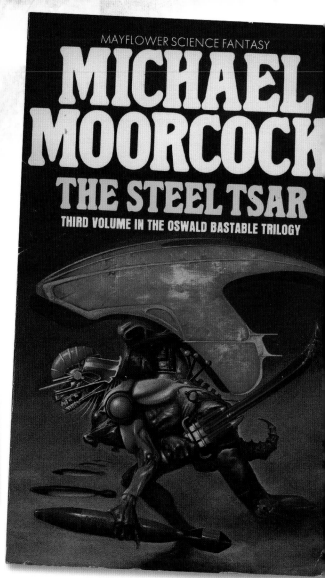

MAYFLOWER SCIENCE FANTASY
MICHAEL MOORCOCK
THE STEEL TSAR
THIRD VOLUME IN THE OSWALD BASTABLE TRILOGY

imperial airships. There is opposition at home, too, with anarchists and socialists plotting to change the future.

Moorcock adopted the Wellsian political approach, rather than that of Verne, the explorer and traveller content with exoticism. Not content with delivering an adventure, Moorcock instead threads his retro-future tale with political comment, criticising the racism celebrated by the original Edisonades, as well as tackling the dark side of imperialism, and even the failings of the anarchists and socialists opposing it. According to Moorcock, this trio of novels was 'intended as an intervention into certain Edwardian views of Empire ... They were intended to show that there was no such thing as a benign empire, and that even if it seemed benign, it wasn't. The stories were as much addressed to an emergent American Empire as to the declining British.'

Moorcock felt he was engaged in a serious enterprise in using the tools of retro-fiction to make salient critical points about the height of British Imperialism. So much of what has followed, argues Moorcock, are simply adventure stories in the style of the old Edisonades that celebrate the very nostalgia he was attacking. 'I'm still not entirely sure what Steampunk is. Most of what I've seen which uses elements I thought pretty much original to me hasn't been used for the same purposes. [It's a] strange feeling seeing my "toolbox" used for purposes other than those I created it for.'

The second book in the series, *The Land Leviathan*, puts Bastable in an alternative 1904 where the Great War appears to have occurred earlier, with the use of futuristic and biological weapons having devastated the West. In its place, Africa has risen to prominence, with the Ashanti Empire dominant. The final volume, *The Steel Tsar*, thrusts Bastable forward to yet another alternative 1941 that sees Britain and Germany allied, thus avoiding the Second World War and the Russian Revolution.

Moorcock essentially crafted a series of anti-Edisonades, highlighting the dangers of technology and the tendency for it to be used by governments in the service of suppression. The Victorian optimism and forward-looking hopefulness is deliberately excluded from these works, replaced instead by Wells-style dire warnings of apocalypse. In Moorcock's retro-future, technology corrupts rather than saves.

The world of the radicalized 1960s and left-wing critiques of old-world attitudes to Empire had come to fantasy fiction. Rather than celebrate the rich and independent (as the explorer-scientists of Verne's work tended to be) or the genius of improbably youthful inventors (as the Edisonades did), Moorcock and his alternative history-writing contemporaries explored the dark side of the not-so-glorious past. Their re-imagined Victorian age is not one of aristocrats and rulers, but instead features anarchists, suffragettes and opposition to taken-for-granted ideas such as slavery, the 'superiority' of white Westerners and unfettered colonialism. This was a world made ready for punk.

Punk has always been used as a derogatory term for a bad attitude, from the teenaged rebels of the 1950s – idealized by the likes of James Dean and Marlon Brando on screen – to the safety-pin-clad rock stars of the mid-1970s in Britain. In the 1960s and 1970s, radicalized science fiction authors adopted these anti-authority attitudes, questioning the 'official' accounts of history and offering alternative viewpoints, especially on the dark side of Empire. These 'punk' writers would not be put in their place and neither would their characters. Theirs was a literature of rebellion that rejected war in particular. Roberts' *Pavane* may have seen the Spanish Armada succeed in its attack on England, but the world he writes about had not experienced the horrors of Passchendaele.

This anti-authoritarian aspect of Steampunk was addressed by critic Jeff Nevins: 'Steampunk, like all good punk, rebels against the system it portrays ... critiquing its treatment of the underclass, its validation of the privileged at the cost of everyone else, its lack of mercy, its cutthroat capitalism ... Steampunk is well aware of the Edisonade boy inventor, and kills him, as villains must be killed, by the end of the story.'

Science fiction had developed into a distinct genre through the 'steam' age, with Verne, Wells and the Edisonades. Now the writers of the late 1960s and 1970s had added 'punk' attitudes to their retro-future fiction, developing a distinctive, politically-driven sub-genre. As the 1970s drew to a close, Steampunk's time had finally come.

2

FROM CYBERPUNK TO STEAMPUNK

How three Californian authors inadvertently invented the Steampunk literary subgenre in the 1980s.

Enter Cyberpunk

While they have many precursors, three specific authors are generally regarded as the founders of the literary movement known as Steampunk. Surprisingly, all three were writing in southern California in the late 1970s and early 1980s rather than in London, where their original Steampunk tales were set.

K.W. Jeter, James P. Blaylock and Tim Powers would all embrace or reject Steampunk to varying degrees, but there is no doubt that their casual collaboration and distinctive work spawned this fertile new subgenre. It was Jeter who gave the movement its name, in an almost casual throwaway comment in a letter to *Locus* magazine in 1987.

Initially, the literary science fiction movement most feted in the 1980s was

Cyberpunk. Coined by Bruce Bethke for the title of his story 'Cyberpunk' (1983), the term became more widely known in association with William Gibson's first novel, *Neuromancer* (1984). Editor of Asimov's *Science Fiction* magazine, Gardner Dozois, used it to group together authors coming to prominence in the early 1980s, including Bruce Sterling, Rudy Rucker, Lewis Shiner and John Shirley. Cyberpunk combined anxieties about the new science of cybernetics with the global domination of (often corrupt) corporations, the growth of information technology (computers were just beginning their invasion of the home in the 1980s) and augmentation of the human body and mind, either through cybernetic additions and replacement, or drugs and biological engineering.

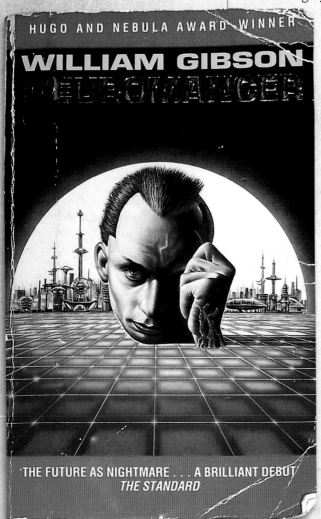

The largely British musical and political movement of the mid to late 1970s, as epitomized by bands like The Sex Pistols, directly influenced the use of 'punk' as a suffix. Although by the time the 1980s arrived, punk had given way to the New Romantics and indie electronica, the word related to an attitude: a streetwise awareness, filtered through youthful alienation and an aggressively anti-establishment mindset. Various largely short-lived literary subgenres would adopt the suffix, with Cyberpunk followed by Splatterpunk (extreme horror) and Biopunk (biologically-based science fiction).

New technology and the growing importance of information and data gave rise to a new wave of science fiction. The acquisition, storage and transmission of digital data became central to Cyberpunk's style. Although the word 'cyberspace' appears to have been coined by Bruce Sterling, it was again Gibson's *Neuromancer* that popularized it. Eventually, it would become attached to the world of virtual reality and the internet, which only became established outside science and academia a whole decade after Gibson's book appeared.

Like Steampunk, Cyberpunk had its precursors: mainly the 1950s work of Alfred Bester, William S. Burroughs and Samuel R. Delaney. Also, as Steampunk would later do, the Cyberpunk ethos branched out from its literary source to become a politically motivated movement with its own design aesthetic. Sterling, in particular, advocated Cyberpunk as a polemical movement tackling the big issues of a rapidly and dramatically changing world, with a cynical eye on the future. By the end of the 1980s, Cyberpunk had reached the mainstream and, arguably as a result, was simply reabsorbed into the mass of general science fiction.

In 1986, writing in Asimov's *Science Fiction* magazine, author Norman Spinrad argued that adherents of the form should be dubbed 'neuromancers' (after the early 1980s pop and fashion movement, the New Romantics, as well as Gibson's novel). He suggested that Cyberpunk was 'a fusion of the romantic impulse with science and technology', an idea that seems now to have more application to the backward-looking Steampunk than to the forward-looking Cyberpunk.

Philip K. Dick (1928-1982)

Dick was a highly productive novelist, from his pulp magazine days in the 1950s through to the appearance of his philosophical novels in the late 1970s. *The Man in the High Castle* (1962) contributed to the alternative history subgenre of science fiction that would eventually feed into Steampunk (one definition of Steampunk might suggest a collision between the science fiction genres of alternative history and Cyberpunk). Tim Powers appeared as the character David in Dick's late novel *Valis* (1981), while Kevin was modelled on K.W. Jeter, who would later write a series of authorized sequels to the movie *Blade Runner* (1982, based on Dick's novel *Do Androids Dream of Electric Sheep?*, 1968).

Jeter jumpstarts a genre

Aspiring author K.W. Jeter got his start on the fringes of proto-Cyberpunk in the late 1970s. Along with his southern Californian writer friends James P. Blaylock and Tim Powers, Jeter was a friend of one of science fiction's Golden Age authors, Philip K. Dick. In the mid-1970s, Dick had an open-door policy to neighbours and friends, but these three aspiring authors became members of a core group that was part of Dick's life until his early death in 1982. He encouraged their ambitions, while their paying homage to him was an ego boost for an author largely underappreciated during his lifetime.

Jeter first met Dick in 1972, when his creative writing teacher showed the young writer's first manuscript to the author. *Dr. Adder* was a proto-Cyberpunk novel in which the United States is divided into competitive areas run by warlords and gang bosses, who are out to control the newly emerging biological and cybernetic technologies. The central character of Adder is an artist-surgeon who modifies clients' sexual organs (anticipating the body modification movement of tattooing and piercing that became mainstream in the 1990s). The controversial novel was not published until 1984, two years after Dick's death, but carried an afterword by the author promoting Jeter.

From the mid-1970s, Jeter was regularly hanging out with Blaylock and Powers. The trio all lived close to one another and near to Dick. Powers noted: 'We would get together and drink Scotch and smoke cigars, and though you'd think that it would have been a lot of writing talk, in fact it was not. Sometimes we'd say, "Oh hell, I got a rejection letter from Ballantine," and Phil Dick would always say, "It's just as well; there's too many books in the world already," which we'd take comfort from!'

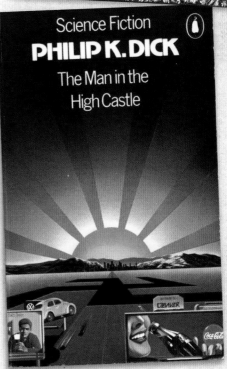

35

Beyond their connection with Dick, the trio regularly met up for beers and would inevitably chat about their writing. 'We used to get together at O'Hara's Pub a lot, over on Orange Circle. And we would have story conferences over many, many pitchers of beer,' Powers said. 'In fact, we concocted a lot of books there. I remember Jeter giving me priceless advice on my first book.'

They would read each others' manuscripts, offering feedback and criticism, helping one another to solve plot problems and work out character kinks and they would toss around ideas for novels. Jeter was the first of the three into print, with *Seeklight* (1975), a pulp science fiction adventure, and *The Dreamfields* (1976), a novel that anticipates computer-generated virtual realities. Powers quickly followed with swashbuckling adventure novels *The Skies Discrowned* (1976, aka *Forsake the Sky*) and *Epitaph in Rust* (1976). Both were writing for Toronto-based pulp publisher Laser Books, a short-lived formulaic imprint that gave new writers an opportunity. Blaylock would join them in the 1980s with a whimsical fantasy series inspired by J.R.R. Tolkien's *The Hobbit* and Kenneth Grahame's *The Wind in the Willows*, starting with *The Elfin Ship* (1982).

All three of the trio had studied English literature at college. 'I read Wells and Verne and Conan Doyle as a kid, and Victorian literature at the university, and as much of [Robert Louis] Stevenson and P.G. Wodehouse as I could get my hands on after I graduated, and the result on my writing is evident,' Blaylock said. 'Because I wrote

Below: *Blade Runner* (1982) brought the Steampunk 'dark city' to the screen in distinctive style. The film was based upon a novel by Philip K. Dick, mentor to Steampunk originators K.W. Jeter, James P. Blaylock and Tim Powers.

the stuff before it became a field or subgenre – before it was anything at all – my connection to it was purely literary. None of us had the idea that we were writing in some subgenre. Cyberpunk had become popular. [*Locus*] asked what Tim and I and K.W. called what we wrote and he said, "Steampunk".'

Jeter felt the trio embodied a 'punk' attitude from the very beginning. 'In the early 1970s there was a vogue for dismissing old "stodgy" works, like those by Robert Louis Stevenson, any of the old school thriller writers' he later recalled. 'I think we were all such contrarians that just to piss people off, we would do a lot of reading of that material ourselves. It was a way of getting under people's skins, saying you were interested in this crazy old stuff. Before we began writing our takes on that material, it was preceded by an interest in the real thing. We had a tremendous respect and enthusiasm for material that at that time nobody was into very much.'

Blaylock read Dickens, old pirate novels, Robert Louis Stevenson's *Treasure Island* and *The Strange Case of Dr Jekyll and Mr Hyde*, and a selection of P.G. Wodehouse. 'I wanted to imagine I was living in 1875 and this is the sort of thing I would write,' he remembered. 'I wanted to play in that era.' He was equally interested in the pulp fiction and dime novels of the past, before scientific discoveries closed off imaginative possibilities, such as the loss of Mars and Venus as imaginary playgrounds. 'I preferred the imaginary science of the late nineteenth century to current science. I loved the trappings of that age. In short, in a literary sense I enjoyed spending time in that world as I understood it. I still do. When Mars had canals, I would have bought real estate there. I know very little about history, and what I do know I stole from Dickens and other writers.'

Powers was on a similar wavelength. 'It came from having a taste for H. Rider Haggard and

MAN HAS MADE HIS MATCH
...NOW IT'S HIS PROBLEM

HARRISON FORD is

BLADE RUNNER

JERRY PERENCHIO and BUD YORKIN PRESENT
A MICHAEL DEELEY-RIDLEY SCOTT PRODUCTION
STARRING HARRISON FORD
IN BLADE RUNNER WITH RUTGER HAUER · SEAN YOUNG
EDWARD JAMES OLMOS SCREENPLAY BY HAMPTON FANCHER AND DAVID PEOPLES
EXECUTIVE PRODUCERS BRIAN KELLY AND HAMPTON FANCHER VISUAL EFFECTS BY DOUGLAS TRUMBULL
ORIGINAL MUSIC COMPOSED BY VANGELIS ASSOCIATE PRODUCER IVOR POWELL PRODUCED BY MICHAEL DEELEY DIRECTED BY RIDLEY SCOTT
ORIGINAL SOUNDTRACK ALBUM AVAILABLE ON POLYDOR RECORDS · PANAVISION ® TECHNICOLOR ® DOLBY STEREO IN SELECTED THEATRES
A LADD COMPANY RELEASE IN ASSOCIATION WITH SIR RUN RUN SHAW
THRU WARNER BROS A WARNER COMMUNICATIONS COMPANY
© 1982 The Ladd Company. All Rights Reserved.

EMINENT VICTORIANS
2ND SERIES OF 50 SUBJECTS
7
HENRY MAYHEW
ALBUMS FOR THESE PICTURE CARDS CAN BE OBTAINED
AT 1/- EACH THROUGH ALL TOBACCONISTS.

London Labour and the London Poor (1840)

Henry Mayhew's epic work was the basis of the limited research that Jeter, Blaylock and Powers did into Victorian London. Mayhew was a social researcher and campaigner and his three-volume work chronicled the lives of beggars, street entertainers, prostitutes, labourers and market traders: anyone who plied their 'trade' (whatever it might be) in London. His emphasis on marginal people and their activities proved to be a treasure trove of detail for the three originators of Steampunk. Details of clothing and even dialect were influential on the fantasy versions of London that the writers developed between them.

Robert Louis Stevenson. If you set it in actual Victorian London and get all your cool research from old books, you don't have to have any intrinsic imagination, just find the details in research! It was borrowing an aura of credibility. Any revision of history we did was accidental, because we didn't know what we were doing!'

Slowly they began to discuss creating stories in the mode of H.G. Wells and Jules Verne, set in Victorian times but filtered through modern attitudes and featuring retro-fitted modern technology. Jeter had read Henry Mayhew's *London Labour and the London Poor*, an extensive account of life in Victorian London published in 1840. 'I believe there were times when we each had a copy of it,' recalled Jeter. 'We'd sit around in O'Hara's and go through sections of it, and someone would go "Dibs! I'm having that!" Jim beat me to one of the best parts, the bit about the tanning industry in Victorian London [used in Blaylock's *Homunculus*].'

The trio repurposed historical details, atmosphere and even the idiom of speech reported by Mayhew in their writing. 'It was a little time machine that had appeared in front of us, a revelation,' noted Jeter. According to Powers: 'Every ten pages is material for a novel. If you read it, you'll be able to say "There's where Jeter ripped it off, there's where Powers ripped it off, there's where Blaylock ripped it off."'

Jeter was a fan of Wells's *The Time Machine* and came up with the idea of fusing Mayhew's first-hand accounts of the real experiences of the Victorian poor with a Morlock-driven sequel to Wells's novel. The 1970s' alternative histories of Michael Moorcock may also have influenced Jeter in his thinking. The result was *Morlock Night* (1979). Jeter's central conceit was simple: what would happen if the Morlocks captured the time machine (the fate of which was left unresolved by Wells) and used it to travel back from their ruined future to Victorian London? The cover of the first edition was adorned with the enticing strapline: 'What happened when the Time Machine returned?' Lacking the overt political sub-text of Wells' original, *Morlock Night* is pure adventure entertainment. Jeter never intended it to be the launching pad for an entire literary subgenre.

Rather, it was with *Infernal Devices* (1987) that Jeter laid claim to the title of one of the original godfathers of Steampunk. Jeter populated his well-researched Victorian world with characters, events and props that would come to be core to definitions of Steampunk. His central character, George Dower, is not an adventurer: quite the opposite. He likes his quiet, safe life, but he is drawn into a series of bewildering events. His father was an inventor, and when Dower is visited by a mysterious stranger with a clockwork device built by his father that needs repairing, he soon finds himself drawn into a peculiar world. Along the way, Dower finds out more about his father, encounters clockwork automata and a device that can peer into the future, and uncovers the existence of strange, Lovecraft-style human-fish hybrids that live in Wetwick, a weird area of London. He also finds himself in the middle of a conflict between the Royal Anti-Society (the remnants of Cromwell's Godly Army), and the Ladies Union for the Suppression of Carnal Vice.

O'Hara's Pub

O'Hara's Old Towne Pub in Orange, California is the spiritual birthplace of Steampunk. That was where K.W. Jeter, James P. Blaylock and Tim Powers spent many hours over drinks working out the details of their pseudo-Victorian worlds. Just a short distance from the Chapman University campus (where Blaylock and Powers are now both professors), the unassuming North Gassell Street tavern does not yet feature a historic site marker indicating its importance in the birth of the fantasy Victoriana known as Steampunk.

If written today, the Steampunk elements would probably be emphasized more than they are in *Infernal Devices*. To Jeter, the setting, characters and props were simply items in a Moorcock-style 'toolbox' used to tell his story. It's a picaresque adventure, with Dower stumbling through a quest for knowledge (about his father) and encountering the remnants of his father's clockwork creations en route, as well as uncovering a hidden history of London.

Between these two novels, Jeter had actually visited London in the early 1980s. During his visit he discovered a shop on the periphery of Covent Garden that had a window display made up of ancient Victorian instruments, for sale as antiques to collectors. The impression of wooden-and-brass technology stayed with him and inspired his approach to *Infernal Devices*. This inspiration would be a key foundation stone in the later widespread use of the Steampunk design aesthetic. 'Modern scientific equipment looks so dull by comparison, although it blows up a lot less often,' said Jeter of the Victorian technology he'd stumbled across. 'The Steampunk design aesthetic is at the far opposite pole from the Apple aesthetic where everything is smooth, white and featureless.'

Although *Infernal Devices* is a key founding text for Steampunk, it would be over twenty-five years before Jeter returned – with belated sequel, *Fiendish Schemes* (2013) – to the genre he'd had a hand in developing and naming. It was left to Blaylock and Powers to further develop the subgenre the three authors had accidentally created.

39

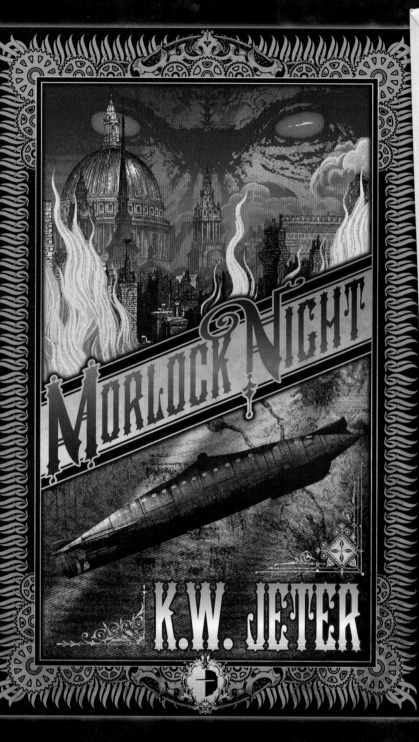

Morlock Night (1979)

Jeter's *Morlock Night* started life as an entirely different project. He and Powers (along with Ray Nelson) had been approached to contribute novels to a series that would follow the adventures of King Arthur reincarnated in several historical eras. The three of them selected periods in which to set their tales, with Jeter choosing Victorian London. They set about writing their respective novels, only to later discover that the prospective British publisher had abandoned the idea. In order not to waste their research, Jeter and Powers set about stripping their stories of any King Arthur-related details and salvaged what they could. Powers's Arthurian research resurfaced in *The Drawing of the Dark* (1979) and *Last Call* (1992), especially elements of the Fisher King legend. Jeter took his planned Victorian novel in a different direction, and the result was *Morlock Night*.

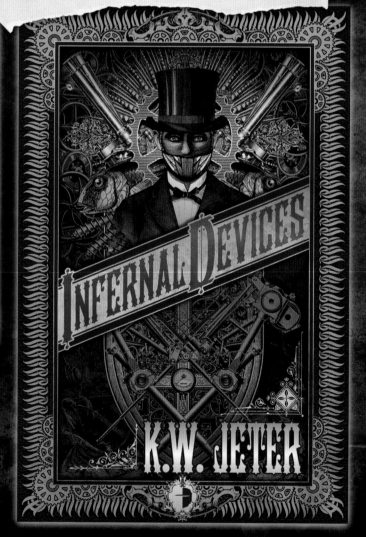

Blaylock blasts back

James Blaylock can claim to have been the first of the group to have a Steampunk work published with the short story 'The Ape-Box Affair' (1978). Blaylock admitted tackling a short story first because it was simply quicker and easier than writing a novel. The earliest expression of the ideas the trio had developed during their sessions at O'Hara's, it was eventually collected, along with three other short stories and two full-length novels, as *The Adventures of Langdon St. Ives* (2008), comprising Blaylock's complete Steampunk works to that date.

The original short Steampunk tale 'The Ape-Box Affair' is set in 1892 and sees an orang-utan landing in St. James Park's duck pond in a spherical flying vehicle (an 'infernal machine'), the unforeseen outcome of scientist and adventurer Langdon St. Ives' attempt to launch the innocent creature into outer space. Immediately mistaken for an alien, the befuddled ape – named Newton – escapes into the city pursued by various horse guards, police and journalists. There follows a Keystone Kops-style chase through town in which toymaker Wilfred Keeble's mechanical ape-in-a-box gets mixed up in the caper, to everyone's confusion. The story features mad scientists, mixed-up monkeys and inexplicable mechanical contrivances and was the first blast of modern Steampunk.

Blaylock followed 'The Ape-Box Affair' with more short stories, including; 'The Hole in Space' (based on a facetious remark from Jeter in O'Hara's about Blaylock's approach to science and C.S. Lewis's Space trilogy) that tells of St. Ives's further attempts to launch a rocket; 'The Idol's Eye' in which St. Ives narrates an adventure in Java; and 'Two Views of a Cave Painting', a whimsical time-travel tale.

Above: The Turk, a chess-playing automaton from the late 18th century, later revealed to be a fake.

41

'Nobody had heard the word Steampunk back when Tim, K.W. Jeter and I were writing our Victoriana,' recalled Blaylock in 'Parenthetically Speaking', the afterword to *The Adventures of Langdon St. Ives*. 'We certainly had no idea that we were inventing a subgenre of science fiction. My idea of science fiction had always had to do with backyard scientists and fabulous submarines and spacecraft that house onboard greenhouses. We were merely writing stories that amused us, and we often had an equally amusing time recounting to each other aspects of amusing stories that we intended to write.'

First published in 1984 by Ace Books, Blaylock's novel *The Digging Leviathan* ignored the expected Victorian setting, but co-opted a host of eccentric Victorian characters who would have fitted right into a work by Wells or Verne. Set in mid-1960s Los Angeles, the novel harks back to the Edisonades as it is based around the misadventures of Jim Hastings, a precocious fifteen-year-old inventor. Fascinated by the pulp fiction of Edgar Rice Burroughs, Hastings and his friend Giles Peach (who sports a pair of gills, in common with everyone in his family) construct a tunnelling vehicle modelled after that in Burroughs's *At the Earth's Core* (1914).

Mentoring the boys are a group of out-of-time Victorian gentlemen who belong to an alternative science-based social club dubbed the Newtonian Society. The idea of a tight-knit community group would be developed further in other Blaylock novels, such as *Homunculus* and ghost story *All the Bells on Earth* (1997). The men in these self-selecting groups are self-styled amateur 'experts' on esoteric subjects. Among the members are Hastings' uncle Edward St. Ives (a descendant of Langdon St. Ives, Blaylock's Victorian adventurer), and the characterfully named Russell Latzarel, Roycroft Squires, and William Ashbless (a different character named after the fictitious poet invented by Blaylock and Powers for *The Anubis Gates*).

Hastings' father – now semi-institutionalized following a breakdown brought on by the death of his wife – fears they have all fallen victim to a Hollow Earth conspiracy. As in Jeter's *Infernal Devices*, there is something fishy (and vaguely Lovecraftian) going on in *The Digging Leviathan*, as the novel's bumbling 'heroes' uncover strange technology, an underground civilization of magical mermen and a carp-based potion offering long life.

STEAMPUNK

While not Steampunk per se, there are enough elements within *The Digging Leviathan* (and enough correspondences to Blaylock's other work, as well as the work of Jeter and Powers) to suggest the book had an impact on the development and growth of the subgenre. In fact, there are references within the novel that anticipate the creative subculture of Steampunk, the actual making of decorative if often useless retro-futuristic items. Blaylock writes of a pair of his characters: 'the two had pieced together a wonderful gadget around an old fan motor. The machine hadn't any purpose, really, beyond gadgetry,' while he describes another item as 'a sort of Art Deco wonder of crenellations and fins and thick, ripply glass, as if it had been designed by a pulp magazine artist years before the dawn of the space age which would iron flat the wrinkles of imagination and wonder.' These are definitely Steampunk sentiments.

A diving bell, intended to be used to explore the mysterious deep, recalls the ape-piloted ship from 'The Ape-Box Affair', as well as any number of vehicles imagined by Verne and Wells, all with rivets and brass valves. Blaylock writes:

> The diving bell itself, borrowed by Professor Latzarel from the Gaviota Oceanographic Laboratory, was round as a ball. It was almost an antique. Hoses led away out of it into great coils, and in a ring around the bell, within the upper one third or so, were a line of portholes riveted shut. There was a hatch at the top, screwed down with what looked like an immense brass valve. The whole thing was etched with corrosion and flaked with blue-green verdigris. It looked to Jim like something out of Jules Verne.

Blaylock's characters come closest to approximating the kind of people who would eventually populate the real-world subculture of Steampunk itself. Edward St. Ives is described as 'a collector of books, especially of fantasy and science fiction, the older and tawdrier the better. Plots and cover illustrations that smacked of authenticity didn't interest him. It was sea monsters; cigar-shaped, crenellated rockets; and unmistakable flying saucers that attracted him. There was something in the appearance of such things that appealed to that part of him that appreciated the old Hudson Wasp [a car produced 1952–54 by the Hudson Motor Car Company of Detroit].' Many Steampunk readers and participants would recognize much of themselves in that description.

In contrast to the underwater and underground adventures of *The Digging Leviathan*, Blaylock took to the skies for his next novel, *Homunculus* (1986),

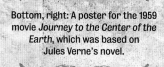

Bottom, right: A poster for the 1959 movie *Journey to the Center of the Earth*, which was based on Jules Verne's novel.

Burroughs's *Pellucidar* and other Hollow Earths

As well as Burrough's *Pellucidar*, Poe's Pym of Nantucket and Hans Pfaall stories and Verne's Journey, Hollow Earth settings featured in George Sands' 1884 novel *Laura, Voyage dans le Cristal*, where giant crystal structures were to be found in the planet's interior. Other nineteenth-century tales included Lewis Carroll's *Alice's Adventures in Wonderland* (1865, originally titled *Alice's Adventures Under Ground*); *The Coming Race* (1871) by Edward Bulwer-Lytton which featured the Vril-ya, a subterranean master race (who, weirdly, gave their name to yeast-based drink Bovril invented in the 1870s); *A Strange Manuscript Found in a Copper Cylinder* (1888), a novel by James De Mille that presented an underground civilization with inverted values in which wealth was derided, poverty lauded and a 'death cult' celebrated death rather than life; and L. Frank Baum's later Oz-set novels featuring the underground Nome Kingdom. As well as the obvious inspiration of Burroughs' work, Blaylock may also have been aware of Willis George Emerson's *The Smoky God* (1908) that told of the exploits of Olaf Jansen, an adventurer who travels into the Earth and discovers an advanced civilization.

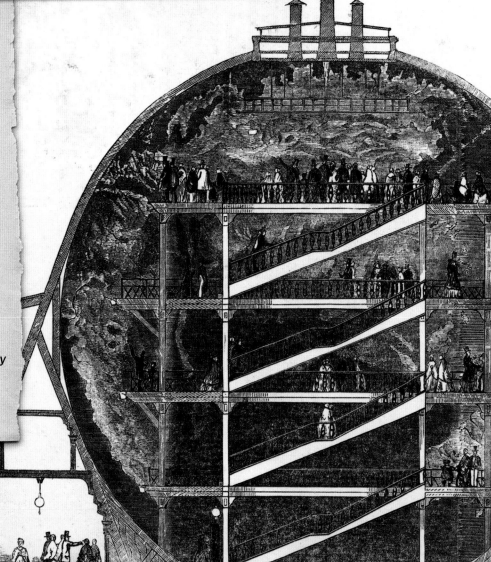

A Hollow Earth

Hollow Earth theories, largely dismissed since the end of the eighteenth century, proposed that the Earth, if not entirely hollow, certainly featured enough interior spaces for civilizations independent of surface dwellers to evolve. One of the most popular examples was the 'Shaver mystery' of the mid-1940s, when pulp magazine *Amazing Stories* editor Ray Palmer colluded in the publishing of supposed 'true' stories by Richard Shaver. These chronicled the existence of degenerate human descendants – the Dero – who use fantastic technology left behind by more sophisticated ancient races. Hollow Earth theories became rallying points for alternative scientific worldviews (largely disproved over time) and growing conspiracy theories. They also became ideal topics for Steampunk-style literature.

JULES VERNE'S

JOURNEY TO THE CENTER OF THE EARTH

STARRING
PAT BOONE · **JAMES MASON**
ARLENE DAHL · **DIANE BAKER**

CINEMASCOPE   COLOR by DE LUXE

CHARLES BRACKETT · HENRY LEVIN · WALTER REISCH and CHARLES BRACKETT

1. Аэростатъ Монгольфье.

3. Аэростатъ Бланшара.

7. Аэростатъ Генлейна.

4. Аэростатъ (bal. captif) Жиффара.

two years later. A dirigible carrying a long-dead pilot (and the seemingly magical title character) has been flying over Victorian London for some time, but its orbit is decaying and it threatens to fall back to Earth. Investigating the mysterious airship are adventurer, scientist and member of the Royal Society Langdon St. Ives, and Shiloh, an untrustworthy evangelist and mastery of the art of fakery. The villain of the piece is mad hunchback Dr. Ignacio Narbondo who, in alliance with the wealthy and unprincipled Kelso Drake, is also after the airship and the secrets its pilot may hold: he believes it could help in his quest to reanimate the dead. A host of other eccentric characters – many of them members of St. Ives' Trismegistus Club – are caught up in the madcap quest for the airship, including young hero Jack Owlesby, his fiancé Dorothy, toymaker William Keeble, Theophilus Goodall and Narbondo's assistant Willis Pule. There is much business about several mixed-up boxes manufactured by Keeble, echoing 'The Ape-Box Affair'. All finally gather on Hampstead Heath to witness the airship's final moments and to uncover the truth ...

Winner of the 1986 Philip K. Dick Award, *Homunculus* is a more obviously Steampunk effort. As with *The Digging Leviathan*, it features a rather loose, freewheeling 'plot' (something the author's critics often point to as a problem with his writing), but much of Blaylock's work is concerned with character and atmosphere rather than with establishing a complicated narrative or even a coherent world. His 1870s Victorian London is as much a fantasyland as Tolkien's Middle Earth. This was something Tim Powers admitted, seeing the trio's lack of research as a virtue. 'Our weird Victorian London was perfect for misunderstood science and misunderstood geography,' he said. 'We weren't hampered by knowledge. Blaylock's London – accurate as it is in its geography and demographics – is a more magical city than the real one could ever have been. Blaylock can't help but impose his own weird and amiable and Byzantine perspective on it.'

Many of the cast of *Homunculus* are reunited for *Lord Kelvin's Machine* (1992), the third in Blaylock's loose Steampunk trilogy and probably the most obviously Steampunk of the three. Expanded from a novella published in Asimov's *Science Fiction* magazine in 1985, Blaylock continues the battle between Langdon St. Ives and Dr. Ignacio Narbondo. Following the death of his wife Alice at the hands of Narbondo, St. Ives and his sidekick Hasbro chase down the mad doctor across Norway, attempting to thwart his plan to detonate a series of volcanoes that will plunge the Earth into the path of an onrushing comet. A mysterious machine invented by Lord Kelvin is pressed into service, only to become a time travel device by the climax.

Lord Kelvin's Machine raises the stakes, replacing the focus of *Homunculus* on magic and alchemy with something more recognizable as Steampunk's alternative science, stretching knowledge in new directions. In Blaylock's world, there are sixteen Maxwell's Equations (instead of the four that form the basis of electrodynamics), while a new unified field theory includes gravity. The revision of the title artefact to become a time machine allows Blaylock to erase any dangling loose ends, while recycling his narrative in a new, more redemptive form. 'They came naturally for me,' Blaylock said of the Steampunk elements in his novels. 'I was crazy for Jules Verne, and so I read *Twenty Thousand Leagues Under the Sea* and thought, "I want one of them submarines.

STEAMPUNK

I'm going to put one of them submarines in my book.'"

There was initial resistance from publishers to Blaylock's flights of fantasy, mainly as they'd not seen anything quite like it before. Del Rey had published his previous more overtly fantasy novels (*The Elfin Ship*, *The Disappearing Dwarf*) but they turned down *The Digging Leviathan*, claiming, according to Blaylock, that they did not publish 'loony' books. Ace Books editor Beth Meacham bought it, saying that *The Digging Leviathan* was the single strangest novel proposal they'd ever received. According to Blaylock: 'Here's Ace saying you can write a nut book for us if you want to. It's a neo-Victorian nut-scientist book, but they had no problem with that.' He would return to the adventures of Langdon St. Ives almost twenty years later in the Robert Louis Stevenson-inspired novella *The Ebb Tide* (2010), making him the first of the original trio to return to Steampunk following the mainstream popularity of the subgenre.

Powers: the reluctant Steampunk

The third godfather of Steampunk was Tim Powers, although he tended to distance himself from the work of the other two, insisting *The Anubis Gates* (1983) 'is a complete fake as Steampunk: there's no "steam", no tech; it does not take place in London; and it does not take place in Victorian times. The London I was writing about in *The Anubis Gates* is kind of an imaginary one.'

The Anubis Gates (1983) owes a debt to H.G. Wells, although the time travel in Powers' novel is achieved through scientific manipulation of holes in time and space seemingly created by magic. However, while his books are more fantasy than anything else, through his close connections with Jeter and Blaylock and his inclusion among the Steampunk originators of Jeter's 1987 letter to *Locus*, he is generally regarded as a contributor to the literary foundations of the genre.

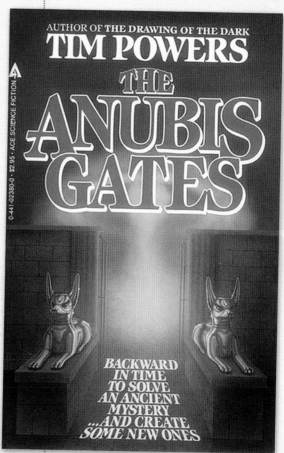

Essentially an old-fashioned rollicking adventure story, *The Anubis Gates* has less of the rough-hewn edges of the work of either Jeter or Blaylock. It's a more polished narrative, perhaps modelled after the pace of 1930s cliffhanger movie serials, and follows the unfortunate professor Brendan Doyle (mentioned in Blaylock's *The Digging Leviathan*). The novel fits well with one of the emerging themes of Steampunk: the resilience of the British Empire. Following a failed plot by Egyptian magicians to bring down the Empire in 1802, there remain around the world a series of magical gates that make time travel possible. A group of millionaires from 1983, accompanied by Doyle as an expert guide, travel to 1810 in order to attend a lecture given by the poet Samuel Taylor Coleridge. Doyle, however, ends up trapped in the nineteenth century and caught up in ongoing battles between magical rivals.

Speaking at a convention, Powers noted that, 'The punk in Steampunk is partly nineteenth-century adventure, which was not self-conscious, crossed with twentieth-century characters who are self-conscious. It's also important to remember that spiritualism was considered a form of science ... ectoplasm, mesmerism, bi-location. As fictional devices, these things are a lot of fun.'

Powers is correct that *The Anubis Gates* lacks the 'steam' of Steampunk – the wacky

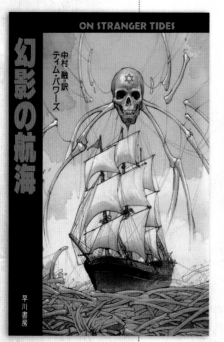

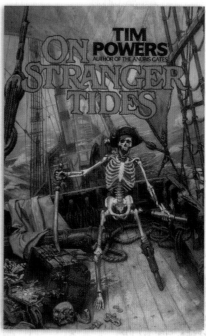

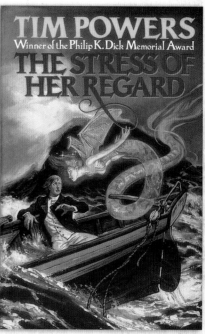

retro-Victorian, often anachronistic technology. However, Steampunk fiction often straddles the time period when what was perceived as 'magic' (as electricity was sometimes regarded) rapidly became part of the new inquisitive movement of 'natural philosophy', or 'science', as it would become known. More centrally, the novel tackles the question Steampunk asks of the Victorian period: what if history (personal, national or scientific) had been different? Through his connection with the mysterious poet William Ashbless, Doyle gets a personal answer to that question, but the entire project of Steampunk goes beyond simple alternative history to viewing Victorian London as a very real turning point in history, from which so many different things could have come – hence the very diversity of the subgenre itself.

Power's later *On Stranger Tides* (1987) unexpectedly became the part-basis for the fourth Pirates of the Caribbean movie in 2010. Like *The Anubis Gates*, this novel features magic in a historical setting, although it is less complex than its predecessor. However, there are enough echoes to make it worth reading when delving into the literary roots of the movement. Featuring pirates who practise voodoo magic and a quest for the Fountain of Youth, it is even more removed from the core tenets of Steampunk than the previous book – although this one falls into the correct time period.

In The Stress of Her Regard (1989), Powers would follow up on his interest in the Romantic Poets first expressed through the characters of Coleridge and Byron in *The Anubis Gates*. Again, the novel orbits the Steampunk aesthetic (of the three originators, only Blaylock really committed to the form in multiple books), as it is set in the correct time period, but lacks the urban London location. The Romantic Poets Byron, Shelley and Keats are all connected to a vampiric female, the Lamia, in a tale that mixes magic and science in the way Powers had done in his previous novels. Here the real and the fantastic merge, with Powers expressing the feel of Steampunk without strict adherence to the subgenre's narrative 'furniture'.

There have been debates about Powers' continuing place within the confines of Steampunk, but removing his work would be to deny the very flexibility that has made the term so useful in describing an entire, growing sub-sector of science fiction, fantasy and horror. The Frankensteinian construction of the word Steampunk itself reflects the wide range of work that can come under the one banner: it's a mash-up, a pastiche of Cyberpunk that can be used in very specific ways, but always conveys to the reader a wider generic idea of what to expect from any given work. It's a single word that encompasses enough degrees of what diverse audiences might perceive it to be that it can be successfully applied not only to literature, but to movies, comic books, games, fashion, art and even music.

There can be no doubt that, despite what may have come before, everything dubbed Steampunk that came after the (largely) 1980s work of these authors owes them a great debt. It wasn't something they set out to create, but a literary subgenre that emerged from the connection between three friends. As Jeter himself noted, 'I don't believe I did any more to get the ball rolling than just to fortuitously come up with a word that works as a more or less convenient label to slap onto a bag that already is splitting down the seams with all the crazy stuff that's coming out of it. One of the biggest benefits that I've derived from my association with the whole Steampunk thing is that working along those lines clued me in on the whole value of historical material.'

Below: A diagram of Charles Babbage's Difference Engine No. 1. Overleaf: None of Babbage's calculating machines were constructed during his lifetime. The Science Museum in London completed this working model of Difference Engine No. 2 in 1991, for the bicentennial of its Victorian inventor's birth.

The Difference Engine: Cyberpunk reacts

Cyberpunk's prime proponents, Bruce Sterling and William Gibson, responded to the arrival of the Steampunk work of Jeter, Blaylock and Powers at the end of the 1980s with *The Difference Engine* (1990), an alternative history take on the creation of the computer in the Victorian age. Their take on Steampunk was essentially reductive, thrusting their Cyberpunk approach back into the Victorian age, complete with a dark, dominating cityscape, totalitarianism, pollution, freedom-denying bureaucracy, the ubiquity of information technology and the birth of self-sustaining artificial intelligence.

At its heart, *The Difference Engine* has a clever conceit. In Sterling and Gibson's alternative history, real-life inventor Charles Babbage completes his analytical engine (a prototype Victorian-era computer he never built in reality). The result is huge social and technological upheaval, as if the computer and information revolution had taken place in Victorian London rather than in the 1980s and 1990s.

Set mainly in 1855, Babbage's mass-produced computing machines are ubiquitous while new technology is still steam-powered. The equivalent of today's computer 'hackers' are the 'clackers', technically

Charles Babbage (1791-1871)

Babbage was a mathematician, inventor and engineer, most famous as an early inventor of the programmable mechanical computer, although his 'difference engine' was not actually constructed until 1991 when it was proved that Babbage's theoretical device was fully functional. Parts of the incomplete mechanism Babbage embarked upon are now on display in London's Science Museum. The computing machines proposed by Babbage were to have been steam-powered and would mechanize the process of calculation. Babbage moved on to design a more complex 'analytical engine' that would use punch cards that he was still working on at the time of his death.

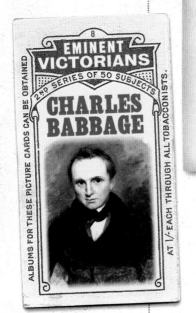

proficient people who can programme Babbage's devices through manipulation of punch cards. Advanced steam technology and computing power has strengthened the British Empire, especially militarily. Victorian engineers and scientists (known as 'savants'), such as Isambard Kingdom Brunel and Charles Darwin, are revered and given prestige within this very different society. American has never united, leading to a series of distinct colonial territories divided between Russia, Britain and the American Confederacy.

This alternative history is populated by a trio of significant characters: Sybil Gerard, prostitute and daughter of a Luddite leader; Edward Mallory, a distinguished scientist and palaeontologist; and Laurence Oliphant, a travel writer and spy who smuggles Edisonade-like works of proto-SF to the Crown Prince of Greater Britain (including one entitled *Wheel-Men of the Czar*). The three protagonists are variously in pursuit of a series of computer punch cards, although these are essentially a Hitchcockian 'MacGuffin' (a generally unimportant item or objective that propels a narrative quest).

By its conclusion, however, *The Difference Engine* attempts to re-establish the hegemony of Cyberpunk over Steampunk. It concludes with a brief coda set in a reimagined 1991, where the Victorian utopianism of Babbage's age has

led to a dystopia in which humanity appears to have been consigned to an ephemeral, digital existence dominated by a capricious sentient artificial intelligence, dubbed The Eye. It's a downbeat conclusion, and in some ways it recolours the preceding narrative as a critique of Steampunk rather than a celebration of it, or even than a serious contribution towards it. It is as though Sterling and Gibson were rejecting the arrival of the new upstart subgenre that threatened to eclipse their own, so they set out to use Michael Moorcock's Steampunk 'toolbox' to reclaim the territory for Cyberpunk.

Despite the novel's questionable relationship to the

purer forms of Steampunk, Sterling and Gibson's *The Difference Engine* did much to popularize the form beyond the work of the California triumvirate of Jeter, Blaylock and Powers among the mainstream. Whether this reactionary volume was the right one to spearhead Steampunk's voyage into the 1990s is a moot point: it got the job done.

The original godfathers of Steampunk were initially unaware of the growth of the later subgenre, both in its literary expansion and as a lifestyle subculture. However, they could not avoid such awareness for long, and all three became set on making new contributions to the subgenre they'd help create. 'Now it's a real big deal,' Blaylock has said of modern Steampunk. 'I think it's an artistic or fashion aesthetic more than a literary thing. I find it heartening and interesting that Steampunk has caught on, but I'd be writing it in any event. It's something that happened to me over the years and that became part of me on a sort of cellular level. As a result, I'm not all that interested in defining the field; I leave that to others. I love watching it develop, however: the aesthetic is immensely appealing. I'm happy to have played my small part, and to continue to play it: emphasis on "play".'

Tim Powers had noticed that contemporary interest in Steampunk moved beyond the novels to such an extent that many participants were unaware of its literary origins. 'There's several Steampunk conventions and they don't really have many books in the dealers' room,' Powers said. 'They have tons of costumes and goggles and ray-guns. It's more of a costume phenomenon, which has always been a big part of science fiction fandom. It seems that it has evolved dynamically into another area and out of dutiful loyalty keeps referring back to me, Blaylock and Jeter.'

Jeter, however, continues to have a special interest in all things Steampunk. 'The enthusiasm is entertaining to me, my having coined the term and all. I'm glad that people are having fun with the various concepts associated with it,' Jeter said. 'There's possibly a deeper element involved – though I don't want to get too pretentious about it – that would be the admiration by Steampunk devotees for the handcrafted aspect of everyday objects from previous industrial periods, versus the cheap plastic crap that lines the store shelves nowadays. There's a humanness, for lack of a better word, to old stuff – and old ways – that the modern world lacks.'

Returning to Steampunk with a long-overdue sequel to *Infernal Devices* called *Fiendish Schemes* (2013), Jeter was slightly concerned about coming back to the subgenre he'd help create. 'There's an intimidation factor involved in picking up a subgenre that I've let lie fallow for nearly a quarter-century; in that time, there have been a lot of really good writers who have been working in that particular Victorian retro-fantasy field, and they've produced a lot of entertaining, interesting books. So the competition has definitely upped its game, so to speak.'

It had been a long journey from Wells and Verne, via Moorcock and Harrison, to Jeter, Blaylock and Powers. However, the distinctive genre of fictional adventures in a high-tech alternative Victorian period now had a name and an agenda. The 1990s would see a slow-burn development of the genre, but the new century would bring with it an explosion of all things Steampunk.

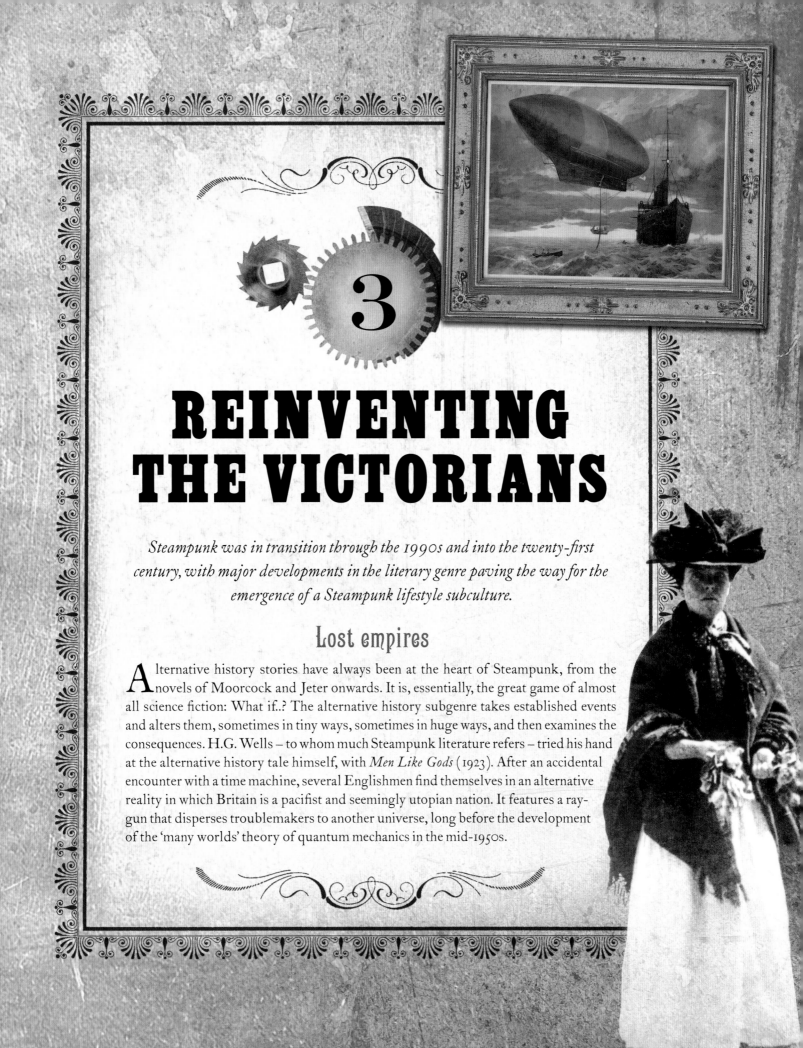

3

REINVENTING THE VICTORIANS

Steampunk was in transition through the 1990s and into the twenty-first century, with major developments in the literary genre paving the way for the emergence of a Steampunk lifestyle subculture.

Lost empires

Alternative history stories have always been at the heart of Steampunk, from the novels of Moorcock and Jeter onwards. It is, essentially, the great game of almost all science fiction: What if..? The alternative history subgenre takes established events and alters them, sometimes in tiny ways, sometimes in huge ways, and then examines the consequences. H.G. Wells – to whom much Steampunk literature refers – tried his hand at the alternative history tale himself, with *Men Like Gods* (1923). After an accidental encounter with a time machine, several Englishmen find themselves in an alternative reality in which Britain is a pacifist and seemingly utopian nation. It features a ray-gun that disperses troublemakers to another universe, long before the development of the 'many worlds' theory of quantum mechanics in the mid-1950s.

The Difference Engine may have been the first Steampunk novel of the 1990s, but it was also intended to be a final word on the genre by writers whose true allegiance was to Cyberpunk. Bruce Sterling's co-author William Gibson rejected the label that was being attached to this particular flavour of Victorian retro-futurism: 'I'll be happy just as long as they don't label this one. There's been some dire talk of "Steampunk", but I don't think it's going to stick.' On that score, at least, this science-fiction prophet proved to be definitively wrong.

It wouldn't be until the middle of the decade that Steampunk rediscovered itself, with the word's first use in a title. Paul Di Filippo's *The Steampunk Trilogy* (1995) consisted of a trio of novellas very much in the Jeter and Blaylock style, if bawdier. The first tale, 'Victoria', unsurprisingly features Queen Victoria, here replaced by a giant salamander. The second is 'Hottentots', in which a Swiss naturalist embarks upon a quest for a stolen fetish object, while the third, 'Walt' and 'Emily', sees poets Walt Whitman and Emily Dickinson embark upon a wild affair while journeying across the astral plane. Adopting the freewheeling whimsical approach of the late-1980s Steampunk pioneers, Di Filippo's 1990s' take foregrounds sex and sexuality. From the replacement Queen Victoria's nymphomania (much to the exhaustion of Prime Minister, Lord Melbourne) to Walt and Emily's unlikely astral tryst, Di Filippo offers a fruity take on a sometimes straight-laced genre.

Charles Dickens (1812-1870)

According to critic John Clute:

There's no getting away from the man who invented Steampunk: Charles Dickens. *Oliver Twist* (1837–39) depicts a London [that is] a kind of apotheosis of the supernatural melodrama popular at the beginning of the century: grand guignol. Similarly, the Gothic fever-dreams of such writers as Monk Lewis or Charles Maturin can be seen to underpin the greatest achievements of Dickens – *Bleak House* (1852–53), *Little Dorrit* (1855–57) or *Our Mutual Friend* (1864-65) – those novels in which the nightmare of London attains lasting and horrific form. For Dickens, that nightmare may be a prophetic vision of humanity knotted into the subterranean entrails of the city machine …

It may have been Di Filippo's work or there may have been something in the air, but the mid-1990s saw the return of the Steampunk literary genre in earnest, with a series of diverse authors picking up the storytelling toolbox abandoned by Moorcock, Jeter, Blaylock and Powers. Among them would be Cyberpunk exponent Neal Stephenson (in *The Diamond Age: Or, A Young Lady's Illustrated Primer*, 1995), children's author Philip Pullman (in his series His Dark Materials, 1995–2000) and *Twin Peaks'* co-creator Mark Frost (in *The List of Seven*, 1993, and *The Six Messiahs*, 1995).

At work here was a nostalgia for Victoriana, perhaps in reaction to British Prime Minister Margaret Thatcher's late-1980s call for a return to 'Victorian values', or the conservatism of US Presidents Ronald Reagan and George H.W. Bush. Additionally, for American authors, Victorian London was a scene of exotica presenting the opportunity to explore a world socially and morally very different from 1980s and 1990s America. It is notable that the entire genre was effectively kick-started by a trio of Californians.

Victorian London

Critic and writer Stan Nicholls proposes that '... in essence Steampunk is a US phenomenon, often set in London, England, which is envisaged as at once deeply alien and intimately familiar, a kind of foreign body encysted in the US subconscious ... It is as if, for a handful of SF writers, Victorian London has come to stand for one of those turning points in history where things can go one way or the other, a turning point peculiarly relevant to SF itself. It was a city of industry, science and technology where the modern world was being born, and a claustrophobic city of nightmare where the cost of this growth was registered in filth and squalor.'

David Lynch's collaborator on the television series *Twin Peaks* (1990–91), American Mark Frost, wrote two novels that evoke the ethos of the genre and are reminiscent of Tim Powers's *The Anubis Gates*. *The List of Seven* (1993) and *The Six Messiahs* (1995) feature Arthur Conan Doyle (creator of Sherlock Holmes and a nineteenth-century spiritualist) as the leading character, alongside Frost's creation, Jack Sparks. Instead of the mysteries of electricity or other pseudo-advanced technologies, Frost's novels expand upon the way that spiritualism (contact with the dead or the spirit world) was once considered almost as a scientific discipline. While Frost adopts a techno-fantasy approach, he makes no use of retro-futurism in technological terms. Light and quick moving, like Blaylock's work, Frost's epic battle between the forces of good and evil has the added strength of witty and clever dialogue honed through years of writing screenplays: his Jack Sparks is a prototype Sherlock Holmes while also being a distant echo of *Twin Peaks'* quirky investigator, FBI Agent Dale Cooper.

Sparks' London base is a Georgian townhouse opposite the British Museum. Within he harbours a comprehensive research library he calls 'The Brain', a set of twelve drawers in a cabinet containing index cards that carry the details of every crime and criminal in London. This and other elements – such as the chemistry set, the collection of exotic weaponry and the tailor's dummy that once took an assassin's bullet instead of Jack – all echo much of Conan Doyle's Holmes stories. In addition, *The List of Seven* (set in 1884) features other real-life eminent Victorians, such as Bram Stoker, author

Above: Basil Rathbone as Sherlock Holmes and Nigel Bruce as Dr Watson in the movie *Sherlock Holmes and the Voice of Terror* from 1942.

Una produzione **GEORGE PAL**

L'UOMO CHE VISSE
(THE TIME MACHINE)
NEL FUTURO
di **H. G. WELLS**

ROD   ALAN   YVETTE   SEBASTIAN   TOM
TAYLOR · **YOUNG** · **MIMIEUX** · **CABOT** · **HELMORE**
Diretto da **GEORGE PAL** · Sceneggiatura di **DAVID DUNCAN** · Dal romanzo di H. G. WELLS   **METROCOLOR**

of *Dracula*, and Madame Blavatsky, a notorious medium and founder of The Theosophical Society. Naturally, Queen Victoria also manages to put in an appearance. *The Six Messiahs* re-teams Conan Doyle and Sparks in 1894 and plunges them into a religious conspiracy sparked by the murder of a rare book dealer. Both books evoke Steampunk without ever engaging directly with its mechanisms.

A trio of British authors put their distinctive individualistic stamps on Steampunk in the 1990s: Stephen Baxter, Christopher Priest and Kim Newman. This was perhaps an attempt to reclaim the legacy of history and the British Empire for the nation against the fantastical explorations of American Steampunk authors.

Left: The Morlocks from the 1960 film adaptation of H.G. Wells' *The Time Machine*. Above: An Italian promotional poster for the movie. Rod Taylor played the Time Traveller.

57

EMINENT STEAMPUNKS

2ND SERIES OF 50 SUBJECTS

1

STEPHEN BAXTER

ALBUMS FOR THESE PICTURE CARDS CAN BE OBTAINED

AT 1/- EACH THROUGH ALL TOBACCONISTS.

Stephen Baxter (b. 1957)

Often seen as the heir to Arthur C. Clarke, alternative history has been a frequent subject of Baxter's work, from his idealistic retelling of the US space programme in *Voyage* (1996) to ancient history in the Time's Tapestry (2006–08) series and the Northland Trilogy (from 2010, ongoing). Two short story sequels to *Anti-Ice* appeared in Asimov's *Science Fiction* magazine. 'The Ice War' (2008) and 'The Ice Line' (2010) are, according to Baxter, 'loosely related' to *Anti-Ice*, with the second story set eighty-five years after the first.

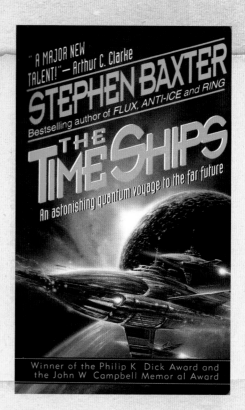

"A MAJOR NEW TALENT!"—Arthur C. Clarke

STEPHEN BAXTER

Bestselling author of *FLUX, ANTI-ICE* and *RING*

THE Time Ships

An astonishing quantum voyage to the far future

Winner of the Philip K Dick Award and the John W Campbell Memorial Award

In two distinctive novels, Baxter tackled the legacies of both Jules Verne and H.G. Wells through Steampunk. In *Anti-Ice* (1993), he attempts to out-Verne Verne with his account of how the discovery of a new element affects Victorian society, while *The Time Ships* (1995) is a sanctioned, official sequel to Wells's *The Time Machine*.

The aptly named Josiah Traveller is the inventor hero of *Anti-Ice*, the man who discovers the new element in Antarctica. When heated, 'anti-ice' releases a huge amount of energy, naturally leading to military interest in exploiting the discovery in the Crimea. Baxter goes beyond just military applications, however, and his novel explores how the addition of this one new element (sourced from a comet which crashed into Earth's moon) fuels the rapid pace of industrialization in Britain in the late 1800s. Essentially a parable about nuclear energy, Baxter adopts the standard Steampunk device of imagining a world in which such technical innovation arrives much earlier.

When Queen Victoria abdicates following Prince Albert's death in 1861, Prime Minister Gladstone consolidates the British Empire's hold on power through the country's monopoly on 'anti-ice'. While the new element is used to power all sorts of vehicles (including a monorail that spans the English Channel), Traveller is interested in only one: his moon rocket, Phaeton. The destination of this first space flight is the 'little moon', the Earth's second satellite created by the comet's lunar impact. Returning to Earth, Traveller is compelled by Gladstone to use 'anti-ice' to develop weapons to defeat France in the looming war. The discovery that the orbiting 'little moon' is composed almost entirely of 'anti-ice' provokes an arms race and a Cold War-style standoff early in the new century.

To Visit the Queen (1998)

Diane Duane's *To Visit the Queen* (1998, *On Her Majesty's Wizardly Service* in the UK) took the development of anomalous weapons as its divergence point from real history. More concerned with anthropological fantasy (Duane's central characters are feline wizards) and magic than with traditional Steampunk motifs, Duane's novel nonetheless posits the invention of nuclear weapons during Queen Victoria's reign and in that respect bears comparison to *Anti-Ice* and *Queen Victoria's Bomb*.

Baxter captures not only the setting of Victorian Britain, but his prose style also emulates Victorian writing. He tells part of the story in epistolary form, while the characters adhere to the types established by Verne and Dickens. While he maintains a 'sense of wonder' throughout his outlandish tale, Baxter also considers the political and social consequences of his 'what if?' question.

It is in *The Time Ships* (1995) that Baxter fully indulges his Wellsian storytelling. Authorized by the Wells estate, this sequel follows Wells's unnamed time traveller back to the future where he discovers that his actions have changed the society he'd previously witnessed. Now, technologically sophisticated Morlocks dominate mankind. Returning to the past, the time traveller attempts to fix this second future, making things progressively more complicated as he encounters his younger self and journeys through various alternative versions of time (including a twenty-four-year Great War and a prehistoric past where groups of time travellers become trapped). Repairing his 'time car', the time traveller once more escapes into the future and sees mankind flee a dying Earth (Stapleton-style). By the end, nanotechnology life forms dominate the universe as well as – thanks to the time traveller's technology – the time lines of past, present and future.

Baxter's outlandish confection combines his own ideas of 'deep time', the long-term survival of humanity and the rise of nanotechnology (expressed in his novels *Time*, 1999, and *Space*, 2000), with those of Wells, especially the latter's pessimistic view of future warfare and the fate of mankind. Many of Wells's works beyond *The Time Machine* are referenced in *The Time Ships*, including the short stories 'The Chronic Argonauts' (1888), 'The Land Ironclads' (1903), and his novels *The First Men in the*

59

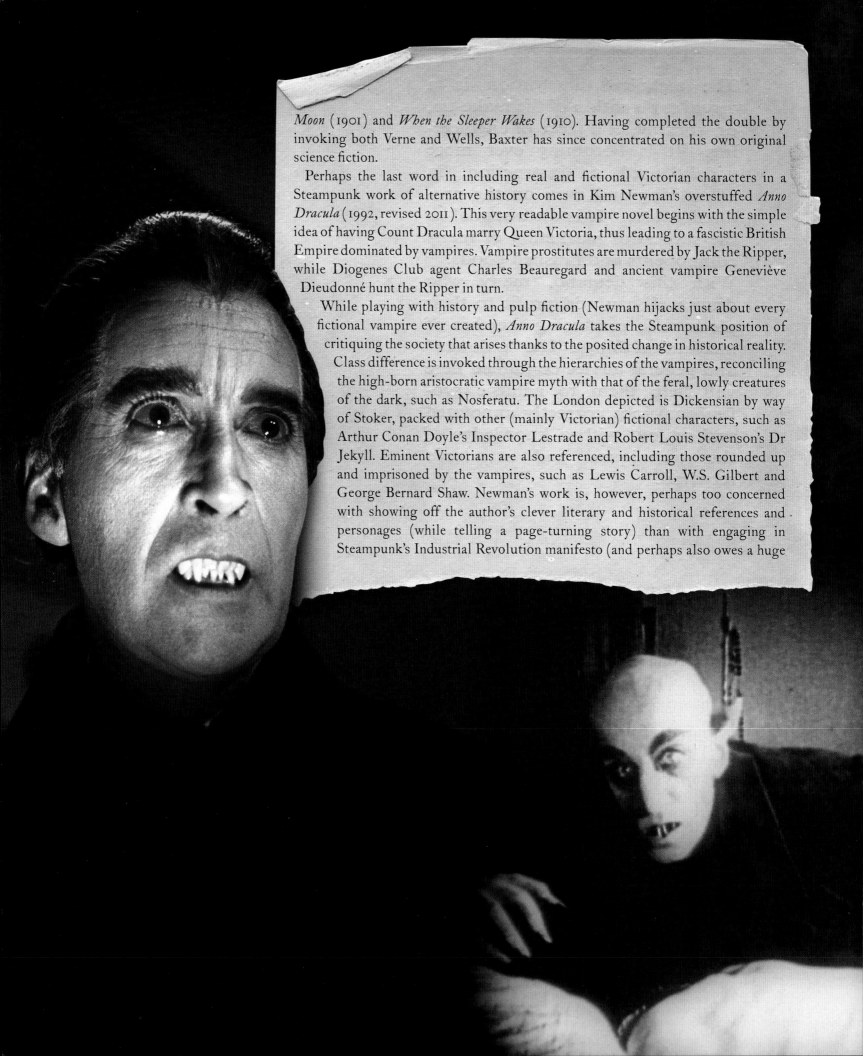

Moon (1901) and *When the Sleeper Wakes* (1910). Having completed the double by invoking both Verne and Wells, Baxter has since concentrated on his own original science fiction.

Perhaps the last word in including real and fictional Victorian characters in a Steampunk work of alternative history comes in Kim Newman's overstuffed *Anno Dracula* (1992, revised 2011). This very readable vampire novel begins with the simple idea of having Count Dracula marry Queen Victoria, thus leading to a fascistic British Empire dominated by vampires. Vampire prostitutes are murdered by Jack the Ripper, while Diogenes Club agent Charles Beauregard and ancient vampire Geneviève Dieudonné hunt the Ripper in turn.

While playing with history and pulp fiction (Newman hijacks just about every fictional vampire ever created), *Anno Dracula* takes the Steampunk position of critiquing the society that arises thanks to the posited change in historical reality. Class difference is invoked through the hierarchies of the vampires, reconciling the high-born aristocratic vampire myth with that of the feral, lowly creatures of the dark, such as Nosferatu. The London depicted is Dickensian by way of Stoker, packed with other (mainly Victorian) fictional characters, such as Arthur Conan Doyle's Inspector Lestrade and Robert Louis Stevenson's Dr Jekyll. Eminent Victorians are also referenced, including those rounded up and imprisoned by the vampires, such as Lewis Carroll, W.S. Gilbert and George Bernard Shaw. Newman's work is, however, perhaps too concerned with showing off the author's clever literary and historical references and personages (while telling a page-turning story) than with engaging in Steampunk's Industrial Revolution manifesto (and perhaps also owes a huge debt to Brian Stableford's alternative history fantasy *The Empire of Fear*, 1990, while in turn influencing Alan Moore and Kevin O'Neill's acclaimed comic book series *The League of Extraordinary Gentlemen*, 1999).

Much more subtly, Christopher Priest's prize-winning *The Prestige* (1995, made into a movie in 2006) entangles the real-world figure of Victorian engineer and inventor Nikola Tesla with a tale of two battling magicians. Very different from most of Priest's other science fiction and fantasy work (except in continuing his focus on unreliable narrators), *The Prestige* introduces one significant technological element into what is otherwise a straightforward pseudo-historical novel (told in the form of an investigation from the present day through journals and letters). One of the magicians, Rupert Angier, appears able to conduct an entirely impossible trick dubbed 'In A Flash', but is revealed to be using Tesla's transportation device to achieve his 'illusion'. This technique has a cost: while it transports a copy of the live magician, it leaves behind a dead husk that must be disposed of. Rival magician Alfred Borden achieves a similar trick, 'The Transported Man', by co-opting his twin brother, Frederick, but when he interrupts Angier's power supply, the maverick magician is split in two. Priest takes a different approach to many of the original Steampunk works that equally combine magic with retro-futuristic technology (*Morlock Night*, *The Anubis Gates*), in that he adds one element of an impossible technology to magic (albeit this is in the form of conjuring and sleight of hand, rather than anything supernatural). In

Left to right: Three faces of Dracula (Christopher Lee, Max Schreck, Bela Lugosi) as featured in Kim Newman's *Anno Dracula*.

doing so, he created a unique work. Previously the author had made his own attempt at a joint-sequel to Wells's classics *The Time Machine* and *The War of the Worlds* in *The Space Machine: A Scientific Romance* (1976), a rare British pre-cursor to the Steampunk of Jeter, Blaylock and Powers.

This 'alternative history' strand in Steampunk is the dominant one, presenting a reflection of the present through Victorian ideas. The 'past' that the best Steampunk novels conjure up is somehow 'better' than the real, historical past (even when it presents weapons of mass destruction the likes of which the Victorians could never have conceived). This imaginary past is made to feel real by mixing invented characters with genuine historical personalities and events, or with figures from the pop culture of the time (the best example being *Anno Dracula*). As well as genuine historical detail (an influence that goes back to Jeter, Blaylock and Powers' use of Mayhew's *London Labour and the London Poor*), many of these novels pastiche the 'Victorian voice' (as in Baxter's *Anti-Ice*), and combine that with the addition of fantastic technology that could not exist but nonetheless feels like part of the reformed Steampunk universe.

One thing these diverse works make clear is that the definition of Steampunk is malleable, viewing the Victorian age through the prism of science fiction. In utilizing the technology made possible by the steam engine ('steam') combined with revolutionary politics ('punk'), the resulting genre of Steampunk resists the limits of either the Victorian period for its setting or Victorian London as its primary geographical location. In fact, some of the finest Steampunk works would encompass space travel and journeys to the moon, while yet others would apply the Steampunk aesthetic to entirely fantastical worlds, yet still fall within the generic boundaries.

Empires in space

Voyages to other worlds have been central to Steampunk, from the earliest works of Verne and Wells to modern masters like Stephen Baxter and Bob Shaw. Initially the moon was the unattainable object of desire, understandably, as it was the Earth's nearest neighbour and very much visible to everyone. It seemed to be within reach, and given civilization on Earth, men wondered what they might find not only on the moon, but on our nearest planetary neighbours Mars and Venus. Space opera and Steampunk share the same roots.

In two novels – *From the Earth to the Moon* (1865) and *Around the Moon* (1870) – Verne sent his Victorian explorers on the greatest journey of them all. *The First Men in the Moon* (1901) was Wells's take on the same subject. In movies and TV versions of the story, the spherical craft that launches Bedford and Dr. Cavor to the moon is kitted out inside like a Victorian gentleman's club, but it is barely described in the novel and suggests little more than an empty sphere. Although Cavor doubts they will meet any people on the moon, positing that it is a dead world, the pair do in fact encounter 'mooncalves' – 'stupendous slugs, huge, greasy hulls, eating greedily and noisily, with a sort of sobbing avidity' – and the Selenites, one described as 'a mere ant, scarcely five feet high. He was wearing garments of some leathery substance ... a compact, bristling creature, having much of the quality of a complicated insect, with whip-like tentacles

and a clanging arm projecting from his shining cylindrical body case. The form of his head was hidden by his enormous many-spiked helmet ... and a pair of goggles of darkened glass, gave a bird-like quality to the metallic apparatus that covered his face.'

This combination of the Vernian voyage to other worlds in impossible craft and the Wellsian encounter with whatever forms of life reside there can be found at the core of Steampunk space opera. This was an extension of the Victorian obsession with exploring the Earth, mapping the entire world and classifying all creatures who lived upon it. The rapid developments of the technology of travel – the railway, ocean-going steamships – and of communication – the typewriter, telegraphy – served to remove many of the restrictions of space and time. There was no reason, it was believed, that these new technologies could not be applied to breaching one more 'great frontier'. Travelling to another world was looked upon in the same way as voyaging to an unexplored continent. The biggest point of differentiation between Steampunk and more general space opera is that Steampunk's explorations tend to be confined to localized, singular worlds within the solar system, while space opera often encompasses a variety of multiple worlds.

The 'planetary romances' of the later Victorian years grew out of the work of Verne and Wells. Beyond the Victorian authors – including Serviss's *Edison's Conquest of Mars* – all these diverse works saw the seemingly unknown universe as simply the opposite: everything was ultimately knowable and understandable to the advanced Victorian mind. As the Earth itself had succumbed to mankind's tender advances, then so would other worlds, the moon, Mars and – prime among them – Venus.

Bottom, left: Isambard Kingdom Brunel, the great Victorian engineer. From bridges and tunnels, to railways and the first propeller-driven transatlantic steamships, his designs revolutionised the era.

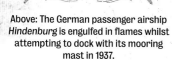

Above: The German passenger airship *Hindenburg* is engulfed in flames whilst attempting to dock with its mooring mast in 1937.

Steampunk spacecraft are open to instant comprehension. Unlike the real world craft of NASA or the high-powered space vehicles of *Star Wars*, Steampunk craft are launched from massive cannons (Verne) or powered by an anti-gravity element (Wells). They are not filled with high-octane rocket fuel or sport massive ion-drives, but rely on easily understood simple technology or straightforward magic. Where the *R-101* and the *Hindenburg* disasters brought the real age of airship travel to a fiery, untimely end in the 1930s, the Steampunk equivalents sail forever onward to the extent that they were in danger of becoming one of the first clichés of the subgenre, alongside the ubiquitous brass goggles. The airship, in fact, may be Steampunk's signature vehicle.

In *Anti-Ice*, Baxter takes over the challenge of Victorian space travel from Verne and Wells. In his description of the capsule that will journey to the moon, Baxter tips a knowing wink to his reader:

> There were chronometers, nanometers, Eigel Centigrade thermometers. There was a bank of compasses set in a three-dimensional array, so that their faces lay at all angles to each other. Traveller sighed over this arrangement.
>
> "I had hoped to use the direction of magnetic flux to navigate through space," he said, "but I am disappointed to find that the effect fades away more than a few tens of miles from the surface of the Earth."
>
> "Damned inconvenient!" Holden called drily.
>
> "Instead you rely on a sextant," I said, indicating a large, intricate brass device consisting of a tube mounted on a toothed wheel. "Surely," I went on, "the

64

Bob Shaw (1931-1996)

Prolific Northern Irish-born author Bob Shaw had a largely unsung influence on the development of Steampunk, pioneering the secondary world and space opera forms of the subgenre in his Land and Overland trilogy of the late 1980s. Plagued by migraines and having almost lost his sight due to illness, much of Shaw's speculative fiction dealt with matters of vision and perception. He claimed to 'write science fiction for people who don't read a great deal of science fiction' and was the author of over thirty novels.

Carthaginians themselves would have recognized such a device ... but could never have imagined it in such a setting."

"Carthaginians in space," Traveller mused. "Now there is an idea for a romance ... But, of course, one could never make such a tale plausible enough to convince the public."

An unsung pioneer of Steampunk space opera was Bob Shaw, a prolific British author in the 1970s and 1980s (best known for his Orbitsville trilogy, 1975–90), often overlooked today. His neo-Steampunk Land and Overland trilogy (1986–89), beginning with *The Ragged Astronauts* (1986), is perhaps as instrumental in establishing Steampunk's modern literary origins as the work of the California trio of Jeter, Blaylock and Powers, if less recognized.

Shaw describes two worlds close enough to one another to share a common atmosphere. Travel between the planets of 'Land' and 'Overland' is perfectly possible but via hot air balloon, instead of space capsule. In *The Ragged Astronauts*, Shaw follows the evacuation of much of the population from Land to Overland, escaping a repressive feudal society and an energy crisis caused by deforestation. The sequel, *The Wooden Spaceships* (1988), sees a conflict erupt between those newly arrived on Overland and those who remain behind on Land. A network of 'fortresses' is constructed between the two worlds, made of super-hard wood called brakka. The final volume, *The Fugitive Worlds* (1989), sees this double planetary system confronted by a strange artefact from space. Writer and critic Orson Scott Card regarded *The Ragged Astronauts* as what 'an eighteenth century hard-SF novel might have been, if Swift or Defoe had paid more attention to Newton'.

Although not set on Earth, Shaw's work features a method of space travel that is even easier than Verne's cannon launch and uses ornate giant balloons (almost airships). His 'ragged astronauts' who make the trip include Victorian-style scientists and liberated women not happy with their place in an ossified society. According to Steampunk creator Jake Von Slatt, *The Ragged Astronauts* 'is almost not fantasy, the science is so good. It's "new Steampunk"'. Shaw's work is Steampunk transposed, and it opened the door to the genre exploring side-step fantasy worlds within wider evolving generic conventions.

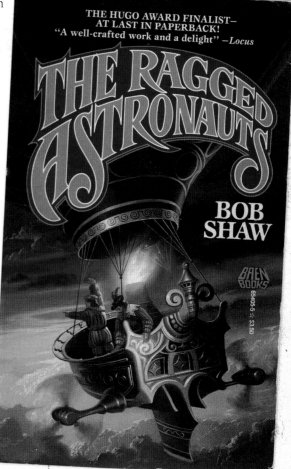

65

Unreal empires

Since its earliest beginnings, one of the main preoccupations of science fiction has been the creation of secondary worlds. Whereas traditional literary Steampunk involved the recreation of a fantasy version of Victorian London, the increasing prevalence of secondary-world Steampunk has allowed for the application of an evolving aesthetic to fully-imagined fantasy worlds unconnected to the real one (as Shaw had pioneered). It was a literary development that would bring Steampunk into the twenty-first century.

Prime among this growing group of Steampunk novels is China Miéville's *Perdido Street Station* (2000), a work that marked out new territory for the genre in the new millennium. Set in the over-industrialized city of New Crobuzon – modelled after the 'dark cities' of *Blade Runner* (1982) and *The City of Lost Children* (1995) crossed with the nightmarish visualizations of Victorian London by Gustav Doré – *Perdido Street Station* attempts to out-Dickens Dickens in a science fiction milieu. Miéville mixes magic and Steampunk 'science' in the same way as Jeter, Blaylock and Powers, but he makes his own unique mark on the subgenre.

Miéville has described the book's setting as 'basically a secondary-world fantasy with Victorian era technology. So rather than being a feudal world, it's an early industrial capitalist world of a fairly grubby, police state kind'. There is perhaps no more obvious setting for a Steampunk fantasy than a giant railway station (from which the novel takes its title), except perhaps a huge airship. Miéville is engaged in the task of world-building in a way that previous Steampunk authors were not. The Victoriana adopted by the founding trio of Jeter, Blaylock and Powers (and their forebears such as Moorcock, Laumer and Harrison) was founded on some kind of basic reality, although altered in significant ways. *Perdido Street Station* certainly draws on real-world parallels, but it imagines an environment, a cast of characters and a society that has as much in common with the Middle Earth fantasies of Tolkien as it does with those original Steampunk works.

As well as Dickens, Miéville invokes that other prominent Victorian, Darwin, in his creation of a cast of creatures unknown on this Earth. Steampunk had previously entertained the idea of mythical mermen or the denizens of a Hollow Earth, but until then few titles had introduced fantasy characters and creatures, and certainly not in the number and diversity that Miéville did. The scientist at the centre of *Perdido Street Station* is Isaac der Grimnebulin, a man concerned with the investigation of 'crisis energy'. He is hired to restore the removed wings of Yagharek, a garuda – a humanoid bird-like being – punished by his tribe. This work causes him to investigate the biology of the inhabitants of New Crobuzon, leading to devastating consequences, both personal and for the city. There's something of the horror fantasy of Clive Barker (particularly *Imajica*, 1991) in Miéville's work, and the novel essentially becomes a 'bug hunt' of the *Aliens* (1986) variety.

From Dickens, Miéville draws eccentricity of character, and he spends time giving his characters (both humans and 'creatures') a depth that escaped most of his Steampunk predecessors, who were largely happy with comic book caricatures in their mad scientists and antagonists. Partly this is due to the fact that *Perdido Street Station* is a more serious work of world-building fantasy. Indeed, the downbeat ending and the overall grimness of the world Miéville created (the story's 'hero' is partially named 'Grim') echo the industrial squalor of Gibson and Sterling's *The Difference Engine* from a decade before, transposed to a overtly fantasy world.

Engaging with social issues and offering various political critiques through setting and character, *Perdido Street Station* echoes the engagement of Steampunk with political questions arising from the Victoriana era (of Empire, class, social justice and living conditions). Although as an author Miéville is associated more with the 'new weird' literary movement than with Steampunk, his adoption of the aesthetic in *Perdido Street Station* marks this work as a transformative one for the subgenre. The city of New Crobuzon is as much a character as anyone in the novel and echoes Victorian London in all its splendour and squalor. Technology – both magical and steam-driven – features heavily, including transportation by rail and airship, and animal-machine hybrids (a form of cyborg) abound.

The politics of Victorian Britain are effortlessly transposed to this new world, including strike action by exploited workers, military-style police actions against

Left: The sprawling, retro-futuristic city of New Crobuzon – arguably the central character in China Miéville's novel *Perdido Street Station*.

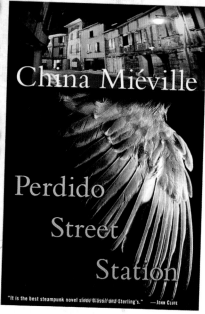

China Miéville (b.1972)

Hailed as a proponent of the 'new weird' movement in fantasy fiction, Miéville has touched on Steampunk concepts beyond his central work of *Perdido Street Station*. *The Scar* (2002) is set in the same universe and features a floating city called Armada made up of thousands of ships. *Iron Council* (2004) is again set in the Bas-Lag universe, against a background of war and the expansion of a steam-driven railway (with some of the book verging on the Weird West). Miéville's Young Adult fantasy novel *Un Lun Dun* (2007) explores an alternative London in a similar way to Neil Gaiman's *Neverwhere* (1996). Miéville is notable for using the Steampunk aesthetic in the service of his own unique brand of speculative fiction.

the oppressed, censorship of speech, electoral fraud and a class that rules in its self-interest. What *Perdido Street Station* offered overall was a new model for Steampunk, one that moved the aesthetic not only off-world, but took with it the social and political concerns writers like Moorcock had previously engaged with. Miéville forced an evolution of Steampunk, the likes of which Darwin might have been proud.

Among those most prominent in picking up the fantasy worlds Steampunk baton from Miéville were Stephen Hunt and George Mann. Hunt's Jackelian series of novels – starting with *The Court of the Air* (2007) – was pitched to publishers as 'Charles Dickens meets *Blade Runner*'. The Kingdom of the Jackals is essentially Victorian Britain in disguise, with steam power replacing oil as the energy driving the economy, and magic widely practised alongside technology. A neighbouring country named Quatérshift is modelled after the Paris Commune of 1871.

Hunt had form in the field of pseudo-Steampunk. His previous novel, *For the Crown and the Dragon* (1994), was set in an alternative Napoleonic period, where European-wide wars were fought via airships, clockwork machine guns and steam-driven tanks. However, that novel had been classed as 'flintlock fantasy'.

Unusually for Steampunk, *The Court of the Air* features a juvenile lead character. Waif Molly Templar witnesses a murder, but comes to realize she had been the real target. With the help of a 'steam man' (Steampunk's robot analogy), she flees her home pursued by enemies of the state. The second major character is also an orphan: Oliver

Brooks lost his parents in an aerostat (airships, essentially) crash, before falling in with otherworldly benefactors. Like Molly, he too is on the run from unseen forces out to kill him.

Hunt's novel starts out like yet another pastiche of Dickens, but becomes ever more outlandish. Secondary world Steampunk allowed authors to go beyond the researched details of Victorian London that had helped Jeter, Blaylock and Powers establish their altered visions of the past. Above and below Hunt's fantasy of Dickensian London there are floating cities and underground civilizations, but he still finds space to fit in riffs on Verne and even Lovecraft's Cthulu mythos (an often overlooked Steampunk precursor). Miéville scores over Hunt in attention to characterization – Molly and Oliver are fairly undeveloped protagonists – but for Hunt, it seems, plot is all.

Each of the subsequent novels in the series explored a slightly different genre within the same Steampunk setting. Hunt described *The Court of the Air* as a 'quest novel', while the follow-up, *The Kingdom Beyond the Waves* (2008), was an 'adventure novel' that drew more on Verne (not least in having a character named Robur) and Burroughs (the lost world of Camlantis has shades of Pellucidar) than Dickens. The third novel, *The Rise of the Iron Moon* (2009), was an 'invasion tale' that saw the Kingdom of the Jackals under attack by the Army of the Shadows, and the return of Molly Templar and Oliver Brooks. The remaining three novels in the series were pitched as a 'murder mystery' (*Secrets of the Fire Sea*, 2010), a 'war story' (*Jack Cloudie*, 2011), and a 'spy novel' (*From the Deep of the Dark*, 2012).

What Hunt achieved with the Jackelian series was a form of genre mash-up, combining the Steampunk aesthetic with other – often pulp – literary forms. Going beyond Miéville's secondary world creation in infusing a Tolkienesque setting with Steampunk attributes, Hunt further uncoupled Steampunk from its founding shapes, showing how as a form it could be more malleable than some restrictive definitions suggest. In doing so, he contributed to the increasing separation of the idea of Steampunk from a singular literary form, allowing for others to move the concept further away from the written word altogether.

George Mann took Steampunk in yet another new direction with his series of novels concerning The Ghost, a superhero character located in a Steampunk-style version of 1920s New York. Mann had previously deployed 'traditional' Steampunk in his rather basic Newbury & Hobbes series, comprising *The Affinity Bridge* (2008), *The Osiris Ritual* (2009), and *The Immortality Engine* (2010). These books had the Victorian London setting, the cameo by Queen Victoria (her life extended by a steam-driven life-support system), airships and clockwork automata. They followed the adventures of Sir Maurice Newbury, an agent of the Queen, and his spirited sidekick, Veronica Hobbes, as they engage with supernatural enemies of the Crown. However, for many critics, these books were Steampunk by numbers.

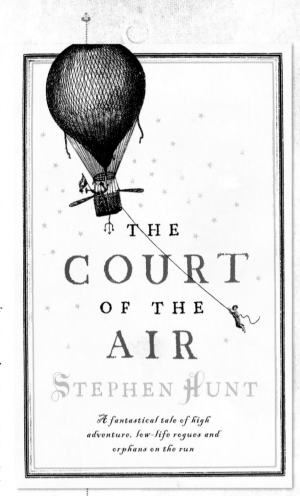

THE COURT OF THE AIR

STEPHEN HUNT

A fantastical tale of high adventure, low-life rogues and orphans on the run

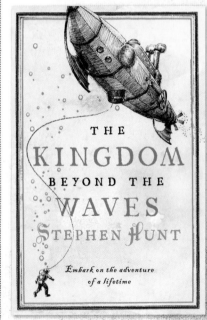

THE KINGDOM BEYOND THE WAVES

STEPHEN HUNT

Embark on the adventure of a lifetime

69

For his second series, however, Mann brought something new to the genre. In *Ghosts of Manhattan* (2010) and *Ghost of War* (2011), Mann crossed Steampunk with the superhero genre (most often explored through comic books and, increasingly, blockbuster movies). Set in the same universe as the Newbury & Hobbes series, The Ghost novels thrust the Steampunk aesthetic into the 'future' of 'the roaring Twenties'. America is in a Cold War with the British Empire (which has just lost Victoria at the artificially extended age of 107). Coal and steam power are still all the rage, but this city has a new breed of hero in a steam-powered Batman figure.

Superhero Steampunk is an interesting literary innovation in extending the generic mash-ups pioneered by Miéville and Hunt. The setting reflects the subject matter, as the American comic book superheroes emerged from the pulp magazines of the 1920s, featuring characters like Zorro and The Green Hornet (although the masked hero idea can be traced back, appropriately enough, to the late-Victorian era The Scarlet Pimpernel). The 1930s would see the emergence of The Shadow and Doc Savage, culminating in the creation of the iconic Superman in 1938. It is amid this milieu that Mann sets his superhero Steampunk.

This superhero, though, sports a series of Steampunk gadgets. Like Batman (developed in 1939, in the wake of Superman), The Ghost has no 'super powers', he's just a skilled vigilante helped by the latest crime-fighting gadgets that steam-driven technology can deliver. As well as dragging Steampunk forward to the 1920s, Mann pulls the tropes of 'film noir' back from the 1940s and applies them to his characters and cityscape. However, as if in thrall to the origins of Steampunk itself, there is more than a touch of Lovecraft in the conclusion of *Ghosts of Manhattan*.

These secondary-world writers pushed the generic reach of Steampunk beyond its fantasy/alternative Victorian London origins in surprising new directions. From Tolkien-type invented world fantasies to steam-driven superheroics, Steampunk's Victorian values were truly turned on their head, giving a whole new lease of life to a genre that until the dawn of the twenty-first century had never really caught fire in the mainstream.

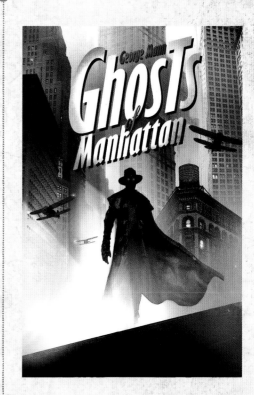

What *Perdido Street Station* and the other secondary-world works achieved was to uncouple Steampunk from London-set Victoriana and use Moorcock's toolbox in a whole new way. This separation of the style from content (location, characters, incident) would lead to the adoption of the aesthetic by film and television, further removing it from its literary origins. Eventually, those movies and TV shows would spawn an entire lifestyle subculture built around Steampunk that was incredibly far removed from its literary origins, and would redefine its meaning for a whole new generation.

4

A YOUNG LADY'S PRIMER

Examining the roles of women in Steampunk, from the fictional Victorian damsels in distress and the strong female protagonists of 'gaslamp fantasy' to the genre's innovative rule-breaking authors.

The Steampunk heroine

It has often been pointed out that science fiction features a masculine bias and an appeal to a male readership. Steampunk, though, with its emphasis on the aesthetic appeals of the Victorian age and more positive representations of women, definitely – and defiantly – breaks the rules. As author Gail Carriger says:

> I believe that is because most female heroines are what I would call 'skinned'. That is, they might be biologically women, but they are gendered male. They are following the classic hero's journey, withdrawal, isolation, return… just like any hero of ancient mythology. They aren't really women at all, they are men with boobs. Writers, like [our] culture, are trapped in a paradigm of unoriginality.

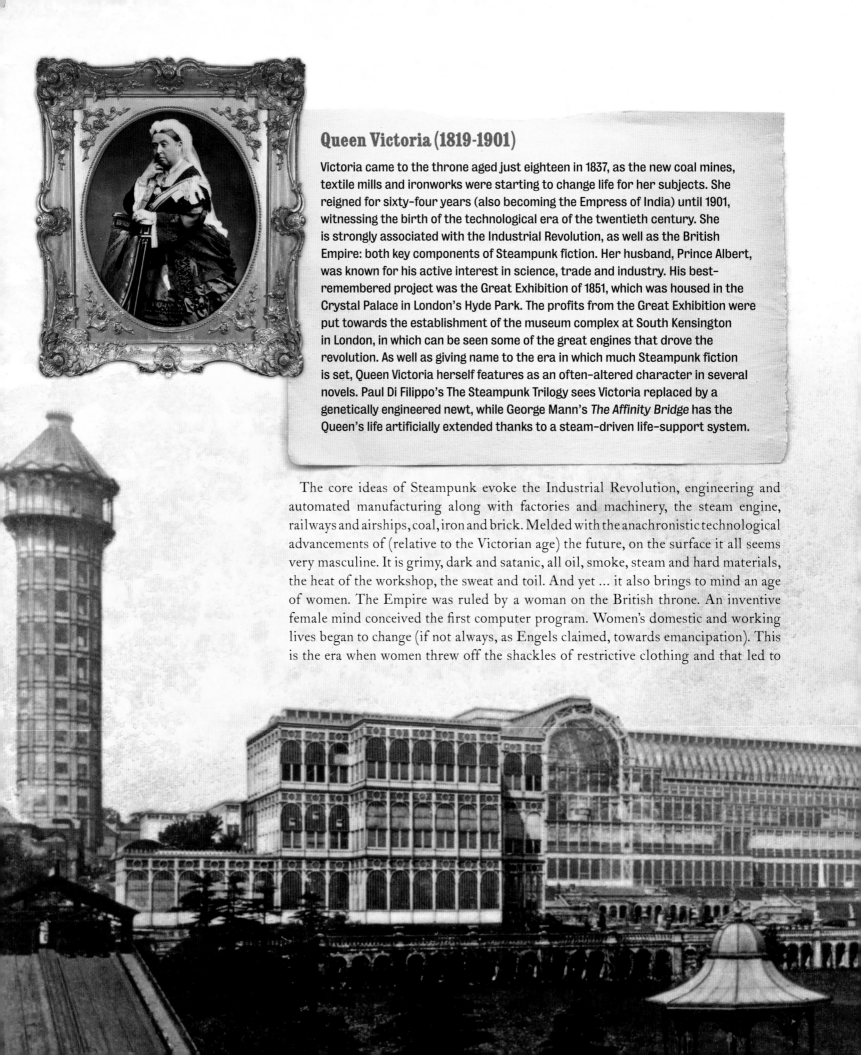

Queen Victoria (1819-1901)

Victoria came to the throne aged just eighteen in 1837, as the new coal mines, textile mills and ironworks were starting to change life for her subjects. She reigned for sixty-four years (also becoming the Empress of India) until 1901, witnessing the birth of the technological era of the twentieth century. She is strongly associated with the Industrial Revolution, as well as the British Empire: both key components of Steampunk fiction. Her husband, Prince Albert, was known for his active interest in science, trade and industry. His best-remembered project was the Great Exhibition of 1851, which was housed in the Crystal Palace in London's Hyde Park. The profits from the Great Exhibition were put towards the establishment of the museum complex at South Kensington in London, in which can be seen some of the great engines that drove the revolution. As well as giving name to the era in which much Steampunk fiction is set, Queen Victoria herself features as an often-altered character in several novels. Paul Di Filippo's The Steampunk Trilogy sees Victoria replaced by a genetically engineered newt, while George Mann's *The Affinity Bridge* has the Queen's life artificially extended thanks to a steam-driven life-support system.

The core ideas of Steampunk evoke the Industrial Revolution, engineering and automated manufacturing along with factories and machinery, the steam engine, railways and airships, coal, iron and brick. Melded with the anachronistic technological advancements of (relative to the Victorian age) the future, on the surface it all seems very masculine. It is grimy, dark and satanic, all oil, smoke, steam and hard materials, the heat of the workshop, the sweat and toil. And yet ... it also brings to mind an age of women. The Empire was ruled by a woman on the British throne. An inventive female mind conceived the first computer program. Women's domestic and working lives began to change (if not always, as Engels claimed, towards emancipation). This is the era when women threw off the shackles of restrictive clothing and that led to women's suffrage. Queen Victoria, Ada Lovelace and Amelia Bloomer could be considered heroines of the day, but more importantly they provided a template – to varying degrees – for the independent, active heroines of Steampunk fiction. It is a feature of this fiction that its characters meet (and are sometimes based on) actual historical people. *The Difference Engine* features Ada Lovelace, while Queen Victoria (albeit incidentally) appears in many novels, including Kim Newman's *Anno Dracula*, George Mann's Newbury & Hobbes series, Gail Carriger's Parasol Protectorate novels and Paul di Filippo's The Steampunk Trilogy.

Science fiction has not always been kind to women or given them very interesting roles, but Steampunk is different, and in producing a plethora of strong, active heroines it opens up the appeal and accessibility of the genre, both for readers and writers. As Suzanne Lazear, writer of Young Adult Steampunk stories, recognizes in her blog: 'When I was part of a panel on Steampunk we got some very interesting questions from the audience, one of which was 'What roles can women play in Steampunk stories, given the traditional roles of Victorian women?'

Her answer boils down to, 'In Steampunk women can do whatever they want.' Steampunk is an extremely flexible genre when it comes to the range of female characters, their professions, their interests and their active lifestyles, not to mention the clothing they wear whilst in action.

The Steampunk heroine has her roots in fantasy literature going back to the 1970s and earlier – as do the other now-familiar conventions of the genre. Women rarely, if ever, feature in the works of Jules Verne. H.G. Wells was an advocate of women's rights, and although his novels often question the roles of women and the family in his contemporary society, they do not include substantive active roles for female characters. Of course, early examples of science fiction such as *Twenty Thousand Leagues Under the Sea* and *The Time Machine* are futuristic reflections of their times and not a retro-futuristic rewriting of the past.

Below: Held in London's Hyde Park and housed in the Crystal Palace, the Great Exhibition of 1851 gathered exhibitors from around the globe to celebrate the innovations of the Industrial Revolution.

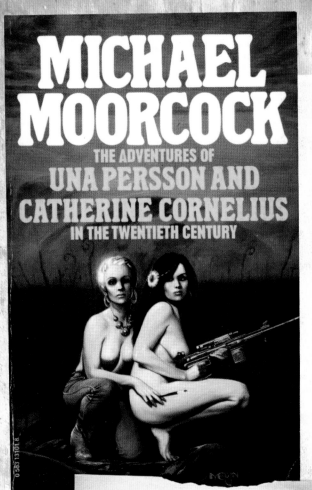

MICHAEL MOORCOCK

THE ADVENTURES OF
UNA PERSSON AND
CATHERINE CORNELIUS
IN THE TWENTIETH CENTURY

Una Persson

One of many characters reproduced across Michael Moorcock's multiverse, Persson is the lover of both Jerry and Catherine Cornelius in the Jerry Cornelius novels and features most prominently in *The Adventures of Una Persson and Catherine Cornelius in the Twentieth Century: A Romance* (1976). As a member of the Guild of Temporal Adventurers she pops up in *The Dancers at the End of Time* (1981) and *The Metatemporal Detective* (2007). Her mystery is deepened by being 'Mrs' Persson, a trait shared by *The Avengers'* Mrs Peel, who similarly has no husband on hand.

Perhaps the female Steampunk archetype is best represented by Una Persson, a female incarnation of the Eternal Hero (in particular of Jerry Cornelius) from Michael Moorcock's multiverse. Featuring in many of Moorcock's works, it is her appearance in The Nomads of the Time Stream series that is most significant.

The world of Oswald Bastable in *The Warlord of the Air* is an Edwardian one, but in the spirit of alternative history Steampunk posits a culture and a technology extrapolated from the steam age into the twentieth century, one defined by airship fleets and Empire. It is a little different from the archetypal later Steampunk, in which the historical era is redefined by anachronistic technology. Moorcock depicts the contemporary world of 1973 extrapolated from Victorian-Edwardian characteristics and mores, making it easier to depict emancipated women. Una Persson is a temporal adventuress, and in Nomads is described as a 'famous chrononaut'. In *The Warlord of the Air* Una is the main female character, an anarchist – although the warlord General Shaw calls her a physicist. Her appearances in the trilogy depict her as beautiful and mysterious, and though she seems an incidental character, she is much more. She acts as a guide to the hero Bastable, and also to some extent in the later novels to 'Moorcock', the character who is the author's great-grandfather. As a guide to the characters, Una is a key to the fiction itself. Her appearance, behaviour and attitude are all telling in respect of the prototypical Steampunk heroine. She is fleeing Britain with Count Von Bek, implicated in an anarchist attack on a leading political figure. She is described as 'a pretty girl' with 'short, dark hair' framing 'her heart-shaped little face', but wearing a serious expression and 'with steady grey eyes'. She is also quite blatantly sexual (described as a 'lady friend' of Von Bek's), yet about as far from a typical love interest as it is possible to get. Bastable is scandalized that she shares a cabin on the airship with a man to whom she is not married, and wonders where Mr. Persson is.

What most marks out this type of female character is her camaraderie with men. Una fights as a political radical and a revolutionary alongside men like Von Bek. Moorcock's Nomads novels are prototypical Steampunk and can certainly be included in the

Adèle Blanc-Sec

Created by graphic novelist Jacques Tardi, Adèle Blanc–Sec is a writer of fiction and journalism who battles monsters such as mummies and demons in what might be described as a supernatural *belle époque*. A total of ten individual *bandes dessinées* have been released in French, with several translated into English, inspiring the 2010 movie directed by Luc Besson. Although the books explore a gaslamp fantasy version of the early twentieth century, it is not strictly a Steampunk prototype in the same way as Moorcock's fiction, but Adèle's attitudes and behaviour make her a Steampunk heroine.

'Industrial Age Victoriana' alternative histories that K.W. Jeter was to label Steampunk, but more importantly Una is a template for later active Steampunk heroines. Certainly, active and complex female characters have increased in importance within the genre.

Like Una Persson, Jacques Tardi's Adèle Blanc-Sec is a prototypical Steampunk heroine in the graphic novel *The Extraordinary Adventures of Adèle Blanc-Sec* (1976). She is a writer, an investigator and an explorer. Although not involved in scientific or technological pursuits, she can certainly be described as an adventuress. She blurs the gender conventions, smoking furiously as she 'tac tac tacs' away on her typewriter. She drinks, smokes and shoots like a man, and is unashamed of it. With her tomb-raiding exploits in Luc Besson's 2010 film version of Tardi's graphic novels, her role is nothing less than a *belle époque* version of Lara Croft. Adèle is no conventional beauty: she is freckled, and frequently surly-looking. She is always practically dressed in warm coats and scarves, and ready for action. She fends off pterodactyls and lives with a mummy: an Ancient Egyptian mummy, not her mother. It may be a cliché, but the word feisty could have been invented for her. She is clearly the godmother of *Girl Genius*.

Clothed for action

Although Amelia Bloomer has little to do with Steampunk, many of the fiction's heroines could surely appreciate her reasons for creating the eponymous Bloomers. They allow the freedom of movement that traditional Victorian-era attire did not. Agatha Heterodyne, protagonist of the comic *Girl Genius* (print 2001–05, online 2005–08), appreciates the comforts of trousers and dungarees when going about her work and adventures. She is often depicted sporting tough leather gauntlets or wielding a huge spanner. Her skills lie with mechanical

PORTRAIT OF Mrs AMELIA BLOOMER FROM A DAGUERREOTYPE BY FFRENCH.

EMINENT VICTORIANS
2ND SERIES OF 50 SUBJECTS
AMELIA BLOOMER
ALBUMS FOR THESE PICTURE CARDS CAN BE OBTAINED
AT 1/- EACH THROUGH ALL TOBACCONISTS.
10

78

Amelia Bloomer (1818-1894)

Like Victoria and Lovelace, Amelia Bloomer was born in the early years of the nineteenth century, though her background was quite different. From New York, she began writing on women's rights for her husband's newspaper in her twenties. She was a staunch advocate of female emancipation and prohibition (the two causes were strongly linked) and published her own newspaper entirely devoted to women's issues. One of her concerns was the restriction of women's fashions and she argued for women's dress reform, giving her name to 'bloomers', loose-fitting, full-length pants gathered at the ankles, with a short skirt over the top. Such garments afforded women freedom of movement, leading to activities that could not have previously been enjoyed.

Girl Genius (2001-08)

Girl Genius is a webcomic, also available in printed comic book format and other spin-off media such as a novel and short stories, by Phil and Kaja Foglio. The comic relates the adventures of Agatha Heterodyne. An alternative history, the Foglios prefer to call it 'gaslight fantasy' rather than Steampunk, though it shares aesthetic qualities and narrative conventions with the latter. It envisages a world in which the Industrial Revolution has led to war between 'Sparks', archetypal mad scientists with superpowers.

and electrical devices. She is often elbow-deep in engineering projects, not to mention trouble, so practical clothing is a must. Similarly, Rebecca Fogg in the television series *The Adventures of Jules Verne* (see Chapter 5) literally discards her encumbering skirts when she needs to leap into action during her exploits as a secret agent for the British crown. With a snap of a button she leaves her amazing pop-off skirt behind to emerge dressed in leggings, boots and corset, like some Steampunk version of British 1960s spy-fi TV series *The Avengers'* Mrs Peel. In Gail Carriger's Parasol Protectorate books, Genevieve Lefoux gets around the issue by dressing (rather scandalously) in men's suits. Not all Steampunk heroines adopt dress reform practices, though. The Girl Genius usually wears a plain and practical-looking skirt paired with a waistcoat. Like Agatha, Katie MacAlister's airship captain in *Steamed* (2010) sports short skirts – relatively speaking – just barely skimming the ankle for ease of movement.

Agatha Heterodyne is no skinny waif. It is refreshing, if not downright unusual, to see a comic book heroine with sturdy curves, and she is typically posed to emphasize the fact. Even more importantly, she looks intelligent and capable with her spectacles and sensible clothes. With her goggles, spanner and sometimes a big gun, she is equipped for work as well as adventure. Agatha is no Victorian dilettante playing at science and technology for pleasure... not that she doesn't have fun, of course. And these Steampunk heroines are certainly renowned for that.

Ada Lovelace (1815-1852)

Ada Lovelace was the daughter of poet Lord Byron, but in Steampunk is most associated with the Analytical Engine. Regarded as the founder of scientific computing, she described herself as 'an Analyst (& Metaphysician)'. Her mother had her tutored in mathematics and music, and the logical nature of these disciplines enabled her visionary thinking. She designed a flying machine in her early teens and began an acquaintanceship with Charles Babbage when she was just seventeen. Babbage was the inventor of the Difference Engine and later the Analytical Engine, both elaborate calculating machines. Ada recognized the possibility of the Analytical Engine for 'developping [sic] and tabulating any function whatever'. She anticipated future developments in computer technology, including computer-generated music. Like many women of her era, her contributions to science have often been overlooked, but she deserves her status as Babbage's 'Enchantress of Numbers'.

Top of the class

Steampunk's heroines are often at odds with the realities of the historical Victorian period. Women's lives were restrictive, as were Victorian social mores generally. But the Steampunk genre has not turned away from confronting these tensions and many novels offer an exploration of women's place in society and how they might escape it. Class is a contentious issue in Steampunk. The nature of the technologies and industry on which it is based requires labour and toil. Yet the attractiveness of the aesthetic is in no small part based on the affluent elite, who can afford to sail the skies in dirigibles and wield control over technology and information alike.

The version of Ada Lovelace in William Gibson and Bruce Sterling's *The Difference Engine*, in keeping with the historical person, is a 'great savant' as well as an inveterate gambler, but also the daughter of the foremost politician in the land (with Lord Byron being Prime Minister). She is described as the 'bride of science', the Enchantress of Numbers and the Queen of Engines, but she is flawed, having 'no more common sense than a housefly'. The ruling classes in Gibson and Sterling's seminal alt-history are marred by pride. Ada 'wants to upset the universe and play at dice with the hemispheres'. Here, it is the Luddites who are the political opposition, advocating the rights of the workers.

The female characters of Steampunk are often women who have fallen on hard times, having descended through no fault of their own to the lower classes, or become ensnared in the underbelly of life as they go adventuring. *The Difference Engine*'s Sybil Gerard is a complex character who reflects the contentious issue of class. She is a 'ruined woman' fallen on hard times, but by background she is the educated daughter of a politician, albeit an executed Luddite. Sybil is living hand to mouth, her father having rebelled against a system that allowed society to be controlled by the Difference Engine. This is a dystopic view of the English class system, a world where 'they can rob a hero's daughter of her virtue', but they can't ever take what she knows.

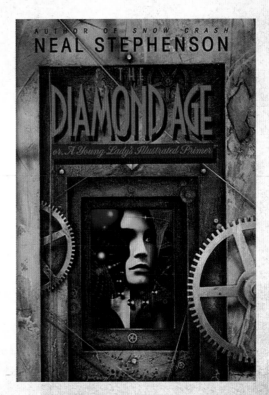

Similarly in *Boneshaker* (2009), Cherie Priest creates an emotionally complex heroine with a past in which family ruin figures prominently: she is both daughter and wife of disgraced men. This seems to have become a running theme in the feminine form of the genre, generally serving to obscure issues surrounding class difference and bringing gender to the fore. *Boneshaker*'s Briar Wilkes is a single mother, struggling financially and working in a job involving manual labour. Briar is a prime example of Steampunk heroines who have to fall back on their own resources. These are not updated fairy stories where the heroine finds her prince and lives happily ever after. Briar's reason for venturing into the zombie-ridden ruins of an alternative Seattle is to rescue her wayward teenage son and rebuild her relationship with him.

81

Knowledge is power

Knowledge is key, too, in *The Diamond Age: Or, A Young Lady's Illustrated Primer* (2000) in which Neal Stephenson turns alternative history on its head and posits a future world where society models itself on the Victorian era. The Young Lady's Primer, designed for the granddaughter of an aristocratic equity lord with the intent not only of educating her but allowing her to develop an inquiring mind, instead falls into the hand of a lower-class girl. A third copy is given to the daughter of its developer, allowing Stephenson to explore the differences between the classes. It is the lower-class Nell who learns the most from the Primer and she rises in life, becoming something of an action heroine and leader of the Mouse Army of young female orphans. The upper-class Elizabeth rebels against the neo-Victorian mores and joins the secretive CryptNet, while the middle-class Fiona abandons her mother to run off with her disgraced father, only to leave him to join a subversive theatre company.

The Glass Books of the Dream Eaters (2008) by G.W. Dahlquist follows a similar pattern of a heroine who breaches convention. Although not the sole focus of the novel – it shifts narrative point of view between the three main characters, two of them male – Celeste Temple is in many ways the prime motivator of the story and the dominant member of the trio. Although she needs help from men, they frequently act on her behalf and in her service.

Writing Steampunk's women

Independent women and themes of emancipation are a key to female-driven Steampunk fiction. What is most promising about the latest wave of this fiction, influenced by the subculture and 'fan productions' such as *Girl Genius*, is the rise of the female author. Gail Carriger, Cherie Priest, Ekaterina Sedia and others are at the forefront of the current wave of female-driven Steampunk.

In Ekaterina Sedia's *The Alchemy of Stone* (2008), Mattie – a female-identified automaton – lives independently, learning a craft as an alchemist, and asserting her personality and her ability to fall in love. Sedia explores gender politics alongside the more obvious questions of artificial intelligence. In an extremely patriarchal society, women were often regarded only as the property of men, first their fathers and then their husbands. Mattie may have been given her emancipation by her maker Loharri – jealous father figure and figuratively abusive husband rolled into one – but she is still beholden to him, since he will not give up possession of the key that winds her clockwork heart. This allegory of women's rights is thus bittersweet – the end of the novel sees Mattie wind down, with scant hope of reawakening.

Gail Carriger's work goes further. Alexia Tarabotti, focus of the Parasol Protectorate novels – *Soulless* (2009), *Changeless* (2010), *Blameless* (2010), *Heartless* (2011) and *Timeless* (2012) – is a direct descendant of Adèle Blanc-Sec. What is most refreshing about her is her unstereotypical appearance and person-ality that match her typically feisty and hands-

on Steam-punk heroine role. Alexia has swarthy Mediterranean looks and is not conventionally beautiful, but what really marks her out is that she has no soul – a quality that makes her immune to the supernatural powers of vampires and werewolves. She is unique, even amongst the paranormals that populate Carriger's Victorian London. In a telling pastiche of historical romance fiction, Alexia is introduced as an unconventional spinster, despised by her mother and vain half-sisters. When we meet her she is killing a vampire – an unfortunate act, since paranormal creatures are an accepted part of society. Investigated by the Bureau of Unnatural Registry, she is thrown into adventure and romance with alpha werewolf Lord Maccon.

Perhaps even more significantly than these amusing plays with the conventions of the adventure-romance, Carriger's novels offer an engagement with feminine culture and gender solidarity. The author has spoken about deliberately setting out to subvert the notion of Joseph Campbell's masculine mono-mythic hero with a thousand faces, replacing it with what she refers to as the Demeter Myth, after the Greek goddess of fertility. Carriger develops her narrative through and alongside the characters, building and maintaining friendships and familial relationships. These women do not complete heroic tasks alone, but network and rely on each other. Carriger feels that it is 'a problem that we often view this type of behaviour as weak. We are obsessed with the idea that in order to succeed a hero/heroine must be strong and independent and act alone. Alexia's greatest strength is in her friends and her relationships, and I always try to ensure that my stories highlight this.'

Alexia has a number of confederates along the way who are certainly no shrinking violets, and are perhaps even stronger female archetypes than Alexia herself. Most notable is Genevieve Lefoux, an accomplished inventor who dresses like a man, her wardrobe even including a top hat and – on occasion – a fake moustache. As Carriger writes on her livejournal page, 'Genevieve Lefoux … is, in essence, Alexia's Q [from the James Bond series]. But as I wrote her she turned into much, much more. Her hidden chamber beneath the hat shop is possibly the most Steampunk element in any of my books.'

Gail Carriger (b.1976)

Gail Carriger is the nom de plume of an academic from California who has constructed a complete alter ego for her fiction. This is in keeping with Steampunk as a subculture invested in role-play, and Carriger herself is a Steampunk heroine. In her publicity, online profile and convention appearances she exudes the typical personality beloved of Steampunks, right down to tea-drinking and other eccentricities. Further, her work has strong female themes including strong-willed women with streaks of intense practicality. There is a focus on alternative lifestyles and breaking the boundaries of social decorum. Her female characters develop strong friendships and strong attachments, whether romantic or otherwise.

Certainly, this chamber puts the Steampunk into the Parasol Protectorate. The conjunction of inventor's workshop below and hat shop above culminates in Genevieve's tool kit, stowed inside – what else – a hat box. Always one to use her parasol as a weapon – when we are first introduced to Alexia, she fights off that vampire with one – the umbrella that Genevieve designs for her contains many weapons and devices (like the hidden gadgets in the TV series and film *Wild Wild West*). As noted in *Blameless*, this parasol:

> ...had been designed at prodigious expense, with considerable imagination and much attention to detail. It could emit a dart equipped with a numbing agent, a wooden spike for vampires, a silver spike for werewolves, a magnetic disruption field, and two kinds of toxic mist, and, of course, it possessed a plethora of hidden pockets. It was not a very prepossessing accessory, for all its serviceability, being

both outlandish in design and indifferent in shape. It was a drab slate-gray with cream ruffle trim, and it had a shaft in the new ancient Egyptian style that looked rather like an elongated pineapple.

It is not simply her equipment that makes this Steampunk heroine such a formidable character. It is her attitude (the 'punk' in Steampunk), much more than the technology and achievements of engineering, that are significant in *Blameless*:

> Despite its many advanced attributes, Lady Maccon's most common application of the parasol was through brute force enacted directly upon the cranium of an opponent. It was a crude and perhaps undignified modus operandi, but it had worked so well for her in the past that she was loath to rely too heavily upon any of the newfangled aspects of her parasol's character.

Steampunk heroines are always resourceful, but that does not mean they cannot be as aggressive or as physical as their male counterparts. They frequently exhibit similar attitudes in their sexual relationships, but more importantly they develop strong friendships with men and other women alike. The Victorian woman may have been the possession of a superior male, be it her husband or her father, and located firmly in domesticity, but Steampunk women like Alexia, Briar, Nell, Mattie, Celeste, Adèle and Una prove that fictional female characters can be anything but.

85

5

NITRATE NIGHTMARES AND SELENIUM DREAMS

Exploring the amazing visions of Steampunk in movies and the expanded Steampunk worlds of television.

Flickering Victorian fantasies

From the earliest days of film there has been something magical about images on celluloid, as if humanity's dreams could be projected onto giant screens. Few captured this dream-like state as well as French filmmaker Georges Méliès, many of whose early silent shorts adapted ideas from Jules Verne, depicting fantastic vehicles that took explorers to the frozen moon and the icy South Pole.

Drawing on his knowledge of the machinery used in his family's shoe-making business, Méliès had pursued a career in magic and was also a builder of automata.

His inventive films influenced other filmmakers in their techniques. He brought his magical view of the world to film, seeing the then-new medium as a way of not simply capturing reality but a way to alter reality itself.

A Trip to the Moon (1902) – his best-known film – came right at the start of the Edwardian era. Loosely based on Verne, with elements of H.G. Wells's *From the Earth to the Moon*, the film has Méliès himself lead six Victorian adventurers on a trip to the moon (launching from a giant cannon, Verne-style). Attacked by 'moon men' (the Selenites, Folies Bergère acrobats representing the traditional 'natives' encountered by Victorian empire builders), the explorers escape in their rocket. The short formed the aesthetic basis for the Smashing Pumpkins' Steampunk-infused 1996 music video 'Tonight, Tonight'.

A sequel followed, with 1904's *The Impossible Voyage* (again loosely based on Verne), in which Méliès played Engineer Mabouloff of the splendidly named Institute of Incoherent Geography. This epic features a variety of Steampunk vehicles, including a super submarine, an impossible automobile, and a railway car filled with ice. A train is launched into space attached to balloons, landing on the sun where the 'ice box' protects the travellers from the heat until they can escape in their solar 'submarine'. The boiler overheats and the sub explodes, depositing the seemingly indestructible travellers back on Earth. This whimsical concoction is a celebration of the Victorian ingenuity for creating new modes of transport. Pioneering film critic Lewis Jacobs hailed the film as packed with 'mechanical contrivances, imaginative settings and sumptuous tableaux'.

Perhaps Méliès greatest Verne-inspired movie was *The Conquest of the South Pole* (1912). Although drawing on real-life explorations, the movie was also influenced by Verne's *The Adventures of Captain Hatteras* (1864) and completed a loose 'extraordinary voyages' trilogy. Rival groups of

Méliès's automata

An automaton is a self-operating machine, an early robot. From earliest times, men built machines in their own image, especially during the Renaissance when chess-playing and musical automata were widespread (some were fakes, operated by concealed people, such as the Turk from 1769). Many of Méliès's automata were sophisticated puppets used in his theatre performances. When Méliès bought the old Robert-Houdin theatre in Paris, he inherited several. His fascination with automata would lead to Méliès building his own movie camera, as depicted in the 2011 movie *Hugo*.

balloonists (in fact, there is a dizzying array of flying vehicles) strive to be first to reach the South Pole, only for one crew – led by Méliès as Mabouloff – to encounter a malevolent frost giant (the decaying head of which could be seen in the Cinémathèque Française's Musée du Cinema in Paris right up to the late 1980s). Méliès laid the groundwork for much of the great cinematic Steampunk that followed.

The imaginary worlds of Jules Verne were brought to the screen again in the 1950s in one of the first recognizably Steampunk movies. Karel Zeman's *The Fabulous Worlds of Jules Verne* (1958) had a unique look, inspired by Méliès. The Czech film combined woodcut-style backgrounds with live action and animation to recount Verne's 1896 novel *Facing the Flag*, although the story liberally draws on Verne's entire body of work. The original Czech title *Vynález zkázy* translates as *A Deadly Invention*, but the movie was retitled for American release in 1961. It is the missing link between the early extraordinary excursions of Méliès and the colourful Vernian romps of the 1960s.

Above: Georges Méliès's *A Trip to the Moon*. Bottom, right: His sequel, *The Impossible Voyage*. Top, right: A French poster for *The Conquest of the South Pole*. Méliès has been a key influence on much of the cinema that is now seen as Steampunk.

89

The story – which sees a professor and his assistant battle the villainous Count Artigas (combining Robur and Nemo) for control of a potentially destructive new energy source – spurs a delightful display of the new technology allowing mankind to explore on land, in the sea and in the air. There are elaborate steam ships, ironclad dreadnoughts, a 'steel juggernaut' steam train, exotic submarines, fabulous airships (taken directly from the illustrations in Verne's novels by Alphonse de Neuville and Édouard Riou), underwater bicycles, and even a steam-powered automobile. There are animated sequences of pistons, cogs and clockwork in action. 'Steam and electricity have discarded the past,' says the film's narrator, seeing steam-powered technology propelling mankind into the future.

Zeman used every cinematic technique available in the mid-1950s. While the main characters are filmed in live action, this is combined with stop-motion animation, miniature models, double-exposures and animation to depict these wonderful worlds. Impressive sequences include the sinking of the sailing ship Amelie by Artigas' submarine, a series of spectacular underwater vistas, a visit to a hellish smoke-choked factory city hidden within an extinct volcano, and a thrilling battle with a giant octopus. In the absence of the computer-controlled special effects of the 1970s or the computer-generated imagery of the 1990s, Zeman pushed the limits of cinema in bringing Verne's Steampunk visions to cinematic life.

Zeman was looking back at the nineteenth-century view of science from a mid-twentieth century perspective, at a time when the atomic age had brought both a new power source and a new threat. In *The Fabulous World of Jules Verne* he simultaneously celebrates the achievements and optimism of the Victorians, satirizing them yet offering a critique of his own period, in which scientific innovation could be turned equally to the benefit or disadvantage of mankind. Zeman created a film that was not only about the Victorian period, but appeared to have come from it.

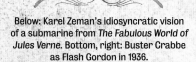

Below: Karel Zeman's idiosyncratic vision of a submarine from *The Fabulous World of Jules Verne*. Bottom, right: Buster Crabbe as Flash Gordon in 1936.

Karel Zeman (1910–1989)

Czech animator Karel Zeman filmed several Jules Verne stories. In 1955 he'd directed *Journey to the Beginning of Time* (*Cesta do praveku*), a version of *Journey to the Centre of the Earth* (released in the US in 1966 with new US-set sequences), while in 1967 he combined *Two Years' Vacation* and *Mysterious Island* in *The Stolen Airship* (*Ukradena vzducholod*), utilizing an Art Nouveau style and featuring Captain Nemo. Each of his movies adopted techniques of combined animation and live action similar to those seen in *The Fabulous World of Jules Verne*.

STEAMPUNK

Steampunk movie serials

The Phantom Empire (1935) was a weird mix of Western and SF serial, featuring a rancher who discovers an entire world of steam-driven technology beneath his feet, including a retro-futuristic robot, moving sidewalks and vacuum tube elevators.

The Undersea Kingdom (1936) drew on Verne, with Ray 'Crash' Corrigan visiting Atlantis in a 'rocket submarine'. Among the Steampunk elements are a land ironclad known as The Juggernaut, and the beautiful Art Deco-styled Volkites, a raygun-wielding robot army. There's also the villain's dirigible-style Vol Planes and the Reflector Plate, an advanced video communicator. Three *Flash Gordon* (1936–40) serials featured airship-shaped spaceships, Gothic-style ray-guns, and an underwater city. *Buck Rogers* (1939) had Buck crash a dirigible in the North Pole, only to be frozen for 500 years.

Elements of Steampunk featured in many 1930s and 1940s movie serials, such as those featuring Buck Rogers, again played by Buster Crabbe.

Steampunk vehicles

Where Méliès had delivered fantastic voyages to the stars, the filmmakers of the 1960s and 1970s followed the Steampunk serials of the 1930s to Hollow Earth, journeying underground and undersea, and then took to the air in fantastic vehicles and airships.

The James Mason-starring Disney movie *20,000 Leagues Under the Sea* (1954) is perhaps the quintessential screen version of Verne's classic. Set in 1868, Mason portrays an initially cold and distant Captain Nemo, reflecting the novel. Nemo intends to submerge the Nautilus while three stowaways (Arronax, Conseil and Ned) are still on the exterior surface. However, in true Disney, family-friendly style this Nemo becomes more heroic, even sinking his beloved submarine by the climax.

The movie is action-packed (though slow for modern audiences) featuring a shark attack, a battle with a warship and a spectacular fight between the crew of the Nautilus and a giant squid. Most memorable, however, is the design of the Nautilus. Nemo and his companions dine in front of a huge Steampunk musical organ, with the salon, dining room and library (as described by Verne) combined into one movie set. The exterior of the Disney submarine is more fish-shaped than the Neuville and Riou illustrations, with the addition of reptile-style fins emphasizing the impression of the unknown ship as a 'sea monster'.

Below and overleaf: James Mason as Captain Nemo in Disney's 1954 film adaptation of Jules Verne's novel *Twenty Thousand Leagues Under the Sea*.

The many versions of *20,000 Leagues Under the Sea*

Méliès created one of the earliest adaptations of Verne's *Twenty Thousand Leagues Under the Sea* in 1907, while a further silent version followed in 1916 (incorporating elements of *The Mysterious Island*). As special effects improved filmmakers returned to Verne, including the 1969 British *Captain Nemo and the Underwater City*. The 1980s and 1990s saw made-for-TV versions, one from Australia (1985) and two from the US (both 1997, respectively featuring Ben Cross and Michael Caine). On television there was the mid-1970s animated series *The Undersea Adventures of Captain Nemo* (1975), featuring a more child-friendly Nemo. The Japanese anime series *Nadia: The Secret of Blue Water* (1990–91) drew on the work of Hayao Miyazaki and was loosely set in worlds inspired by Verne. In 2010 director David Fincher announced a still-unmade remake for Disney, describing it as a 'gigantic Steampunk science fiction movie from 1873'.

93

Disney's Nautilus

Verne's hi-tech, luxurious submarine featured in his novels *Twenty Thousand Leagues Under the Sea* (1870) and *The Mysterious Island* (1874). The Disney version of the super-sub was described as powered by nuclear energy (a big concern of the 1950s: the US Navy's USS Nautilus SSN 571 nuclear-powered submarine launched in 1954, the same year the movie was released). Disney designer Harper Goff art-directed the movie and was responsible for the appearance of the Nautilus, both externally and internally. His design has been so influential that most subsequent versions have followed his distinctive lead. The movie won two Oscars for colour art direction and best special effects.

The movies have presented some weird and wonderful Steampunk vehicles, from inevitable airships to drilling leviathans aimed at the centre of the Earth. Combining Verne's *Robur the Conqueror* (1886) and its sequel from 1904, the otherwise dull movie *Master of the World* (1961) features a fantastic 'ship of the air', the Albatross. Vincent Price plays Verne's Robur, who believes his superior technology can force the world to peace.

Unusual flying vehicles were something of a theme in 1960s cinema, with both *Those Magnificent Men in Their Flying Machines* (1965) and *Chitty Chitty Bang Bang* (1968) presenting unusual craft featuring Steampunk designs. *Those Magnificent Men* features a race from London to Paris. Essentially a lament for a lost period of derring-do pilots and their self-built vehicles, the film ends on the note that with jet aircraft, flying had lost some of its romance. Similar hi-jinks in late-Victorian, early-Edwardian vehicles followed, including *The Great Race* (1965) and *Monte Carlo or Bust* (1969).

Chitty Chitty Bang Bang featured a far more fanciful vehicle altogether: a flying car. Based on a children's novel by James Bond creator Ian Fleming, the film was co-written by Roald Dahl and starred Dick Van Dyke as inventor Caractacus Potts. Set in 1910, the movie features a host of Potts' wacky contraptions including

H.G.WELLS'

THE TIME MACHINE

in futuristic METROCOLOR

STARRING

ROD TAYLOR

ALAN YOUNG · YVETTE MIMIEUX

SEBASTIAN CABOT · TOM HELMORE

STEAMPUNK

a prototype vacuum cleaner, an automatic hair-cutting machine and an early television – 'inventions' designed by the cartoonist and artist Rowland Emett.

Potts rebuilt the car (named for the noises it made) from a junked Grand Prix racer, adding his own modifications. These include a fine array of brass fittings and a pair of elaborate, colourful wings that, when extended, allow the car to fly. Although much of the movie is an imaginary fantasy, it does feature Steampunk touches, including lots of brass, gears, goggles and even an airship. The real-life location of the Scrumptious Sweet Co. factory was Kempton Waterworks in Middlesex, now a steam museum.

Airships seem to have been all the rage in 1970s cinema, from Michael York's pulp wartime adventure *Zeppelin* (1971), via *The Island at the Top of the World* (1974) and disaster movie *The Hindenberg* (1975). *The Island at the Top of the World* sees four turn-of-the-century adventurers embark upon an expedition in the airship Hyperion to the North Pole, only to discover a lost colony of Vikings.

Even Hammer Films attempted to get in on the airship act, with their unmade aerial thriller *Zeppelin v Pterodactyls*. The movie – which only survives as a speculative poster – was to feature a German Zeppelin blown off course during a bombing raid on London only to end up in another 'lost continent'. These airship movies may have been related to the near ubiquity of the Goodyear advertising blimps that were touring the world at the time.

Time traveller triumphant

Verne's contemporary, H.G. Wells, made a dramatic comeback with the 1960 movie of *The Time Machine*. The title vehicle was a Steampunk concoction of brass and chrome, featuring chunky levers, a fantastic spinning disc and a rather comfortable Victorian barber's chair. This was in complete contrast to the machine as described by Wells, which was based around a distinctly less comfortable bicycle saddle.

The machine plunges the traveller (Rod Taylor) into the far future from New Year's Eve 1899, with stop-offs in 1917, 1940 and 1966 – all notable as times of war (with the 1960s in the grip of the Cold War). Eventually, the traveller arrives at the far-flung date of 802,701 where he encounters the remnants of humanity divided into the simple, peaceful Eloi and the seemingly devolved, animalistic Morlocks. The time machine prop was designed by MGM art director William Ferrari, with input from director George Pal. The basic shape was inspired by a horse-drawn sleigh that Pal recalled from youthful sleigh rides, while the barber's chair was intended to be reminiscent of an aircraft pilot's seat.

The end of the 1970s saw Wells himself as a character in Nicholas Meyer's *Time After Time* (1979). Malcolm McDowell plays Wells, who uses his time machine to pursue David Warner's Jack the Ripper from Victorian London to 1979 San Francisco. Jack finds himself in his element in this violent future, declaring, 'Ninety years ago, I was

Top, left: Dick Van Dyke as inventor Caractacus Potts in *Chitty Chitty Bang Bang*. Above: A real-life Potts, cartoonist Roland Emett's kinetic sculptures included the *Visivision Machine* (pictured) and *The Forget-Me-Not Computer*, featuring a bone and a lampshade as part of its operating system. In 1976 *Time* magazine dubbed Emett a 'Gothic-kinetic Merlin', describing his profession as that of 'Fantasticator'.

97

Above: Malcolm McDowell embodied one of Steampunk's founding fathers, H.G. Wells, in 1979's *Time After Time*.

a freak. Now ... I'm an amateur.' While the main Steampunk element is the time machine design, this movie was able to contrast the late Victorian period with modern times, showing the 'present' in the worst light. A big attraction of Steampunk is its depiction of the Victorian period as a time of technological progress, while often ignoring its social problems. As an escape from a troubling present (whether 1979 or today), Steampunk's 'retro-Victorian scientific fantasy' can give a past age an attractive gloss through temporal distance. *The Time Machine* was remade in 2002, directed by Wells's great-grandson Simon Wells, but the new design failed to capture viewers' imaginations.

Steampunk TV gets wild

In the 1960s, Steampunk found a new home on television. *The Wild Wild West* was the grandfather of modern movie and TV Steampunk, running on CBS for four seasons between 1965 and 1969. It centred on the adventures of two Secret Service agents, straightforward law enforcer James T. West (Robert Conrad), and his sidekick Artemus Gordon (Ross Martin), an inventor, gadgeteer and master of disguise, between 1871 and 1875.

The pair travelled the West laying down the law on a seemingly anachronistic train, tricked out with a luxurious interior and a variety of handy gadgets. It featured concealed pistols, a secret escape door in the fireplace and a variety of weaponry in hidden panels. There were carrier pigeons in hidden cages for emergency communication and decorative lion heads that sprayed knockout gas when activated.

West himself was also kitted out with a selection of often-deadly items, many of them created by Gordon, including a 'sleeve gun' (a concealed Remington derringer), explosive devices and a spring-loaded knife blade concealed in a boot. Episodes featured exploding billiard balls, a cue stick that fired bullets, a stagecoach with a James Bond-style ejector seat and a blowtorch disguised as a cigar.

The series showcased an array of comic book villains with elaborate plans to take over the world. The recurring villain was Dr. Miguelito Loveless (Michael Dunn), a genius megalomaniac dwarf who functioned as Moriarty to West and Gordon's Holmes. The writers admitted they often developed the gadgets first and constructed the stories around them, heavily influenced by the works of Wells and Verne. As a result, the bad guys had their own Steampunk gadgets including devices that caused earthquakes, a steam-driven cyborg (in 'The Night of the Puppeteer'), a steam-powered tank known as The Juggernaut, and a potion that allowed a human to move so fast he became invisible (after Wells's 'The New Accelerator', 1901). Other episodes featured a homing torpedo disguised as a dragon, a mechanical exo-skeleton patterned after a suit of armour, and a sonic device that converted paintings into gateways to different dimensions, as well as another train armed with a huge battering ram. One character (in 'The Night of the

Brain') occupied a steam-powered wheelchair, not due to any disability but because he believed he needed all his energy for thinking up evil schemes.

In combing two of the most popular television genres (the Western and the espionage show), the series creators were filtering the present through the prism of the past. They brought then-modern (1960s) technological concepts and ideas (especially James Bond gadgets) to the Old West, and in doing so they sowed the seeds for what would blossom over twenty years later as Steampunk.

The Wild Wild West returned to TV in the late 1970s in two reunion movies, in the wake of Jeff Wayne's H.G. Wells concept album and Jeter's *Morlock Night*. *The Wild Wild West Revisited* (1979) and *More Wild Wild West* (1980) reteamed Conrad and Martin, with Paul Williams playing Loveless Jr., the son of their arch-enemy. *The Wild Wild West Revisited* saw Loveless Jr. attempt to substitute clones for the crowned heads of Europe, while *More Wild Wild West* introduced Jonathan Winters as Albert Paradine II, planning world conquest through his formula for invisibility. Both television films arrived just when Steampunk was becoming established as a recognized literary form, although it would be another twenty years before *Wild Wild West* returned to the screen.

Above: *The Wild Wild West* brought Steampunk to American television, mixing 1960s spy-fi thrills with Western adventure.

99

Above: The Iron Mole drilling machine from *At the Earth's Core*. Right: The impassive, spear-wielding Guardians from *Warlords of Atlantis*.

1970s Steampunk pulp

Edgar Rice Burroughs's writings inspired *The Land That Time Forgot* (1975), *The People That Time Forgot* (1977) and *At the Earth's Core* (1976), produced by Amicus, who were also behind the similar *Warlords of Atlantis* (1978). These four films formed a mini-canon of underground civilization movies with distinctive Steampunk pulp trimmings. Burroughs fan and literary Steampunk instigator Michael Moorcock scripted *The Land That Time Forgot*. A captured U-Boat and a crew from a British merchant ship arrive in a lost world populated by dinosaurs and cavemen. Sequel *The People That Time Forgot* sees the launch of a rescue expedition. Doug McClure starred in the first and made a cameo appearance in the second. He was also the co-lead in *At the Earth's Core*, based around the Pellucidar stories. Peter Cushing is a Victorian scientist who drills into the Earth in his Iron Mole. They discover an underground world inhabited by flying telepathic lizards and primitive people. *Warlords of Atlantis* drew on Burroughs's themes and again starred McClure as a Victorian archaeologist searching for Atlantis. Reptilian sea monsters, a giant octopus, a huge millipede monster and flying fish all attack the adventurers. *Doctor Who* author and magic realist Paul Magrs recognized the relevance of these films: 'I want Steampunk to conjure the wonderful atmosphere of Cushing and McClure in *At the Earth's Core* – that's the world I want to vanish into.'

DOCTOR WHO AND STEAMPUNK: VICTORIAN STYLE

The long-running British fantasy adventure TV series has always had something Victorian about it. From its debut in 1963, the show was heavily influenced by the kind of Victorian science fiction that would be reworked in Steampunk. It had initially been intended as an educational adventure series influenced by H.G. Wells's *The Time Machine* and the Narnia stories of C. S. Lewis.

The Doctor's TARDIS has shown Steampunk tendencies since its very first appearance in 1963. Right: The console from the 1996 TV movie, starring Paul McGann as the eighth Doctor. Below: The latest interior of the cantankerous space-time machine.

Portrayed as cold and aloof (to begin with), the alien time-travelling Doctor often dressed in Victorian-style clothes (emphasized during his third, fifth and eighth incarnations – the Doctor can 'regenerate', renewing his body) and piloted his bigger-on-the-inside space-time vehicle the TARDIS from a central console that, if not exactly steam-powered, certainly often featured valves and pumps. There is definitely something of Captain Nemo about the Doctor and something of the Nautilus about his TARDIS.

Over the years the central console would evolve, with the fourth Doctor (Tom Baker) using a secondary console room during the show's fourteenth season (1976–77). This room was lined with warm wood and featured a smaller console (resembling a Victorian writing desk) surrounded by polished brass rails, with the controls concealed behind wooden panels, while the traditional 'roundels' on the walls featured patterned stained glass.

However, it was the 1996 TV movie (featuring Paul McGann) that introduced the first truly Steampunk console to the series. The expansive new console room was still centred round a six-sided control podium, but this one was much more Gothic in style. This console tended more heavily towards the brass-and-wood look of the earlier secondary console room, with the levers, switches and valves of the earliest 1960s version emphasized. Additionally, this TARDIS featured an expansive library area in which the Doctor is seen reading Wells's *The Time Machine*.

When the regular TV show returned in 2005, it was the McGann console room that inspired every variation thereafter, making more than a dash of Steampunk central to the series' ongoing look. Christopher Eccleston's ninth and David Tennant's tenth Doctors' console featured a variety of anachronistic elements, including an old telephone, glass paperweights, a bell, a locomotive water sight glass and a bicycle pump – each a stylized control for different functions. For example, the bicycle pump was once identified as the 'vortex loop control'.

The 2010 reinvention of the control room for Matt Smith's eleventh Doctor was perhaps the most overtly Steampunk to date, with multiple levels and an 'engine room' area beneath the console which itself was positioned on a glass floor. As before, each of the weird anachronistic contraptions had a specific function: a physical handbrake was the 'lock-down mechanism'; a spinning, spiky ball was an 'atom accelerator'; while an old computer keyboard was the 'spatial location input'. Other items included a Bunsen burner, a microphone, a water dispenser and an analogue typewriter.

Costume drama

Across the years, individual episodes of *Doctor Who* contained specific Steampunk ideas, concepts and visualizations. An early example is the Patrick Troughton-starring second Doctor adventure 'The Evil of the Daleks' (1967). This seven-episode tale sees the Doctor and companion Jamie McCrimmon (an out-of-time eighteenth-century Scottish clansman, played by Frazer Hines) arrive in

1966 London and become embroiled in the experiments of Edward Waterfield. His time machine transports them back to 1866 and an encounter with the Daleks (mutants who inhabit armoured travel machines, the deadly enemies of the Doctor). Victorian time travellers Waterfield and Theodore Maxtible have been using their alchemical machine to transport new items to the future to sell as 'antiques', while also being complicit in a Dalek plan to lure the Doctor into a trap. Waterfield's daughter Victoria is seen in traditional Victorian dress and environments, only to be confronted by the out-of-time technological monstrosity that is a Dalek. Maxtible and Waterfield's time machine has attracted the dreaded Daleks to Victorian England, as well as the Doctor and Jamie.

In 'The Talons of Weng-Chiang' (1977), the fourth Doctor and his companion Leela (Louise Jameson) arrive in Victorian London (drawing on all the benefits of BBC period design), where the Doctor adopts a Sherlock Holmes role, complete with deerstalker and cape, and investigates Chinese magician Li H'sen Chang and his anachronistic technology. While more a pastiche of Victorian generic elements (Sherlock Holmes, Jack the Ripper, Fu Manchu, *My Fair Lady*, *Pygmalion*, *Dracula*, *The Phantom of the Opera* – all later used by Alan Moore in his comic books), this was screened at a time when Victoriana was on the increase in the popular imagination with the BBC variety retro series *The Good Old Days* (1953–83) at its height, followed by Jeff Wayne's *The War of the Worlds* concept album (1978) and Jeter's *Morlock Night* (1979), sowing the seeds of Steampunk more widely. With a disfigured time-travelling villain, a killer ventriloquist's dummy, a giant rat in the sewers and a huge dragon statue with laser beam eyes, 'The Talons of Weng-Chiang' is a Chinese puzzle box that when unpacked is open to multiple readings. For example, is Mr Sin – the ventriloquist's dummy described as 'a computerized homunculus with the brain of a pig' – actually a Steampunk cyborg or automaton?

Elements of what is now recognized as Steampunk (at the very least in design, but often in concept) reoccur throughout *Doctor Who*'s history. The Doctor often lashes up a gadget or two from whatever available technology a given time period has to offer. In 1975's 'The Pyramids of Mars' (set in 1911), he helps construct a Marconiscope (a table-top radio-telescope) 'forty years early', and the serial featured 'service robots' disguised as Egyptian mummies, while 1983's 'Enlightenment' (with the fifth Doctor, Peter Davison) featured seemingly 'real' historical sailing ships that are revealed (in a memorable episode cliffhanger) to be star-traversing spaceships using solar wind propulsion.

The 1985 story 'The Mark of the Rani' (featuring sixth Doctor, Colin Baker) included George Stephenson (builder of the steam-driven Rocket) and alien-controlled Luddites, while 'Timelash' featured H.G. Wells as a character and combined plot elements from Wells's works *The Time Machine*, *The War of the Worlds*, *The Invisible Man* and *The Island of Doctor Moreau*. The final two episodes of the epic 'The Trial of a Time Lord' in 1986 saw the Doctor trapped in a virtual reality re-creation of Victorian London, including a venue called The Fantasy Factory seemingly run by an endless series of duplicates of a petty, Dickensian bureaucrat called Mr Popplewick. Items and vehicles are disguised in appropriate Victorian style, with The Valeyard (the Doctor's enemy) wielding a particle disseminator (looking like a piece of Victorian technology) and the Master (yet another of the Doctor's enemies!) disguising his TARDIS as a statue of Queen Victoria herself.

Empires in time

Aside from the Steampunk-infused TARDIS consoles, the revived series from 2005 has offered several Steampunk-related episodes. 'The Unquiet Dead' (2005) is set in Cardiff 1869 with the ethereal alien Gelth possessing human corpses, while 2006's 'Tooth and Claw', set in 1879, features Queen Victoria (Pauline Collins). Having been targeted in 'Ghost Light' (1989), this time the Queen is under threat from a race of alien lycanthropes (werewolves, or more accurately 'a lupine wavelength haemovariform') that wants to infect her and create a new 'Empire of the wolf'. The Doctor (Tennant) uses the Queen's Koh-i-Noor diamond and a strangely advanced telescope in an attic observatory to concentrate the light of the moon and so destroy the alien wolf.

Other Tennant episodes featured significant Steampunk tropes just as the genre was catching on in popularity: a parallel Earth was identified in 'The Age of Steel' (2006) due to the airships hovering over London, while 'The Girl in the Fireplace' (2006) featured a group of humanoid clockwork robots (inspired, according to writer Steven Moffat, by The

Left: The fourth Doctor, played by Tom Baker, makes use of the wood-panelled secondary console room, in 1976. Below: Mr Sin, originally known as the Peking Homunculus, from the 1977 *Doctor Who* story 'The Talons of Weng-Chiang'. Sin has all the appearances of a Steampunk automaton.

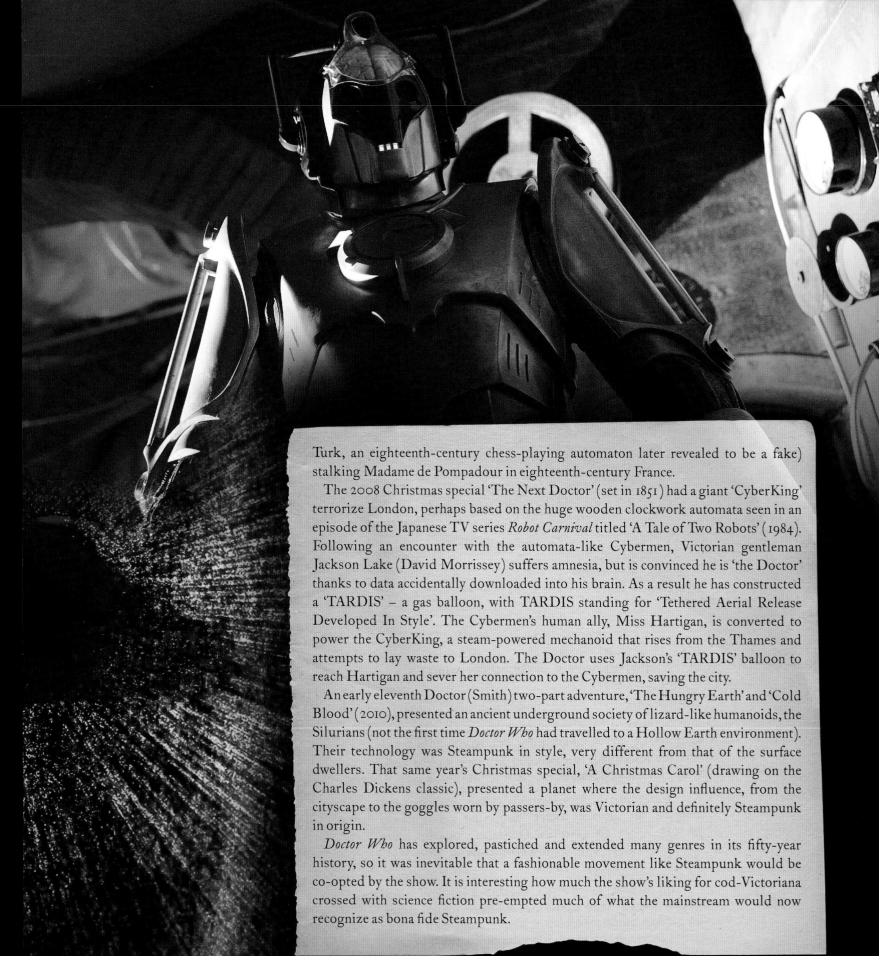

Turk, an eighteenth-century chess-playing automaton later revealed to be a fake) stalking Madame de Pompadour in eighteenth-century France.

The 2008 Christmas special 'The Next Doctor' (set in 1851) had a giant 'CyberKing' terrorize London, perhaps based on the huge wooden clockwork automata seen in an episode of the Japanese TV series *Robot Carnival* titled 'A Tale of Two Robots' (1984). Following an encounter with the automata-like Cybermen, Victorian gentleman Jackson Lake (David Morrissey) suffers amnesia, but is convinced he is 'the Doctor' thanks to data accidentally downloaded into his brain. As a result he has constructed a 'TARDIS' – a gas balloon, with TARDIS standing for 'Tethered Aerial Release Developed In Style'. The Cybermen's human ally, Miss Hartigan, is converted to power the CyberKing, a steam-powered mechanoid that rises from the Thames and attempts to lay waste to London. The Doctor uses Jackson's 'TARDIS' balloon to reach Hartigan and sever her connection to the Cybermen, saving the city.

An early eleventh Doctor (Smith) two-part adventure, 'The Hungry Earth' and 'Cold Blood' (2010), presented an ancient underground society of lizard-like humanoids, the Silurians (not the first time *Doctor Who* had travelled to a Hollow Earth environment). Their technology was Steampunk in style, very different from that of the surface dwellers. That same year's Christmas special, 'A Christmas Carol' (drawing on the Charles Dickens classic), presented a planet where the design influence, from the cityscape to the goggles worn by passers-by, was Victorian and definitely Steampunk in origin.

Doctor Who has explored, pastiched and extended many genres in its fifty-year history, so it was inevitable that a fashionable movement like Steampunk would be co-opted by the show. It is interesting how much the show's liking for cod-Victoriana crossed with science fiction pre-empted much of what the mainstream would now recognize as bona fide Steampunk.

The Steampunk city

Just as the literary movement bloomed in the 1980s, Steampunk elements in mainstream movies remained few and far between. David Lynch went Victorian in *The Elephant Man* (1981), starring John Hurt as the deformed John Merrick. The lush black-and-white photography and set dressing evoked a near-fantasy Victorian world of steam-driven machines, grime and grit, although the film was unusual in taking a Steampunk approach to a real-life story. Lynch had an affinity for the aesthetic and went on to employ it heavily in the retro-future of Frank Herbert's *Dune* (1984), especially in the court of Emperor and the Guild Navigators. Although a flop, the movie has since been reassessed as a prime example of the creation of a fantasy world on screen, alongside Ridley Scott's near-contemporary *Blade Runner* (a prime example of the Steampunk city, projected into the future). Through these movies Lynch created diverse steam-driven industrial environments and visuals.

While very different aesthetically, Terry Gilliam was another director whose 1980s work is shot through with Steampunk. Although moments in Gilliam's previous movies – *Jabberwocky* (1977) and *Time Bandits* (1981) – might tick Steampunk boxes, it was his take on George Orwell's *1984* in *Brazil* (1985) that fully explored a retro-futuristic aesthetic. The film is riven with superfluous duct-work leaking steam, retro-computer screens and augmented typewriters. Amid the depiction of bureaucratic routine and sadistic torture, Gilliam's *Brazil* is a prime example of Steampunk applied to a movie outside the usual Victorian setting. Nonetheless Steampunk author Paul Di Filippo

Left: The Cyber Leader from the 2008 *Doctor Who* Christmas special 'The Next Doctor'. The piston-like sound effects which accompany them and their Art Deco design betray the Cybermen's Steampunk influences. Above: John Merrick, the Elephant Man, as portrayed by John Hurt in David Lynch's nightmarish Victorian vision from 1981.

107

Left to right: The Steampunk aesthetic in David Lynch's *Dune*, Fritz Lang's *Metropolis* and Terry Gilliam's *Brazil*.

recognized Gilliam's contribution: '[Gilliam] gets too little credit as an outlier of the Steampunk movement. Films such as *Time Bandits* and, essentially, *Brazil*, certainly share affinities with hardcore Steampunk [in] an environment that offers glimpses of magic and wonder.'

The maverick Gilliam would go on to apply magic and wonder to *The Adventures of Baron Munchausen* (1988), a movie that drew directly on Karel Zeman's 1961 *Baron Prásil* (*The Fabulous Baron Munchausen*), which used similar techniques to his 1958 Jules Verne movie. A hot air balloon features, as do clockwork and other mechanical contrivances. There's a flight to the moon, an encounter with the Lunar King and Queen, and a clash with an enormous sea creature. While it is based on Raspe's eighteenth-century tall tales, there are many echoes of Verne. Gilliam's interest in cogs, pipes and steam-driven machinery and in imaginative retro-gadgetry was again evident in the fantasies *12 Monkeys* (1995), *The Brothers Grimm* (2005) and, especially, *The Imaginarium of Doctor Parnassus* (2009). Gilliam went full-Steampunk with the short *1884: Yesterday's Future* (2012).

One of the key tropes of Steampunk explored by Lynch and Gilliam is the industrialized city, essentially projecting the cities that grew during the Industrial Revolution into the future or sideways into fantasy. In movies, the Steampunk city had come into its own with Fritz Lang's *Metropolis* (1927). This German Expressionist film depicted a futuristic urban dystopia based on New York, divided between ultra-rich industrialists and workers who toil underground. Under the city a workers' revolution is fomented by Maria (Brigitte Helm), while Rotwang – a mad scientist with one mechanical hand – creates a robot in her image to sow discord.

Drawing on then-recent developments in Modernism and Art Deco, Lang created a stylized city through models, forced perspective and other special effects (tiny

STEAMPUNK

aeroplanes fly between the huge buildings and vehicles cross the 'skybridges' between the city's towers). Equally, the interior sets featured elements that would later make up the Steampunk aesthetic: Rotwang's Art Deco laboratory is a prime example of 'ray-gun Gothic'.

Depictions of dark cities have become key to many recent Steampunk movies, but the source is *Metropolis*. *Alphaville* (1965) and *Blade Runner* (1982) depicted their retro-futuristic steam-wreathed dystopic cities prominently. Others followed, including Gilliam's *Brazil* (1985), the French *The City of Lost Children* (1995), the fantasy-noir *Dark City* (1998), and *City of Ember* (2008). In Japanese animation, Steampunk cities featured in *Akira* (1988), *Ghost in the Shell* (1995) and – completing the circle, at least in title – *Metropolis* (2001).

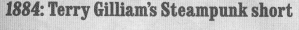

1884: Terry Gilliam's Steampunk short

Written by animator Tim Ollive, Terry Gilliam's *1884: Yesterday's Future* (2012) purports to have been made in 1848 (over forty years before film was invented) and looks ahead to the wonderful future age of 1884. Described as 'a story of outstanding heroism in the face of deception, subterfuge and treachery', the film mixes puppets, animation and CGI. A promotional trailer included an opening theatre-set sequence featuring a coal-powered 'steam-motion image projector' that shows a capsule held together with rivets heading for the moon and concluded with the triumphant exclamation: 'The moon is now a colony of Great Britain!'

Extraordinary voyagers

Since *The Wild Wild West* in the 1960s, television had been slow to take advantage of the possibilities of Steampunk. In 1982 there was *Q.E.D.*, a short-lived series following the exploits of American inventor and investigator Professor Quentin E. Deverill (Sam Waterston) in Edwardian England. Deverill often foiled the plots of his arch-nemesis Dr Stefan Kilkiss (Julian Glover). Created by John Hawkesworth (ITV's 1980s *Sherlock Holmes*) and Robert Schlitt (*Hawaii Five-O*) for CBS, *Q.E.D.* may have developed a stronger Steampunk direction if it had lasted longer. In the pilot, Deverill demonstrates a television-like device to his sceptical Harvard colleagues, before opting to carry on his esoteric research in England. He soon hires Cockney cab driver Phipps (George Innes) as his sardonic general factotum, and sets up a lab in a country manor house. The six episodes involve a plot to destroy London with rockets, an international car race with new-fangled engines, remote control bombs, deadly nerve gas, a ghost-capturing camera, and a new drug that threatens London's opium users. Inventions Deverill demonstrates include a rocket-powered bike, shatterproof glass and a complicated tea-making machine.

Where *Q.E.D.* was light-hearted but aimed at adults, *Voyagers!* (1982–83) was made for children but concealed a serious educational purpose. Airing on NBC for twenty episodes and created by James D. Parriot, *Voyagers!* starred Jon-Erik Hexum as time traveller Phineas Bogg and Meeno Peluce as his young sidekick, orphan Jeffrey Jones. The hand-held Omni device allows Boggs to travel through time to ensure history unfolds correctly. The opening episode saw the pair arrive in an alternative Great War France in 1918 where the war is concluded without the use of airplanes – necessitating a further trip back to 1903 to inspire the Wright brothers to invent the first aircraft. Each subsequent episode saw the travellers arrive where history has gone wrong – where Isaac Newton has failed to discover gravity, Wernher von Braun is taking space travel to the Russians, and Franklin D. Roosevelt is making it big in Hollywood instead of becoming President – before setting things back on course. Although these tales of alternative history had a definite Steampunk vibe, *Voyagers!* was largely lacking in steam-powered or clockwork technology, beyond the bronze pocket watch time-travel device. There are a few touchstones (Verne is inspired to name his adventurer Phileas Fogg after meeting Phineas Bogg) and many Steampunk-ish technological inventions are made due to the intervention of Bogg and Jones.

The mid-1990s saw a televisual resurgence in Steampunk. Square-jawed Bruce Campbell was the title character in *The Adventures of Brisco County, Jr.* (1993-94), an offbeat retread of *The Wild Wild West*. Created by Jeffrey Boam and Carlton Cuse (writers of *Indiana Jones and the Last Crusade*, an influence on the show), this twenty-seven-episode series ran on Fox. In 1893 Campbell's Brisco County is a lawyer-turned-bounty-hunter hired by a group of industrialists to track down John Bly and his outlaws. The first hint of the unusual comes when Chinese workers unearth a long-buried UFO (Unidentified Flying Orb), giving them super-strength.

Each episode pulled off the same trick attempted by *The Wild Wild West* thirty years before, mixing the Western genre with technological gadgets. Steampunk inspirations included a rocket-powered rail cart, early forensic science, and a helium-filled Zeppelin – many of them courtesy of 'mad scientist' Professor Wickwire (John Astin). Campbell was clear about the show's roots: 'It's Jules Verne meets *The Wild Wild West*,' while Cuse cut to the heart of his genre mash-up: 'Our characters just happen to be living in the [Old] West with 1990s sensibilities.'

After a strong start, *The Adventures of Brisco County, Jr.* was cancelled at the end of its first season, during which ratings had declined despite positive critical reaction and a vocal fan following.

There was more Weird West Steampunk in 1995's *Legend*, starring MacGyver's Richard Dean Anderson as Ernest Pratt. He's a dime novel author who falls in with the Nikola Tesla-like Janos Bartok (John de Lancie), whose inventions allow Pratt to bring his heroic alter ego 'Nicodemus Legend' to life. A single season of twelve episodes saw Pratt travel the Old West in a steam-driven car or a steam-powered balloon using the various gadgets built by Bartok to get them out of scrapes. *Legend* was light-hearted stuff, but it – along with several episodes of George Lucas's *The Adventures of Young Indiana Jones* (notably those set in 1917 and 1918) – put Steampunk visuals in front of young audiences, many of whom would grow up to adopt the look as a subcultural lifestyle.

111

Back to the *Wild Wild West*

Through the 1990s movies occasionally dipped into Steampunk, but it wasn't until the end of the decade with *Wild Wild West* (1999), based on the 1960s TV series, that Steampunk pushed into the mainstream in the wake of several movies that dabbled in the aesthetic.

The Steven Spielberg-produced, Barry Levinson-directed *Young Sherlock Holmes* (1985) pre-empted the 1990s movies with its use of computer-generated imagery (CGI) in the 'stained-glass man' sequence, although overall it veered more in the direction of a mad inventor Victorian fantasy with Gothic overtones. The attic laboratory of Sherlock's mentor Professor Waxflatters has enough gadgetry to qualify, and the film also features a flying machine and an underground wooden pyramid built by the remnants of an Egyptian death cult.

Similarly, the old inventor's (Vincent Price) lab in *Edward Scissorhands* (1990) – set in the modern day, although this suburban neighbourhood features a Gothic castle – has a clockwork aesthetic and is packed with steam-driven gadgetry, even if the ultimate product of this labour is the old man's breakfast. Edward, as a manufactured man (an automata?), echoes some of the Frankenstein attributes

Left to right: Steampunk vehicles come in all shapes and sizes, from the flying machine in *Young Sherlock Holmes*, the giant mechanical spider from *Wild Wild West*, and the jet pack in *The Rocketeer*.

to be found in Steampunk, while his anachronistic gadget-packed hands fit. Another incidental Steampunk movie was the conclusion of the time-travelling Back to the Future trilogy. *Back to the Future III* (1990) took a Weird Western Steampunk detour, featuring a time-travelling steam train and a host of homages to Verne.

In 1991 *The Rocketeer* drew on 1930s serials and comic books for its inspiration. Creator Dave Stevens had developed the comic book in the 1980s as a homage to his favourite serials. While the suit originated in the serial *King of the Rocketmen* (1949) – a bullet-shaped helmet, back-mounted rocket-pack and chest-mounted control knobs – Stevens reshaped it through an Art Deco prism, adding fins and curves to the helmet for movie hero Cliff Secord (Billy Campbell). Director Joe Johnston later brought that film's Steampunk aesthetic to his superhero blockbuster *Captain America: The First Avenger* (2011).

A century of films featuring Steampunk (starting with Méliès) climaxed at the millennium with the Will Smith-starring *Wild Wild West* (1999). For Smith, this was just the latest in a series of hugely popular summer blockbusters built around his larger-than-life personality, but that was not enough to make it a success. He was teamed with Kevin Kline as the late nineteenth-century United States secret service agents, out to foil the plans of Dr. Loveless (Kenneth Branagh) in a movie unfortunately obsessed with cross-dressing and crude humour.

Director Barry Sonnenfeld packed *Wild Wild West* with a host of clockwork and steam-driven machinery including a jet-powered penny farthing bicycle, a steam-powered tank and – most famously – the Wanderer steam train. The villainous (and legless) Loveless

had a steam-powered wheelchair and giant 80ft mechanical spider. *Wild Wild West* popularized the Steampunk aesthetic, becoming its most widely seen realization. However, in packing the movie with Steampunk props the creators forgot the importance of script, character and story. Arguably, the six-and-a-half minute promotional music video for Will Smith's *Wild Wild West* title track was a much better representation of Steampunk than the actual movie.

Superhero Steampunk

The twenty-first century would see Steampunk grow dramatically as a literary subgenre, accompanied by a similar profusion of Steampunk movies and TV shows. The films were aided (sometimes hindered) by CGI special effects, making the depiction of Steampunk worlds easier, but lessons had not been learned from the failure of *Wild Wild West*. These new technologies would lead to cheaper visions and several poor movies, and a few gems.

Critical failures on the scale of *Wild Wild West* were *The League of Extraordinary Gentlemen* (2003), a misguided reworking of Alan Moore's comic book that put the familiar characters (and two new ones) in a generic action-adventure plot, and *Van Helsing* (2004), a monster mash-up featuring the classic Universal monsters. They drew on similar sources, Victorian icons of terror and horror, but both smothered their storytelling in a sea of CGI. Despite the visual appeal of Steampunk, their failure demonstrated that story matters.

Both *Hellboy* (2004) and the sequel *Hellboy II: The Golden Army* (2008) – based on the Mike Mignola comic book – were Steampunk-infused superhero fairytales. The first outlined Hellboy's birth, mixing Nazis and Cthulu to good effect, while the second pitched Hellboy (Ron Perlman) into a battle with the world of faerie. Two characters in Hellboy inhabit environment suits: the amphibian Abe Sapien and the SS agent Kroenen, with the latter featuring a wind-up clockwork heart and a mechanical hand.

The Steampunk city. Left: Going underground with Hellboy. Right: The New York vistas of an alternative 1939 in *Sky Captain and the World of Tomorrow*.

115

Ironically, Kroenen is killed when Hellboy drops a giant cog on him. The second film featured the disembodied gaseous spirit Johann Krauss, also encased in a survival suit covered in valves and pipes. Similarly the entrance to the resting place of the Golden Army is accessed via a clockwork-driven mechanism. These may be fantasy superhero movies, but there is enough in the design (giant clockwork cogs feature throughout the second instalment) to call them Steampunk.

Perhaps lo-fi effects better suit Steampunk's retro-Victorianism? *Sky Captain and the World of Tomorrow* (2004) presents a pulp adventure set in an alternative 1939, opening with a Zeppelin docking on the Empire State Building (a use originally intended for the building), and featuring giant flying robots (inspired by the 1941 Fleischer Superman cartoon *The Mechanical Monsters*), deadly rayguns, a robotic Ninja assassin and a flying aircraft carrier. Jude Law is the heroic Sky Captain, while Gwyneth Paltrow is his newspaper reporter sidekick. Investigating the disappearance of several scientists, the pair are soon on the trail of Dr. Totenkopf (a digital Laurence Olivier), whose demonic machines threaten the world.

Right: Replete with arcane and unsettling machinery, *The City of Lost Children*, by Marc Caro and Jean-Pierre Jeunet, inspired a wave of French Steampunk cinema.

The Mysterious Geographic Explorations of Jasper Morello

A hand-made aesthetic infuses the Oscar-nominated short film *The Mysterious Geographic Explorations of Jasper Morello* (2005), made by Anthony Lucas. Using silhouette animation, Lucas depicts a fully-realized Steampunk world starting in the heavily industrialized city of Gothia. The story follows Morello (Joel Edgerton), a navigator who joins Captain Griswald (Thomas Dysart) on a trip carrying a single passenger, the mysterious biologist Dr Claude Bergon (Helmut Bakaitis). His task is to monitor the ship's crew, as it seems airmen are immune to a plague ravaging the city. The crew encounter an abandoned airship and discover a mysterious floating island populated by fierce creatures that offer a cure to the Gothia plague. Another three voyages for Morello were promised, but none has yet appeared, despite an Oscar nomination and a website (the Gothia Gazette) that provides much 'in-universe' background.

STEAMPUNK

Kerry Conran's film was shot using a 'digital backlot' in which live actors are supplemented by digital environments, recalling Zeman's work. Conran drew on 1930s' design influences, including Norman Bel Geddes and German Expressionism. The director's approach was to immerse himself in the environment of the movie: 'We tried to approach it almost as though we lived in that era. We wanted the film to feel like a lost film of that era.'

Secret adventures in infinite worlds

Steampunk on television in the twenty-first century became more confident thanks to an appreciative audience primed by the novels. Two of the most prominent shows even showcased the original touchstones of Jules Verne and H.G. Wells.

Taking as its conceit that Verne not only wrote fabulous adventure tales but actually lived many of them, *The Secret Adventures of Jules Verne* (2000) was a twenty-two-episode series made by CBC in Canada. BBC documentary filmmaker Gavin Scott drew upon his experience writing for *The Young Indiana Jones Chronicles*. He created a fantasy Verne, asking, 'What if there was a lot more truth behind Verne's stories than anyone had believed? What if, in fact, he had actually experienced them as a young man...?'

Scott's inspiration led to a series of outlandish tales in which Verne (Chris Demetral) accompanies Phileas Fogg (Michael Praed) and valet Passepartout (Michel Coutemanche) around the world on the luxurious airship Aurora. Like the train in *Wild Wild West*, the Aurora

French Steampunk movies

The City of Lost Children (1994), directed by Marc Caro and Jean-Pierre Jeunet, led a wave of French cinematic Steampunk. Evil mad scientist Krank (Daniel Emilfork) kidnaps children to steal their dreams. When the little brother of circus strongman One (Ron Perlman) is taken, he sets out on a rescue mission. Along the way he encounters the members of a bizarre cult, all of whom have replaced a single eye with a biomechanical equivalent, and a series of clones who cannot agree on which is the original. Kranks' dream-draining machine is definitely Steampunk, as is the fish tank containing the talkative brain of Uncle Irvin. The entire timeless environment of Krank's dark island seems to have been put through a Steampunk filter. Other examples of French cinematic Steampunk include *Vidocq* (2001), *Micmacs* (2010) and the delightful *The Adventures of Adèle Blanc-Sec* (2010).

117

is stuffed with handy gadgets and deadly weapons. 'Ever seen inside one of those gentlemen's clubs in London's Pall Mall?' asked Scott. 'It's just like one of them – all deep armchairs and leather-bound books and brass fittings – except that it can fly. And it's jam-packed with hidden devices that only Victorian Steampunk could create.'

Their recurring antagonist was the League of Darkness, out to retain power in the hands of the nobility by promoting conflict in Europe. Their leader is Steampunk cyborg Count Gregory (Rick Overton), rebuilt with Victorian technology having died over 500 years before. Among the plots enacted by the League is an attempt to use a Giant Mole digging machine to kidnap Queen Victoria. Later, the League construct their own airship, the Prometheus, in an attempt to shift the balance of power during the American Civil War. Taking dramatic liberties with history, the show pitched the adventurers into confrontations with Cardinal Richelieu (also Praed), Mark Twain, and on a quest for the Holy Grail. They also tackled aristocratic vampires, undead anarchists, and encouraged a young Thomas Edison (who invents a hovering tank). Appropriately, the show was shot in an old Victorian engine repair shed in Montreal that still had railway tracks running through it.

The second show was *The Infinite Worlds of H.G. Wells* (2001), taking the author of *The Time Machine* as its central character. Based on a series of Wells's lesser-known short stories, this three-episode mini-series was framed as the recollections of the older Wells in 1946. Flashing back to 1893, each feature-length instalment adapted two short stories, depicting Wells as a young scientist studying at college. The stories adapted were: 'The New Accelerator' (a favourite of Steampunk) and 'The Queer Story of Brownlow's Newspaper', 'The Crystal Egg' and 'The Remarkable Case of Davidson's Eyes', 'The Truth About Pyecraft' and 'The Stolen Bacillus'. In a style similar to the preceding Verne series, *The Infinite Worlds of H.G. Wells* adopted the usual cavalier attitude to the historical and biographical realities.

Impossible illusions

By the mid 2000s, Steampunk cinema was on a major comeback. The elements that made up the Steampunk style had become so recognizable to audiences that they were often used as simple set-dressing. Christopher Nolan's *The Prestige* (2006) hits Steampunk touchstones through some of the magicians' equipment and the inclusion of mysterious electrical wizard Nikola Tesla (David Bowie), who may be helping one of them achieve an impossible illusion.

There was more fantasy in *The Golden Compass* (2007), based on Philip Pullman's novel trilogy collectively known as His Dark Materials. Set in a parallel universe, the most prominent Steampunk element is heroine Lyra Belacqua's truth-revealing alethiometer, the 'compass' of the title. When used correctly, the hands on the device can be positioned in relation to thirty-six arcane symbols to ask a specific question. The prop in the movie is a lovely clockwork device and became a favourite item for Steampunk fans to reproduce.

The Golden Compass features a variety of fantastic vehicles, although none of them is steam-powered, relying instead on this alternative universe's source of 'ambaric' power contain in 'armillary spheres'. A three-wheeled carriage features a huge spinning sphere in the front section, replacing what would have been horse-power. A sky vehicle is held aloft by two balloons augmented by a pair of armillary spheres, as is a giant dirigible. The film was a prime case of the Steampunk aesthetic applied to a fantasy world.

The same applies to both *Watchmen* (2009) and *Sherlock Holmes* (2009, and the sequel *Sherlock Holmes: Game of Shadows*, 2011). *Watchmen*, based on another Alan Moore comic book, is a superhero movie that critiques the very notion of superheroes, but the visual style of the film includes much metaphysical Steampunk, especially in the section dealing with Dr Manhattan's exile to Mars. There are also touches in Nite Owl's flying vehicle and in some of the other gadgets and set-design, but *Watchmen* is another movie that latched onto the aesthetic as little more than nice set-dressing. Equally, director Guy Ritchie brought an action-movie feel to the Victorian adventures of *Sherlock Holmes*, with a climax in which a Steampunk device is set to release a poison gas into Parliament.

Similarly, *The Three Musketeers* (2011) takes an old story – as Ritchie had done with Conan Doyle's detective – and gives it a Steampunk make-over featuring airships and weapons built from lost plans by Leonardo da Vinci. A movie like *Sucker Punch* (2011) demonstrates all too well what can go wrong when a Steampunk aesthetic is adopted

Above and right: With its clockwork alethiometer and 'ambaric' airships, *The Golden Compass* fused the Steampunk aesthetic with fantasy storytelling.

119

(in costume, as much as in vehicles) and a seemingly endless torrent of CGI is thrown at it. Much anticipated and then derided when it arrived, *Sucker Punch* was Steampunk trying to be sexy, but without much in the way of heart.

Going mainstream

A new breed of twenty-first-century television shows have shown differing degrees of fidelity to the core of Steampunk, but each brought some degree of the visual aesthetic to a broader audience.

The quirky *Eureka* (2006-12) was set in an isolated town populated by eccentric scientific geniuses. A light comedy-drama, it featured a few Steampunk elements during its six-year run, such as the school named after Nikola Tesla. Many of the show's inventions and gadgets had a Steampunk sheen, such as a levitation machine that uses magnetism.

More obviously paying attention to Steampunk aesthetics in its design was Syfy's *Sanctuary* (2008-2011). The show starred *Stargate SG-1*'s Amanda Tapping as Dr Helen Magnus, a Victorian scientist who enjoys advanced longevity due to an injection of vampire blood. In the modern era, she and a team of specialists run the Sanctuary, a safe haven for the world's 'abnormals' (super-powered non-human creatures). Originally, Magnus was a member of 'the Five', a group of Victorian innovators that included (inevitably) Nikola Tesla (a vampire), Nigel Griffin (the model for Wells's *The Invisible Man*), James Watson (inspiration for Conan Doyle's Watson), and John Druitt (a real-life suspect in the Jack the Ripper case). By the later seasons *Sanctuary* featured a huge Hollow Earth city called Praxis, home of many abnormals. Show

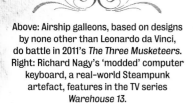

Above: Airship galleons, based on designs by none other than Leonardo da Vinci, do battle in 2011's *The Three Musketeers*.
Right: Richard Nagy's 'modded' computer keyboard, a real-world Steampunk artefact, features in the TV series *Warehouse 13*.

creator Damian Kindler called *Sanctuary* 'cool, retro, Steampunky sci-fi stuff.'

Perhaps the television series with the biggest claim to authentic Steampunk is Syfy's *Warehouse 13* (2009–present). The premise features a team of misfit agents charged with the recovery of weird artefacts on behalf of the US government. Showrunner Jack Kenny admitted in *Wired* magazine that '[In] creating this show, Steampunk was our mantra.'

The fictional history of *Warehouse 13* saw it established in 1914 by Steampunk icons and real-world inventors Nikola Tesla, Thomas Edison and artist M.C. Escher. The show features the thirteenth warehouse, the first having been established by Alexander the Great and the second being the legendary Library of Alexandria. Warehouse 12 was located in nineteenth-century Britain and staffed by H.G. Wells (here the author's sister, played by Jaime Murray). This Wells is 'bronzed' (cryogenically frozen) and revived in the present day where she proceeds to wreak havoc before being co-opted by Warehouse 13. 'In figuring out the kind of world [the show] inhabits, we talked a lot about Verne and Steampunk,' said producer David Simkins. Many of the props were designed to look good onscreen and convey the Steampunk aesthetic, including a huge airship hanging from the ceiling of the cavernous warehouse. 'We're not quite sure at this stage what a lot of these things do,' Simkins admitted of the background props.

Among the range of artefacts encountered by the agents are the lab coat and goggles of Allesandro Volta (eighteenth-century inventory of the battery) that give the wearer temporarily increased 'biomagnetic attraction'. Other Steampunk artefacts include: Bell & Howell's spectroscope and 3D projector; a bracelet belonging to Carlo Collodi

121

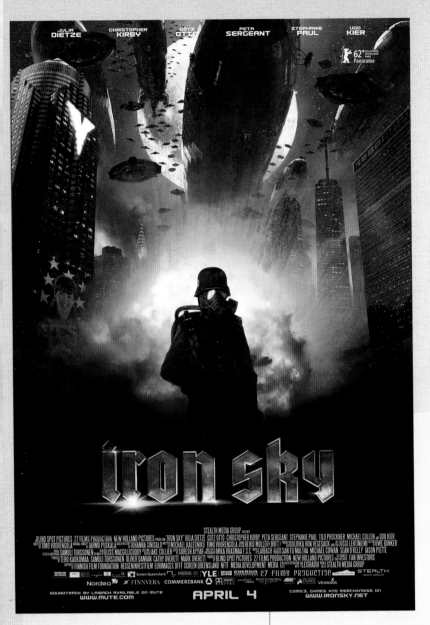

(creator of Pinocchio); Leonardo da Vinci's perpetual motion machine; Lewis Carroll's looking glass (a gateway to an alternative dimension); H.G. Wells's imperceptor vest (which speeds up the wearer in the manner of 'The New Accelerator'); a death-ray lantern used by Victorian serial killer Jack the Ripper; Victorian-born psychologist Max Wertheimer's mind transference zoetrope; Edgar Allan Poe's quill pen and notebook that demonstrates the pen is mightier (as a weapon) than the sword; and Robert Louis Stevenson's lion and eagle bookends which can cause people to swap minds and change personality like Dr Jekyll and Mr Hyde. Many of these artefacts drew upon eminent Victorian literary names or prominent inventors, falling within the realm of Steampunk in their inspirations.

Each of these contemporary shows drew on Steampunk iconography after the genre achieved widespread popularity. The earlier 1980s and 1990s shows were directly inspired by the earliest Steampunk literature, while *Eureka*, *Sanctuary* and *Warehouse 13* debuted when Steampunk was a thriving subgenre of science fiction boasting its own creative communities. These shows paid varying degrees of attention to the genre, occasionally drawing upon a Steampunk aesthetic or idea in design elements, or – in the case of *Warehouse 13* – making Steampunk central to its look. While sometimes irritating to die-hards, these shows did do much to further advance the popularity and acceptance of Steampunk as a mainstream visual style.

Back to Méliès

Although there will be many more Steampunk movies and television shows, Martin Scorsese's acclaimed *Hugo* (2011) felt like a final word on the first incarnation of the cinematic exploration of the genre. Based on Brian Selznick's graphic novel *The Invention of Hugo Cabret* (2007), it's the story of orphan Hugo (Asa Butterfield) who lives in Montparnasse station in early 1930s Paris, working to maintain the clocks. The heart of the story – and the theme Scorsese's film builds upon – is his involvement with filmmaker Georges Méliès, who actually did run a toy stall within the station. This is Scorsese's cue to explore the magical, mechanical origins of cinema and Méliès's lost automata. Between the train station, the clockwork, the broken automata that Hugo repairs, and the role of Méliès (Ben Kingsley), Scorsese's movie is an excellent use of Steampunk in the service of a moving story.

The film (making great use of the 3D format and judicious CGI) takes the viewer inside a clockwork world – both the actual mechanics of the clocks and the orderly life of the station. It's also about the creation and consumption of magical images,

thanks to the mechanical and chemical nature of early cinema. A tribute to the rapidly vanishing world of celluloid, *Hugo* uses the latest technology and an aesthetic based on some of the oldest to create a unique cinematic world that was justly rewarded with five Academy Awards for design and cinematography.

Hugo neatly brought Steampunk cinema and television full circle back to Méliès. Many of the best cinema and television versions of Steampunk predate the term: as with the varying degrees of Steampunk adopted by film and television, each viewer knows it when they see it. Steampunk on screen succeeds when it is embraced wholeheartedly by filmmakers, and fails when there is hesitancy. It thrives when the entire world is a Steampunk one, not just a fantasyland with Steampunk elements attached. As Steampunk band Abney Park's lead singer Robert Park notes: 'We've had Steampunk movies for just as long as we've had movies … it's just recently been given a name.'

123

6
CLOCKWORK GRAPHICS

The unique worlds, characters and technology of Steampunk have lent themselves to graphic novels and videogames.

Steampunk's graphic iconography made it a natural aesthetic for visual media beyond films and television. The worlds of comics, graphic novels, computer and videogames have all drawn on Steampunk for inspiration, and some have made a considerable contribution to the expansion of the genre.

Like its literary equivalent, the ever-spreading world of Steampunk comics had its roots in the 1970s with a connection to Michael Moorcock. Writer and artist Bryan Talbot didn't set out to create the first modern Steampunk comic, but that's what 1976's *The Adventures of Luther Arkwright* became. Talbot admits to being inspired by Moorcock's work, but by the Jerry Cornelius tales rather than the proto-Steampunk novel *The Warlord of the Air* (1971). Riffing on the Cornelius character, Talbot created Luther Arkwright for a short comic strip called 'The Papist Affair' (1976) in *Brainstorm Comix*. Talbot described this first outing – featuring cigar-smoking, stocking-wearing nuns in pursuit of the sacred relics of St. Adolf of Nuremberg – as an 'unutterably silly tongue-in-cheek romp ... my apprenticeship in the comics medium'.

"Although, in general, figurative and decorative art is banned in England, there is a notable exception. Amidst the sea of black and white puritan garments, (coloured clothing is prohibited), and surrounded by the strict no-nonsense architecture, the visitor to London will be struck by the huge statues and illustrated government hoardings. This surprising anomaly is easily explained. It was Matthew Cromwell, father of the current Lord Protector, who said: "Art is a cog in the machine of repression". That this philosophy is adhered to is evident in the wealth of propaganda posters and stone effigies of past heads of state such as the giant statue of Oliver Cromwell by Landseer that overlooks Westminster Square."
"An American Innocent In London"
Oliver North
U.C.A. Ambassador to England 1978-1984

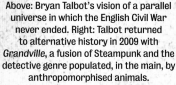

Above: Bryan Talbot's vision of a parallel universe in which the English Civil War never ended. Right: Talbot returned to alternative history in 2009 with *Grandville*, a fusion of Steampunk and the detective genre populated, in the main, by anthropomorphised animals.

Within this false start, Talbot perceived something else: the beginnings of a more serious, more in-depth story, one that would be his own and would reflect his views of mid-1970s Britain filtered through an alternative world. This atheist world would be dominated by logic and science, but open to a wider multiverse (shades of Moorcock) that continually threatens to upset the balance of harmony and unleash the corruption of the Disruptors.

Starting as an ongoing serial in British underground comic *Mixed Bunch* published by Alchemy in 1976, *The Adventures of Luther Arkwright* came to an abrupt halt in 1982, only halfway through Talbot's planned epic. Returning to his alternative universe in 1987, Talbot completed his tale by 1989, with the entire story republished as nine standard format comic books by Valkyrie Press. Comic writer Warren Ellis called *The Adventures of Luther Arkwright* 'probably the single most influential graphic novel to have come out of Britain to date ... [an] important experimental work.'

Luther Arkwright appears to be unique in his ability to move between multiple parallel worlds through his own force of will. Arkwright is aided by Rose Wylde, a telepath who exists in several variations across the parallel universes. Their point of origin is the one stable point in this multiverse, known as zero-zero. As a result of this stability, it is a peaceful, high-technology world free from the malign influence of the Disruptors.

Bryan Talbot (b.1952)

Talbot won the Eagle Award for Best Artist, Best New Comic, Best Comic and Best Comic Character for *The Adventures of Luther Arkwright* in 1988. The collected edition was one of the first 'graphic novels' published in Britain. Talbot explored his emerging Steampunk sensibilities by providing the art in comic *2000 AD* to Pat Mills' *Nemesis the Warlock* storyline, 'The Gothic Empire', in which a far future empire has modelled its technology heavily on Victorian Britain. The 'young Goths', a rebel faction, reinvent themselves, taking their fashion and subculture influences from twentieth-century television.

The comic's principal location is a parallel world trapped in the English Civil War, which has been prolonged indefinitely by the interference of the Disruptors. They have also unleashed 'Firefrost', an ancient artefact causing instability across the multiverse. Arkwright is charged with battling the Disruptors, while also locating and destroying Firefrost. In the course of the story, the hero is killed only to return enhanced.

Talbot first came across what he now recognizes as Steampunk in Moorcock's tales of Oswald Bastable, defining the term as 'retro-SF ... with a Gothic or Victorian element. There weren't many Steampunk books around in 1978 when I plotted Arkwright. I'd read Keith Robert's *Pavane*, so that was probably influential. I'm aware of the phenomenon and have looked at some of the Steampunk sites. I think you can say that it's come of age as a literary genre.'

Unusual in comics of the time, Talbot's work is quite heavy on text while still presenting a series of striking monochrome images, including steam-driven tanks, flying machines, and the continuation of the never-ending 'Britannic Empire'. The Armstrong-Siddeley Vibro Beamer is Arkwright's weapon of choice. The style of

Talbot's work was very experimental, partly as he didn't know any better ('I made all my mistakes in print'). The plot is complex and the artwork detailed, but the rough edges bring something extra to Talbot's unusual tale.

Over a decade after concluding the first instalment, Talbot returned to the worlds of Arkwright with *Heart of Empire: The Legacy of Luther Arkwright* (1999), set twenty-three years after the title character had renounced violence, and focusing on his daughter Victoria. The sequel is a simpler, more straightforward tale. Despite this more accessible approach, Talbot still filled the story with references to historical events, mythology and politics, and makes use of much symbolism and hidden images.

127

Heart of Empire: The Legacy of Luther Arkwright (1999)

In *Heart of Empire*, the long Civil War has finally come to an end with the British Empire emerging as the dominant world power under the command of psychic Queen Anne. Mixing the Victoriana of Steampunk with Elizabethan and Restoration styles, Bryan Talbot's magpie approach to sources sees him using whatever works for the story. Arkwright's daughter Victoria is the heir to the throne, an accomplished engineer, who suffers from recurrent headaches. A threat to the Crown puts Victoria and her mother in mortal danger, while she searches for her long-believed dead twin brother, Henry. Under the influence of accidentally ingested psychedelics, Victoria takes a trip across parallel worlds, eventually meeting her long-missing father and uncovering the true horror hidden at the heart of the Empire.

The Doctor's Graphic adventures

Although Steampunk has not often featured in *Doctor Who* comic strips or graphic novels, a couple of early strips display some attributes of the genre. 'The Iron Legion' (1979, written by Pat Mills and John Wagner and illustrated by *Watchmen*'s Dave Gibbons) depicts a futuristic empire modelled after the Romans', complete with anachronistic robots (the 'iron legion' of the title), while 'Junkyard Demon' (1981) saw the Doctor (Tom Baker) encounter a Cyberman that has been reprogrammed by scrap merchants as a domestic servant (something similar happened to the Daleks in the TV adventure 'Victory of the Daleks', 2010). The story also features a robot with a windmill-powered brain called Dutch.

EXTRAORDINARY GENTLEMEN

Perhaps the most authentic Steampunk work in the world of comic books is writer Alan Moore and artist Kevin O'Neill's ongoing series *The League of Extraordinary Gentlemen* – it certainly captured the mainstream imagination. From 1999 Moore chronicled the offbeat adventures of a group of Victorian characters brought together by the British government to battle threats to Crown and country. Moore repurposed some of the Victorian era's finest fictional personalities, including Mina Murray (better known as Mina Harker, from Bram Stoker's *Dracula*), H. Rider Haggard's adventurer Allan Quatermain, Verne's Captain Nemo, Wells's 'invisible man' Griffin and Stevenson's Jekyll and Hyde. They worked for Campion Bond (an invented ancestor of Ian Fleming's Bond) and the mystery figure of 'M' (revealed as Sherlock Holmes's nemesis Professor Moriarty).

The first two volumes dealt in Wellsian and Vernian pastiche. Volume One is set in 1898 and dealt with an attempt to recover the anti-gravity compound cavorite (from Wells's *The First Men in the Moon*) from the clutches of Fu Manchu (never named for copyright reasons). Volume Two matched the Extraordinary Gentlemen (and one woman) against Wells's Martian invaders from *The War of the Worlds*, with a little help from Dr. Moreau. Germ warfare defeats the Martian invaders, with the 'common cold' explanation from Wells's novel employed as a public cover story. Although more Victorian instalments were promised, these two are the only ones authentically set in that era.

Moore's declared original intention was to produce a 'Justice League of Victorian England', modelled after DC's Justice League of America (a superhero super-group). However, Moore got carried away by his creation, co-opting not only his public domain (out-of-copyright) central characters, but hundreds of others from multifarious sources. In this, he was following in the footsteps of Philip José Farmer's Wold Newton family concept or even Kim Newman's mash-up *Anno Dracula*. Although over-extended in later years (and further developed by other creative talents), the Wold Newton universe of interconnected fictional characters was admitted by Moore as 'a seminal influence upon the [creation of] the League'.

The comic book was hugely popular, with the untangling of Moore and O'Neill's inclusion of myriad minor characters a popular pastime. The publication of the first series coincided with the rise of the internet as a major tool used especially by

ALAN MOORE • KEVIN O'NEILL • BEN DIMAGMALIW • BILL OAKLEY

VOLUME **THE LEAGUE OF** ONE
EXTRAORDINARY GENTLEMEN™

STEAMPUNK

dedicated fan groups, such as comic book fans. Moore's retro-Victorian science fantasy was eagerly dissected in great detail, not least by writer Jess Nevins who extensively annotated the first (and subsequent) series online (the first was later revised and collected as *Heroes & Monsters: The Unofficial Companion to The League of Extraordinary Gentlemen*, 2006).

In constructing his vast imaginary world, Moore did more than just spoof the Victorian Boy's Own adventure fiction that much of *The League of Extraordinary Gentlemen* drew upon. He used the Victorian period – as does the best Steampunk – as a framing device for an exploration of a series of very contemporary takes on some classic characters. Moore was not just poking fun at the pulp fiction originals, but was actually celebrating that style of storytelling from a late-twentieth-century perspective. Despite the depth of Victorian arcana uncovered by Nevins and others, *The League of Extraordinary Gentlemen* remained hugely accessible – the first truly wide success for Steampunk in comics.

Catalogues of contraptions

Humour is often overlooked in Steampunk, and not all graphic approaches to the genre were necessarily narrative-based. Greg Broadmore's *Doctor Grordbort's Contrapulatronic Dingus Directory* (2008) started out as a thirty-two-page catalogue full of imaginary items, but expanded to encompass an entire pulp-based universe. Broadmore was a concept designer for Weta Workshop in New Zealand. Between creating dinosaurs for *King Kong* (2005) and designing alien weapons for *District 9* (2009), Broadmore painted a series of retro-futuristic rayguns for his own amusement. Each weapon was wonderfully detailed and given crazy names like the 'Infinity Beam Projector' and the 'Man Melter'. Showing his work to Weta's Effects Supervisor

Above: Kevin O'Neill's rendition of a Martian tripod from the second volume of *The League of Extraordinary Gentlemen.*

131

Richard Taylor, the potential for a line of distinctive collectibles was clear. With the resources of Weta, Broadmore was able to construct several of the rayguns, weathered to look suitably antique.

Bringing his paintings to life as models wasn't enough for Broadmore, however. In his imagination he began to conceive of the people who might have used the weapons he'd built. 'I started to fill in the back story of the world where these guns came from,' he explained, 'and it started with advertising. I wanted to explore the social world of Grordbort via the ads he created for his guns.'

Part crazy catalogue of impossible items, *Doctor Grordbort's Contrapulatronic Dingus Directory* included promos for a variety of contraptions including weird weapons, metal men, incredible ironclads and rampant rocketships. An illustrated short story introduced a key user of these

Left: The extraordinary hardware of Alan Moore and Kevin O'Neill's 'Justice League of Victorian England': Professor Moriarty's airship rains fire from the sky and Captain Nemo's *Nautilus* surfaces.

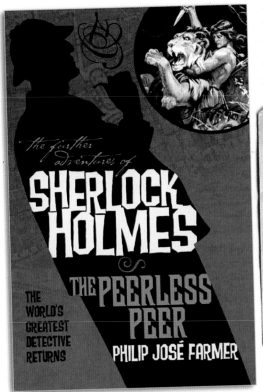

Philip José Farmer's Wold Newton

Farmer created a genre of crossover fiction that connected various pulp fiction characters through their shared ancestry, including Tarzan, Doc Savage, Sherlock Holmes and Lord Peter Wimsey. Farmer suggested that a real-life meteorite that crashed in Wold Newton, Yorkshire in 1795 was radioactive and caused genetic mutations among the descendants of the occupants of a passing coach. Oddly, all these descendants turned out to be world-famous fictional characters, among them such Victorian favourites as Verne's Phileas Fogg, Wells's Time Traveller, Conan Doyle's Professor Challenger, H. Rider Haggard's Allan Quatermain and even Sax Rohmer's Fu Manchu.

Scarlet Traces

In 2002, writer Ian Edginton and artists D'Israeli explored the consequences of the failed Martian invasion of H.G. Wells's *The War of the Worlds* in comic book *Scarlet Traces*. Harnessing the Martian technology, Victorian Britain is reborn as a world power. The alien technology allows the Empire to dominate the world as never before, just as the Martians had attempted to dominate Earth. A sequel, *Scarlet Traces: The Great Game* (2006) moved the story on to the 1930s and on to Mars, with humanity launching a counter-invasion of the red planet.

objects, Lord Cockswain, and his imperialist view of the world. Broadmore described Cockswain as 'the great white hunter'. A trip to Venus for Cockswain is not one of wonder and awe, but simply a chance to shoot at more exotic wildlife. 'He has a very human-centric view of the universe, a classic colonizer. Venus for Cockswain is what Africa was for the English.' Although received as Steampunk by fans, Broadmore's work is often more atomic- and radio wave-powered. Like Alan Moore, he set out to spoof and reinvent pulp fiction, citing Wells and Verne as inspirations, alongside twentieth-century pulp adventures.

A follow-up, *Doctor Grordbort Presents Victory*, featured 'picture strips of unimaginable escapades on the frontier, never-seen-before portraits of dazzling damsels and monstrous villains, and laudable accounts of man and robot pitted against our greatest enemy', expanding the universe of the mysterious Doctor Grordbort and the unreconstructed Lord Cockswain. A series of short animated films depicting Cockswain's exploits in their full-blooded glory featured on Broadmore's Grordbort website.

In his approach to Steampunk, Greg Broadmore united the physical creation of retro-futuristic objects with an imaginary backstory and a set of characters to use them. Another graphic creation that was spun-off into a wider narrative was Boilerplate, a fictional Victorian-era robot created in 2000 by artist Paul Guinan. Originally intended to feature in a series of comic books, the character instead became central to a fictional historical website. Slowly, across the decade, the story of Boilerplate was developed, becoming the basis for a planned movie.

Packed with 'archival' images of Boilerplate in his contemporary Victorian-era (and beyond) settings, the website chronicled the 'history' of a robot, supposedly constructed in the late nineteenth century, that enjoyed a degree of independent

134

Steampunk Batman

Two unique comic books put DC's vigilante hero Batman into the Victorian era. *Gotham by Gaslight* (1989) and *Master of the Future* (1991) see Bruce Wayne becoming a Victorian version of Batman battling Jack the Ripper (a variation on the Joker) and Alexandre LeRoi, an airship pirate (with a mechanical manservant) out to avert the coming environmental pollution of the twentieth century. Inventor LeRoi – who echoes Verne's Robur – is, however, shown to have been simply the tool of a manipulative landowner. The Mike Mignola-drawn comics were later seen as the launching point for DC's Elseworlds alternative histories series of comic books.

artificial intelligence. This 'mechanical man' was developed by Professor Archibald Campion during the 1880s and unveiled at the 1893 World's Columbian Exposition. Built in Chicago, Boilerplate was originally a prototype soldier who fought in the Spanish-American War and the Boxer Rebellion. The mechanical man also led an expedition to the Antarctic. The rudimentary robot becomes a celebrity in this alternative world, mixing with Mark Twain and Nikola Tesla, and appearing in several silent movies. Boilerplate goes missing during the Great War, possibly captured by the Germans, thus explaining their technical advancements between the wars. Following the Second World War there are occasional reported sightings of Boilerplate in the Chicago area. So effective was Guinan's pseudo-history and accompanying doctored images that some people were fooled into believing that Boilerplate actually existed, including comedian Chris Elliot who included the 'robot' in his comic novel *Shroud of the Thwacker* (2005).

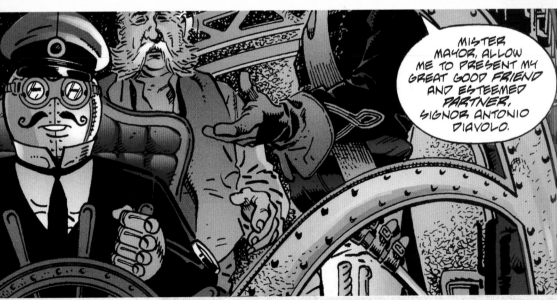

  CLOCKWORK GRAPHICS

Guinan noted: 'I put this thing across as trying to be real, and people bought into it. So, that's a success! But, as an amateur historian, I feel a responsibility to get the story right. So I felt bad about some people being "hoaxed".'

Along with his wife Anina Bennett, Guinan chronicled the Boilerplate story in a coffee-table book, *Boilerplate: History's Mechanical Marvel* (2009), depicting his twenty-five years of adventure and his impact on popular culture. The pair also expanded their website to cover the 'history' of robots in the Victorian era, mixing imagined characters like Boilerplate with real attempts to manufacture mechanical men.

Just as the images and graphic appeal of Steampunk attracted the creators of movies and television, so comic book writers and artists have found themselves drawn to the Steampunk aesthetic. Whether truly Victorian alternative history in the meta-fictional *The League of Extraordinary Gentlemen* or the fantasy-driven other worlds of Luther Arkwright, Steampunk comics range from straight-ahead adventure narratives to oddball creations like Doctor Grordbort and Boilerplate, proving there is little that can't be achieved on a comic book splash page with a decent writer and artist involved.

Warren Ellis's *Aetheric Mechanics* (2008) and *Ministry of Space* (2001–04)

Created by comic book writer Warren Ellis, *Aetheric Mechanics* was set in an alternative 1907 in which a steam-driven space programme has allowed the British Empire to conquer other worlds. On Earth, the Empire is engaged in a conflict with Ruritania using combat mecha (giant robots). This world is not what it seems, though. It is a wonderfully clever meta-fiction that is the inadvertent creation of a scientist from the future, attempting to reconcile two divergent time streams.

The earlier *Ministry of Space* three-part Image Comics series depicted a world in which Britain co-opted Nazi rocket technology before the US or Soviets, giving the country a huge lead in exploring space. Packed with retro-technology and inspired by 1950s' Dan Dare adventures, the series saw Britain's Ministry of Space establishing a foothold off-world, but bringing social problems (such as racial segregation) with it.

Mike Mignola's *The Amazing Screw-On Head* (2002)

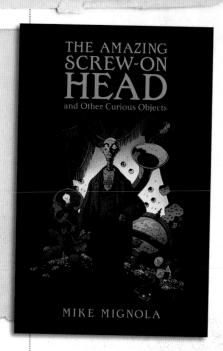

Comic book artist and animator Mike Mignola featured Steampunk elements in his alternative superhero comic book series *Hellboy* (1994–present). Mignola liked drawing mechanical contraptions heavily influenced by the Nautilus in Disney's *20,000 Leagues Under the Sea*. A one-off side project, *The Amazing Screw-On Head* (2002) allowed Mignola to explore his interest in Victorian retro-futurism. He created a robot head – simply known as Screw-On Head – that swaps bodies depending on need. An agent operating on behalf of President Lincoln, Screw-On Head is sent to track down an undead occultist known as Emperor Zombie, who is after a giant supernatural jewel that will allow him to conquer the world. A one-off animated twenty-two-minute television short followed in 2006, written by Bryan Fuller, but changed the story and characters considerably; Emperor Zombie (David Hyde Pierce) is Screw-On Head's (Paul Giamatti) manservant who turns to evil.

Game on

Inevitably, role-playing game and videogame creators found the settings and iconography of Steampunk as equally irresistible as graphic artists. However, the first major Steampunk game didn't require a computer, just a vivid imagination. In 1988, Frank Chadwick created role-playing game (RPG) *Space: 1889*. The scenario hailed back to the Edisonades that pre-dated Steampunk and saw Thomas Edison journey to Mars via his 'ether-flyer'. This pioneering effort expanded through participants' game play to take in exploration of the inner solar system and colonial exploration.

Left: Paul Guinan's fictional mechanical adventurer Boilerplate.

137

Jacques Tardi (b.1946)

French comic book artist Tardi is now best known for his creation of heroine Adèle Blanc-Sec (largely due to the 2010 Luc Besson movie). Set in Paris either side of the Great War, *The Extraordinary Adventures of Adèle Blanc-Sec* is a gaslamp fantasy following the heroine, an author of pulp fiction, in a series of unlikely adventures involving mummies, pterodactyls, demons and mad scientists. Tardi had explored Steampunk in comic books (*bandes dessinées*) with 1974's *Le Démon des Glaces* ('the demon of the ice', published in English in 2011 as *The Arctic Marauder*), set in the 1890s and concerning a mad scientist, monsters from the deep and Steampunk-style flying vehicles and submarines. The hero, Jérôme Plumier, finds himself inside a giant artificial iceberg, complete with an elaborate engine that generates the ice. The lush black-and-white artwork is packed with detail, making this one of the earliest and most important European Steampunk comic books.

Space: 1889 (the title was a spoof of the mid-1970s Gerry Anderson TV series *Space: 1999*) grew out of Chadwick's long experience of *Dungeons and Dragons* (D&D) role-playing games that he'd been involved with during the 1970s and 1980s. Chadwick's gaming exploration of Victorian space travel first came out around the time that the Jeter-Blaylock-Powers triumvirate were making their mark in Steampunk fiction.

Chadwick's core rulebook established an alternative history within which gamers could explore their own scenarios. D&D-style games are run by a 'gamesmaster' who decides how the scenario will play out. Players adopt characters within the game world that have particular attributes and belong to certain classes (in most fantasy games this includes wizards, dwarves and elves). Mostly, these games are played with pencil and paper, with the roll of dice determining the outcomes of conflicts. These initial role-playing games, first developed in the 1970s, were interactive storytelling that long pre-dated the popularity of home computer games or the internet, and depended upon players exercising their imaginations.

The core rulebook for *Space: 1889* suggested that Edison's more outré ideas had come to fruition, including the 'ether propeller' that could drive vehicles through the 'luminferous ether', the universal medium that permeates space. Accompanied by Scottish mercenary Jack Armstrong, Edison travelled to Mars in 1870, paving the way for colonization of the planet by Earth's great powers (a process that by 1889 has also extended to Venus). Life exists throughout the solar system, but it is soon subject to the vagaries of Empire, just as native peoples across Earth had been. *Space: 1889* featured the pulp versions of the planets celebrated in the age before the space probes, with Venus represented as the classic swamp world inhabited by prehistoric giant reptiles and lizard men, while Mars is an ancient, declining desert world with the infamous canals. Chadwick managed to work in the Martian equivalent of dirigibles, with the

Space 1889: Sounds of Mars

In 2005 and 2006 audio drama production company Noise Monster Productions released a short-lived series based on Frank Chadwick's *Space: 1889* RPG. These full-cast dramas were launched by Jonathan Clements' *Red Devils*, the opening salvo in a Martian trilogy of Victorian space adventures in which Germany and Britain battle for domination of Mars, continued and concluded by James Swallow's *The Steppes of Thoth* and Marc Platt's *The Siege of Alclyon*. A fourth instalment, *The Lunar Inheritance* by Andy Frankham-Allen and Richard Dinnick, wrapped up the series. Frankham-Allen would go on to kick-start a series of *Space: 1889* e-books from Untreed Reads Publishing in late 2011.

anti-gravity plant 'liftwood' propelling giant floating platforms, later replaced by armoured, steam-powered flyers.

Various writers extended and deepened Chadwick's game worlds through additional scenarios, including Lester Smith's *Beastmen of Mars* and Marcus Rowland's *Canal Priests of Mars*. Chadwick added more detail in his imaginative Conklin's *Atlas of the Worlds and Handy Manual of Useful Information*, a gazetteer to the solar system's explored worlds.

The *Space: 1889* universe developed and thrived through further gaming expansions, a range of table-top miniature figures and vehicles, a computer game, audio dramas and e-books.

Named after a real but unbuilt Bavarian fortress, Mike Pondsmith's RPG *Castle Falkenstein* (1994) was subtitled 'High Adventure in the Steam Age'. Dispensing with dice, the outcomes of events in this game were dictated through a set of cards, while scenarios were structured as a series of diary entries by game characters including Tom Olam, a game designer from our world transported to the alternative world of New Europa. Swashbuckling adventures modelled after *The Prisoner of Zenda* unfold during the 'Age of Steam', an alternative 1870s.

This is a world where magic has powered the Industrial Revolution, giving rise to steam-powered automobiles, ironclads and dreadnoughts patrolling the seas, and where Babbage's Difference Engine works. Into this world are added the denizens of

139

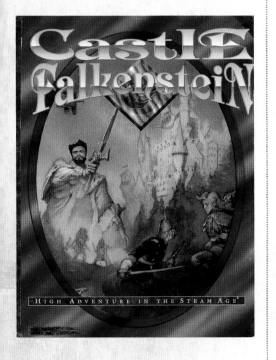

faerie, ambulatory dragons and engineer dwarves. Britain's powerful industrialists are known as the Steam Lords, and their antagonist is the Prussian Chancellor out to unite the German states under one iron fist. A series of expansion rulebooks added to the world of *Castle Falkenstein*, with Steam Age adding all manner of Steampunk vehicles, while *Sixguns & Sorcery* offered a Weird West scenario. A pair of spin-off novels featured characters such as Ada Lovelace (*Masterminds of Falkenstein* by John DeChancie), and Sherlock Holmes and Fu Manchu (*The League of Dragons* by George Alec Effinger, apparently never published). Although a heavily fantasy-infused game setting, *Castle Falkenstein* has proved to be a popular and well-liked Steampunk RPG.

There's more Western-influenced Steampunk adventure in the RPG *Deadlands* (1996) by Shane Lacy Hensley. Set in the Wild West of 1876–79, *Deadlands* is a pulp horror RPG with Steampunk stylings. In this scenario history diverted from its usual course due to a Native American spiritual invocation, which was meant to repel the European settlers but instead opened a conduit to another realm (echoes of *The Anubis Gates*). Into our world came the Reckoners, powerful and malicious entities that feed on negative emotions. The Reckoners use the undead as their tools, prolonging the American Civil War as the dead continue to fight, while their unearthly power sources allow for the creation of advanced technology, making this gaming scenario a horror-Weird West-Steampunk mash-up.

Several game creators took advantage of the Generic Universal Role-playing System (GURPS) developed by Steve Jackson Games, producing such Steampunk variations as *GURPS Steampunk* and *GURPS Girl Genius*. Another variation was the *Iron Kingdoms* RPG, based around Warhammer-style tabletop figure war-gaming. Other Victorian era/Steampunk-focused RPGs included *Victoriana*, *Etherscope*, *Hollow Earth Expeditions*, space opera *Full Light, Full Steam* and *Dark Harvest: The Legacy of Frankenstein*.

From *MYST* to *BioShock* and beyond

One of the earliest Steampunk-inspired videogames was the complex and intriguing *MYST* (1993), developed by brothers Robyn and Rand Miller. Initially released for Apple Macintosh computers (since available across platforms), this graphically driven, puzzle-led adventure game deliberately set out to take advantage of the graphic capabilities of a new generation of computers in the 1990s.

Fittingly, in that it transposed ideas from Steampunk literature to videogames, the player (designated only as 'the Stranger') travels to the world of MYST through the pages of an arcane book. Within the game, ancient books created by lost explorer Atrus function as gateways to mysterious worlds. As the player journeys further into MYST by solving puzzles, more of the backstory is slowly revealed, leading to one of several possible endings.

MYST was a uniquely immersive game back in the mid 1990s. The first-person style (previously the preserve of violent 'shoot-em-up' games) and the involving, often clockwork-driven puzzles made for a captivating experience. Access to areas of the seemingly deserted island of MYST

can only be achieved through solving puzzles, while the 'Ages' (mini-worlds accessible through the mysterious books) represent a particular technology or attribute indicated by the name of each Age: Selenitic, Stoneship, Mechanical and Channelwood. Packed with Steampunk artefacts, including brass telescopes, submarines, airships and steam-powered gadgets, as well as levers and pumps galore, *MYST* may be one of the most important visual sources for Steampunk outside of cinema.

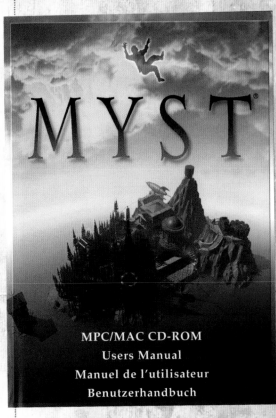

MPC/MAC CD-ROM
Users Manual
Manuel de l'utilisateur
Benutzerhandbuch

As the game unfolds, it becomes clear the player is caught in a battle between estranged brothers, Sirrus and Achenar, the sons of Atrus, author of the linking books. By finding the missing pages from these books and a series of video messages from the brothers, the player can solve the game at their own pace. According to the brothers who developed it, the name and unique atmosphere of the game was inspired by Verne's *The Mysterious Island*.

MYST was one of the earliest games to explore the new worlds of digital multimedia, and although the way the game engine was constructed is primitive compared to twenty-first century digital tools, it was groundbreaking and proved the appeal of intelligent, puzzle-driven and atmospheric worlds to adult game players. Follow-up titles included *Riven* (1997) and *MYST III: Exile* (2001), each deepening and extending the backstory.

One of the most popular Steampunk-influenced computer games was *Final Fantasy VII*, released in 1997, half a decade after *MYST*. This was the first of the Japanese games released in Europe, and was a breakthrough title in terms of the popularity of role-playing games on home computer consoles. The storyline followed Cloud Strife and his allies in a battle against Shinra, a mega-corporation exploiting an energy source that is damaging the Earth's 'life force'. In the process, Cloud also confronts Sephiroth, an experimental life form created by Shinra from extraterrestrial cells, who now aims to dominate the world as a god.

Drawing heavily on Cyberpunk, as much early Steampunk did, *Final Fantasy VII* doesn't feature a cohesive Steampunk worldview. Robots and vehicles often appear to be steam-powered, while an Art Deco approach is evident in the design (both elements were further refined in prequels developed for the later handheld PSP console). While *Final Fantasy VII* was the franchise's breakout title, the previous entry, *Final Fantasy VI* (1994, although not released in the US until 1999) had introduced Steampunk elements in its late nineteenth-century Industrial Revolution-style fantasy setting. Railroads and mining featured, while long-distance communication was limited to carrier pigeon.

The theme would be further developed in *Final Fantasy IX* (2000), where the main characters travel a war-torn world in an airship named the Prima Vista, masquerading as a theatre troupe. Taking a more fantasy-based approach, *Final Fantasy IX*'s medieval-style world is in the early stages of developing steam-driven advanced engines. The character design appeared much more cartoon-like than those in previous games, reflecting the fantasy setting.

Although only a few entries in the Final Fantasy series actually display degrees of Steampunk, the franchise as a whole did much to popularize the computer console

141

version of role-playing games, bringing them to a whole new audience and helping to spread the acceptance of Steampunk.

Other videogames followed *Final Fantasy* in exploring the uses (and sometimes abuses) of Steampunk iconography, including the Wild Arms series (from 1998 in Europe) and the *Thief: The Dark Project* (starting in 1998) franchise. The latter falls within the 'stealth' gaming genre in which players must sneak around environments avoiding detection in order to achieve mission objectives (sometimes dubbed a 'sneak-em-up', rather than a 'shoot-em-up'). Professional thief Garrett is charged with infiltrating a Steampunk metropolis known only as The City, described by game project director Greg LoPiccolo in Steampunk movie terms as '*Brazil* meets *City of Lost Children*'. Garrett has been trained by a secretive order in stealth techniques and is tasked with the theft of The Eye, a powerful artefact that is then misused by the thief's mentor. By the conclusion of the game, the main character has been augmented with a mechanical replacement for a lost eye, amid ominous warnings of a forthcoming 'metal age'.

The Steampunk world of *Thief* was developed further in a series of sequels. *Thief II: The Metal Age* (2000) reduced the magical elements of its predecessor, emphasizing the urban technology of steam-powered robots ruled over by the Mechanists, a powerful religious faction now running The City. Garrett is co-opted in an effort to save The City from the malevolent influence of the out-of-control technology of the Mechanists.

A third game, *Thief: Deadly Shadows*, followed in 2004 opening up The City to free-roaming between missions. A major environment is The City's dominant clocktower where Garrett has to sabotage the giant clockwork mechanism, bringing about the collapse of the tower. This event sees Garrett on the run from various forces that want to control him. Despite the collapse of the company behind the games, a fourth instalment has been promised and is expected to make even more of the Steampunk city at its centre.

Arcanum: Of Steamworks and Magic Obscura (2001), a PC RPG, is widely regarded as one of the most Steampunk of all videogames. Set in a fantasy world that has just undergone an Industrial Revolution, the game begins with the crash of a Zeppelin leaving the main player the only survivor. The player is charged with a mission from a dying goblin: deliver a silver ring to 'the boy'. The game doesn't rush the player into pursuing the mission, allowing him to explore the wider world in a freeform style, taking part in sub-missions. The choices made result in the game taking different directions. Side quests can shape the outcome of the main quest, as can the player's choices whether to use magic or (often steam-driven) technology to solve problems. In the world of Arcanum, the new technologies (including Tesla guns) are beginning to eclipse the older powers of magic. Magic and technology can interact in weird ways, so a wizard travelling by steam train may be relegated to a third-class compartment

as his presence might affect the steam engine. It's a neat conceit that plays to some of the themes of the conflict between new technology and older ways of life that have emerged through Steampunk literature.

Steampunk iconography even influenced 'survival horror' videogame *BioShock* (2007), despite being based in the 1960s rather than the Victorian era. Set in a failed undersea utopia called Rapture, *Bioshock* features a decaying facility now inhabited by aggressive, genetically mutated humans, who exist alongside mechanical robots. The world of Rapture is sufficiently divorced from any real-world concerns for it to constitute a fantasy environment, a Gothic world within which anomalous technology exists. One of the 'boss' villains of the game is a genetically enhanced human grafted into a biomechanical diving suit. Although a dystopic vision drawing on the philosophy of Ayn Rand and concerned with genetic manipulation gone wrong, *BioShock* (and its sequels) has enough Steampunk-related graphic imagery and style to be worth exploring. While *BioShock 2* (2010) further developed the underwater world of the original, the third game, *BioShock Infinite* (2012) takes place aboard a collapsing 'air-city' (held up by blimps and balloons) and features a roller-coaster-style Skyline rail transport system, foregrounding the series' Steampunk credentials.

Games like the Steampunk-influenced *Fable III* (2010) highlight many of the problems for videogames: as with movies and television, few of them wholeheartedly adopt Steampunk as core to their gameplay, simply using the aesthetic as a decorative add-on. Some of the games have done a better job than others: ironically some of the earliest (such as *MYST* and *Final Fantasy VII*) have been the best, hailing from the 1990s, before Steampunk reached widespread mainstream attention. Perhaps it comes down to the fact that, unlike graphic novels, videogames are simply not yet a great medium for stories. The comic books that adopted Steampunk in their look have also made it central to their storytelling (particularly in the work of Bryan Talbot and Alan Moore). The comic books widely seen as Steampunk owe much to their literary forbears in a way that cannot be said of the often-superficial nature of Steampunk videogames.

Left: One of the Little Sisters, who are 'harvested' for the valuable ADAM mutagen, in the nightmarish world of *BioShock 2*. Above: The dystopian *Final Fantasy VII*, which has sold over 10 million copies worldwide and mixes both Cyberpunk and Steampunk elements to create an immersive role-playing experience, in which players battle to save a planet on the brink of environmental collapse.

143

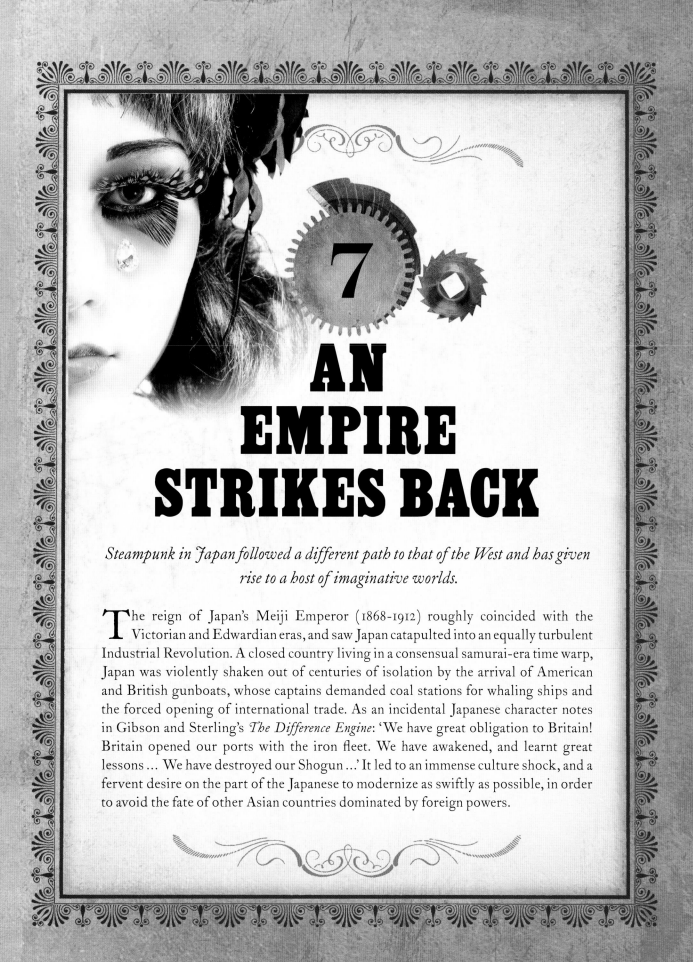

7

AN EMPIRE STRIKES BACK

Steampunk in Japan followed a different path to that of the West and has given rise to a host of imaginative worlds.

The reign of Japan's Meiji Emperor (1868-1912) roughly coincided with the Victorian and Edwardian eras, and saw Japan catapulted into an equally turbulent Industrial Revolution. A closed country living in a consensual samurai-era time warp, Japan was violently shaken out of centuries of isolation by the arrival of American and British gunboats, whose captains demanded coal stations for whaling ships and the forced opening of international trade. As an incidental Japanese character notes in Gibson and Sterling's *The Difference Engine*: 'We have great obligation to Britain! Britain opened our ports with the iron fleet. We have awakened, and learnt great lessons … We have destroyed our Shogun …' It led to an immense culture shock, and a fervent desire on the part of the Japanese to modernize as swiftly as possible, in order to avoid the fate of other Asian countries dominated by foreign powers.

In Japan, the Great War was an excuse for a land-grab in Asia and the Pacific, a validation and later an excuse for mounting militarism. In some senses, Japan was spared Europe's Great War trauma, thereby extending the lifespan of locally set Edisonades. As a result, Japan's Steampunk settings often extend into the reign of the Taisho Emperor (1912-26), before the coronation of his son, Hirohito, heralded the beginning of a different and unfortunate age.

Empire has a different narrative in Japan than that widely perceived in the West. Some Japanese still regard modernity as something thrust upon them by unwelcome foreign powers, a sudden instruction to tinker with new technologies that briefly created sprawling overseas Japanese colonies in Korea, China, Manchuria and south-east Asia. But Japan's empire was brought to a sudden halt in 1945 by the very foreign powers that the Japanese began the period emulating. Its agents were rounded up and imprisoned or executed. Its god-emperor read out a prepared statement saying that he was not really a god after all.

This all served to impart an extra layer to Japanese fiction set in the Meiji and Taisho periods. The imperial reigns that spanned 1868 to 1925 are parsed as a truly golden age (similar to America's *belle époque*), when Japan was on the rise and striving to be accepted as one of the world's Great Powers – Japan was winning, Japan was admirable, and Japan was untainted with defeat. Japanese Steampunk adopted the style of Jules Verne, H.G. Wells and Arthur Conan Doyle, but also rediscovered the period pieces of the likes of Shunro Oshikawa and Juza Unno. Like the genre in English, the Japanese variant captures a sense of the enthusiasm and optimism of the age of steam, even as it punkishly questions some of its assumptions, beliefs and consequences.

Lost in translation

One of the odd characteristics of the Japanese reading public is its ready access to immense fields of foreign literature, translated into Japanese, but from which Japanese characters are largely absent. The Japanese perspective on the early Victorian period is that of urchins on the outside, their faces pressed against the windows of Western culture, gazing in rapt but slightly baffled admiration at the activities of elegant ladies and noble adventurers. In the worldview of the early Victorians, Japan is yet another remote island awaiting the arrival of modern civilization, a mysterious, decadent empire shut off from the rest of the world. Hence, it's not all that surprising that an entire section of Japanese Victoriana

keeps Japan itself at a distance from such stories.

Moreover, foreign science fiction arrived in Japan out of order and out of time, frequently translated into a modern idiom that made it seem fresher than it may have to its home audiences. Science fiction in Japan grew out of legal and pirated versions of European detective fiction, particularly Arthur Conan Doyle's Sherlock Holmes stories, and imitators such as Juza Unno's *Soroku Homura*.

The greats of Japanese science fiction in the period include Shunro Oshikawa (1876–1914), who was strongly inspired by Verne in his *Submarine Warship: A Mysterious Story of Island Adventure* (1900). It features the driven Captain Sakuragi, an eccentric inventor and military man who strives to perfect his steam-powered underwater ram-ship, the Denkosen, before the inevitable clash of the white and yellow civilizations. As befits a pulp story written after Japan's victory in the Sino-Japanese War of 1894–95, *Submarine Warship* features numerous flag-planting adventures in the Pacific and Indian Oceans, before the Denkosen puts its superior Japanese technology to use against dastardly foreign pirates. Oshikawa would follow up with several more books on submarine themes, but died before he could truly fulfil his potential as an author. His legacy divided into two distinct directions; some of his stories of military derring-do were prophetic enough to be adapted as straightforward, contemporary propaganda films by the 1920s. Others were skewed into even more fantastic realms, emphasizing undersea kingdoms and sea monsters. Hence, the most recent and visible incarnation of his work is the anime series *Super Atragon* (1995), in which the lost empire of Mu returns from below the Earth's surface, taking on the modern-day military with Vernian contraptions such as giant magnetic weapons.

By dying before Japan's plunge into full-blown twentieth-century militarism, Oshikawa was spared the sight of the true implications of his right-wing futures. No such mercy awaited

Top: Promotional artwork for *Super Atragon*, an anime series based on the work of Japanese science fiction pioneer Shunro Oshikawa.

the 'father of Japanese science fiction' Juza Unno (1897–1949), whose early tales of innovative SF were co-opted into the imperialist military machine. Unno's early work was often subversive, such as his chilling short story 'The Music Bath at 1800 Hours' (1937), in which the citizens of Japan are brainwashed by a signal broadcast every day at a predetermined time. By the Second World War Unno was conscripted as a propagandist, and wrote story after pan-Asian story about bold Korean inventors assisting the Japanese war effort, or Chinese secret agents spying on the evil British. As a result of their wartime output, Unno and writers like him fell out of favour in the 1950s, exposing Japan to a wave of foreign SF in translation, and to some extent denying that the period between the death of the Taisho Emperor and the bombing of Hiroshima ever existed.

Japanese science fiction from the 1950s onwards was as obsessed with the modernity of the atomic age as fiction in other countries. As in the West, a sense of retrogressive science, or an appeal to the seemingly less problematic futures of yesteryear, arrived in the last quarter of the twentieth century in reaction to modern obsessions with computers and digitization. Japanese Steampunk was one of the longer-lasting reactions to Cyberpunk. Steampunk became a feature of manga (comic books), anime

(animation), games and prose fiction, revisiting the Meiji and Taisho periods when Japan was on the rise, before the ordeal of the Second World War defeat. Japanese authors excelled at retelling the prelude to that war with baroque machinery and alien invaders – this last idea particularly common, as it skewed the story of the twentieth century from one of global warfare to one of a unified Earth-based resistance to a new, truly external enemy.

Steam fantasies

Steampunk fantasy is the most visible element of the Japanese genre to gain worldwide attention, thanks to countless videogames that strive for newness by using design elements from the past. Partly as a reaction against the completely digital twenty-first century technology that powers the games themselves, the likes of the Final Fantasy series often come steeped in cogwheels, gaskets and regulators, almost as if hoping to conceal the chips and hard drives that actually produce them.

While working in the 1970s on the World Masterpiece Theatre series of cartoon adaptations of foreign books, the director Hayao Miayzaki concocted a story called 'Around the World Under the Sea', based on two Jules Verne novels. Nothing came of the idea immediately, although Miyazaki would subsequently put some of his interest in Victoriana to use in 1984 in an Italian co-production based on Sherlock Holmes. An initial plan to animate *The Hound of the Baskervilles* was scrapped amid concerns it would be too frightening for children, leading Miyazaki and his collaborators

Left and below: 2004's *Steamboy*, by Katsuhiro Otomo, is arguably the definitive animated take on Steampunk to come out of Japan.

Hayao Miyazaki (b.1941)

Hayao Miyazaki's love of old-world technology stems in part from his love of the old world values it evokes. Subsequently world famous as the director of many acclaimed anime features under his own Studio Ghibli brand, Miyazaki regularly returns to elaborate Heath Robinson designs, coal-fired technology and absurd extrapolations of outmoded technical assumptions, such as helicopters with a dozen propellers. In everything from the rickety mobile fort of its title to the military hardware of its antagonists, his *Howl's Moving Castle* (2004) is quintessential Miyazaki Steampunk. Although based on the novel of the same title by the British novelist Diana Wynne Jones, *Howl* also draws on Miyazaki's own politics, and functions as an extended allegory of the Gulf War – enemy forces invade a hapless kingdom in search of a magical MacGuffin. Many of Miyazaki's other films harbour old-fashioned technology, for various reasons. In *Kiki's Delivery Service* (1989), a culture based on magic has little need of modern technology and remains trapped in what, for some, would be an idyllic Edwardian time warp. In Miyazaki's Oscar-winning *Spirited Away* (2001), the lead character's entry into a magical otherworld exposes her to sights born of Japanese tradition, much of which is deliberately evoked with the nineteenth-century technology of a haunted bath-house. In *Spirited Away*, the world of the dead is parsed as a world in which dead technologies persist and flourish.

to reconceive the entire thing as a fantasy of wild Victorian contraptions and adventure, in which the entire cast were dogs. *Famous Detective Holmes*, released in English as the episodic series *Sherlock Hound* (1984–85), mixed original themes from Doyle with Steampunk submarines and airships.

However, Miyazaki's original Jules Verne proposal languished, forgotten, at the Toho Studios for an entire generation, until it was dusted off by a new group of animators, Studio Gainax. In a greatly altered form it was brought to life as *Nadia: The Secret of Blue Water* (1990), in which a French inventor teams up with Captain Nemo's daughter to prevent the masters of Neo-Atlantis from taking over the world.

Elements of what would become *The Secret of Blue Water* could also be seen in one of Miyazaki's own movies, *Laputa: Castle in the Sky* (1986). The Vernian influences are still readily apparent, as is the presence of a central character whose necklace and its attached crystal form an important catalyst for the plot. *Laputa* and *The Secret of Blue Water* also share a merry mood, where even Victorian-style villains such as pirates and thieves appear relatively unthreatening, imparting a childish sense of fun rather than the grim Victorian reality.

Perhaps the simplest application of Steampunk in manga form can be seen in Kia

Above: *Sherlock Hound* was a quirky view of Victorian adventure. Left: The eponymous fortress from *Howl's Moving Castle*.

151

> THE STREETS HERE ARE CONTINUALLY ENSHROUDED IN WHITE MIST. STEAM RISES FROM EVERYWHERE OBSCURING THE STREETS AND BUILDINGS.

> BECAUSE COAL IS THE ONLY FUEL AVAILABLE...

Asamiya's *Steam Detectives* (1994). Later also adapted into an animated series, the story is a pastiche of Sherlock Holmes, set in the aptly named Steam City, where the only available fuel is coal. As a result, an entire modern society has evolved with steam-based machinery, even extending to the inevitable giant robots that fight in the battle scenes.

ANIMERICA EXTRA GRAPHIC NOVEL

STEAM DETECTIVES

VOL. 4

STORY AND ART BY KIA ASAMIYA

Steamboy (2004)

It took Katsuhiro Otomo, the director of the post-apocalyptic masterpiece *Akira* (1988), fourteen years to make another full-length animated feature. For much of that time, his much-delayed project was *Steamboy*, a caper movie set in Britain, in which a family of inventors try to keep a miracle energy source out of the hands of dastardly entrepreneurs. Had *Steamboy* been released in the mid 1990s as originally intended, it might have formed a core text of Steampunk. Ironically, it was delayed by developments in modern technology, as Otomo tinkered and retinkered with newly available computer graphics packages.

Steamboy is set in 1866, when Japan was still barely open to the West, in an alternative universe where the Crystal Palace is sited in London's Docklands, and where Scarlett O'Hara is a gun merchant. Weapons are the all-important subject at a world exposition where the nations of the world, except Japan, gleefully display the new inventions that will turn the approaching twentieth century into an industrialized hell. But while *Steamboy* has all the necessary ingredients for Steampunk, and while it might clothe its characters in Victorian garb, its basic plot of a race to attain a quasi-magical, dangerous energy source is suspiciously similar to its predecessor *Akira*. Its title, however, evokes that of another sci-fi classic, Osamu Tezuka's *Astro Boy* (manga 1952–68, TV 1963–66, movie 2009), and may have always been intended as the origin for a different kind of story. By the closing credits of *Steamboy*, its hero has liberated a jetpack from the ruins, and is fighting crime as a Steampunk superhero.

STEAMPUNK

Steam pastiches

The science fiction author Masaki Yamada is best known in English for the anime version of his fantasy *Kishin Heidan* (*Kishin Corps*, 1990–94), which sees the Second World War reimagined with additional alien invaders and giant, petrol-driven robots. He is the most thought-provoking and complex of Japan's Steampunk authors, having created two books of immense imagination, intricately connected to the world of European fiction.

The protagonist of *Ada* (serialized 1991–3, published in book form 1994) is Ada Byron, the daughter of Lord Byron, whose adventures in an alternative London bring her into contact with Sherlock Holmes and Charles Babbage. It's Babbage who is the key, as Ada becomes a vital cog in the construction of the first working 'difference engine' – it is, perhaps, no coincidence that *The Difference Engine* was published in Japanese in the year that *Ada* first began serialization.

The setting of *Ada* tests boundaries of prose narrative to its limits. It is an alternative vision of Victorian London because we are really in the distant future, at a point where a massive information singularity has caused the worlds of fact and fiction to crash together. Ada is indeed Lord Byron's daughter within the story, but she is also an avatar of a far-future super-computer who must be stopped unless her meddling between fact and fiction cause the universe to implode and human history to be plunged into chaos.

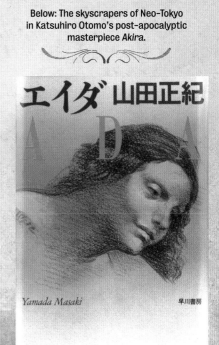

Below: The skyscrapers of Neo-Tokyo in Katsuhiro Otomo's post-apocalyptic masterpiece *Akira*.

ILLUMINATIONS

山田正紀

MASAKI YAMADA

イリュミナシオン

君よ、非情の河を下れ

早川書房

Yamada returned to mind-bending Victorian pastiche in *Illuminations* (2009), a novel that he jokingly called 'widescreen Baroque'. Taking the life and poetry of Arthur Rimbaud as his inspiration, Yamada suggests that the French author's gun-running African misadventures were part of an elaborate interdimensional clash between conflicting time streams, and that his symbolist poems were a garbled attempt to explain time travel and alternative universes to an unsuspecting Victorian readership. Rimbaud is joined in his adventures by Emily Brontë, whose own writings of 'a chainless soul' are also reconceived as attempts to explain quantum cosmology using the vocabulary of the nineteenth century.

STEAMPUNK

Steampunk! (1999)

Steampunk! Three Creatures Tame the Railroad (1999) by Hitoshi Yoshioka uses the now-familiar genre tag as the title to a light-hearted sci-fi adventure novel. In a bizarre action-adventure riff on *Thomas the Tank Engine*, it is set in the distant future on the human colony world Junky Leo, a Wild West analogue crisscrossed by railway lines and traversed by artificially intelligent steam engines. Maverick human adventurers try to make an honest buck with their own locomotive, against hostile natives and scheming fellow humans.

   Steampunk! is in love with the locomotives themselves, and often reads as if it were spun off from a resource management game as its characters bicker over the logistics of coal and water. In his afterword, author Yoshioka fixates on three topics guaranteed to press the right buttons with his readers: trains, technology and dinosaurs. 'Steam locomotives in particular,' he writes, 'hark back to the period of "enriching the nation and strengthening the army", when technology and military hardware from progressive Britain led the way for Japan ... First we copied British products. Only then did we have the wherewithal to create our own.'

Steam class

The Japanese also find a surety and familiarity in the fashions used to denote class in the Victorian system. 'Gothic Lolitas' adorned with frills and aprons like scullery maids and governesses form a recognizable part of the Japanese fashion scene, as do their male equivalents, kitted out like Edwardian dandies and Victorian butlers. Exotic, otherworldly, dangerous London is a recurring setting in Japanese fiction, from the non-genre upstairs-downstairs manga tale *Emma: A Victorian Romance* (2002–06) by Kaoru Mori, to the duelling 1890s 'Frankensteins' of Nobuhiro Watsuki's manga *Embalming* (2005), in which the wonderfully named teenage hero Fury Flatliner is resurrected to fight similar homunculi brought to life using the 'science' first revealed by Mary Shelley.

   As the names suggest, historical accuracy is not a primary concern, nor is it in Yana Toboso's manga series *Black Butler* (2006–present), in which the wealthy young London orphan Ciel Phantomhive sells his soul in a desire to avenge the deaths of his parents. As a result, his handsome manservant Sebastian Michaelis is a fully equipped demon, who works as a secret agent on behalf of Phantomhive and Queen Victoria.

   Black Butler is merely the latest in a long string of hellish fantasies of Britain in manga or anime form, in which Dickensian London in particular is set up as a fantasy 'dark city'. Its roots lie in the likes of 1993's *Earl Cain* by Kaori Yuki, whose titular detective begins investigating his own imminent death when he discovers that someone has been poisoning him with arsenic. Cain's nemesis is his evil half-brother Jizabel Disraeli,

155

a pet-tormenting dastard. His best friend, on the other hand, is Riff the loyal butler ... or so he thinks! In fact, Riff is a member of a secret organization called Delilah, dedicated to the successful reanimation of corpses. Notably, Yuki's manga work began as a simple character piece, its artwork mainly in close-ups with backgrounds largely forgotten. It was only as the *Earl Cain* series brought her fame and fortune that she was able to afford research trips to the exotic land of Britain, in turn encouraging her to add a sense of place to her artwork's ever-present sense of menace.

Sakura Wars (1996–present)

Beginning as a computer game, but soon diversifying into novels, comics, a cartoon series, an animated movie and even an all-girl theatrical musical, Oji Hiroi's *Sakura Wars* (1996) is one of the most influential works in the history of Japanese Steampunk. It reimagines the 1920s with the world under attack by demons, held at bay by virginal sorceresses in clunky steam-powered machines who form new and attractive units of national armies. The original game centred on the fortunate male officer who got to command a squad of international, demon-hunting lovelies. Other incarnations of the franchise came to fixate more on period detail and local colour, including outmoded period slang and popular culture, even to the extent of printing Japanese with old-form characters, right-to-left instead of the more modern left-to-right. An elegant and classy fan club, the Taisho Romantic Society, became the nexus of much subsequent fan activity in Steampunk fiction, art and costume.

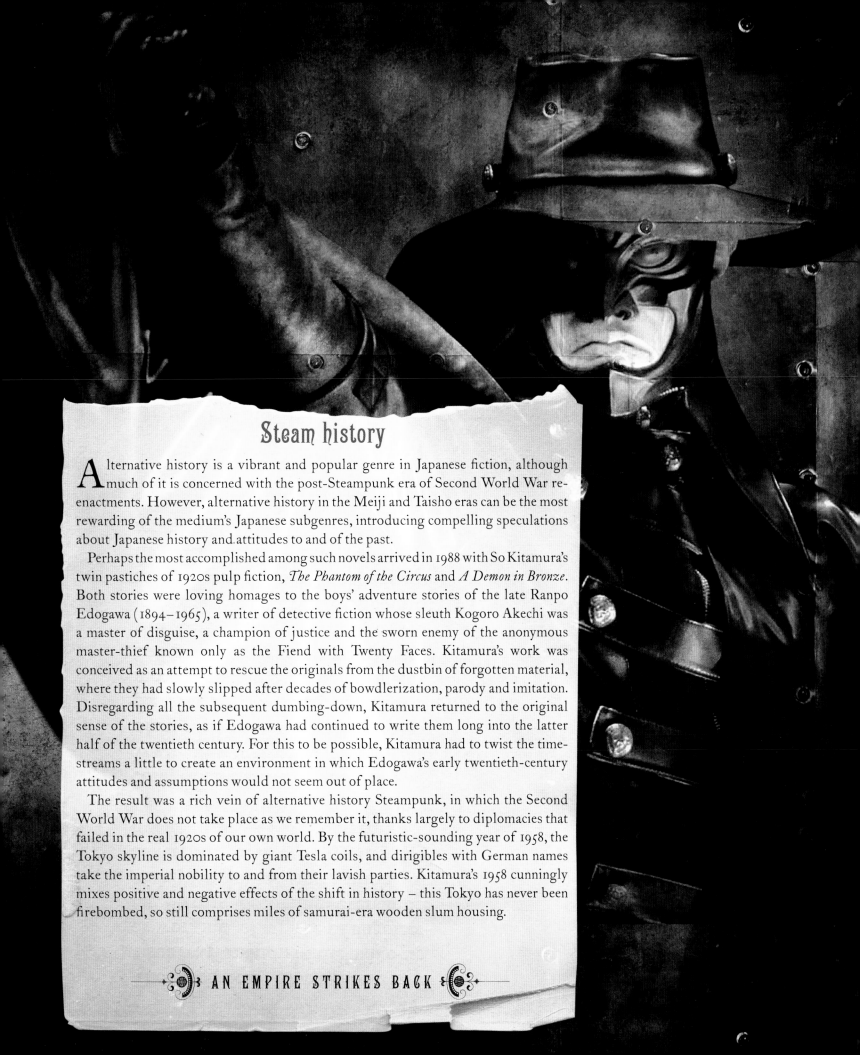

Steam history

Alternative history is a vibrant and popular genre in Japanese fiction, although much of it is concerned with the post-Steampunk era of Second World War re-enactments. However, alternative history in the Meiji and Taisho eras can be the most rewarding of the medium's Japanese subgenres, introducing compelling speculations about Japanese history and attitudes to and of the past.

Perhaps the most accomplished among such novels arrived in 1988 with So Kitamura's twin pastiches of 1920s pulp fiction, *The Phantom of the Circus* and *A Demon in Bronze*. Both stories were loving homages to the boys' adventure stories of the late Ranpo Edogawa (1894–1965), a writer of detective fiction whose sleuth Kogoro Akechi was a master of disguise, a champion of justice and the sworn enemy of the anonymous master-thief known only as the Fiend with Twenty Faces. Kitamura's work was conceived as an attempt to rescue the originals from the dustbin of forgotten material, where they had slowly slipped after decades of bowdlerization, parody and imitation. Disregarding all the subsequent dumbing-down, Kitamura returned to the original sense of the stories, as if Edogawa had continued to write them long into the latter half of the twentieth century. For this to be possible, Kitamura had to twist the time-streams a little to create an environment in which Edogawa's early twentieth-century attitudes and assumptions would not seem out of place.

The result was a rich vein of alternative history Steampunk, in which the Second World War does not take place as we remember it, thanks largely to diplomacies that failed in the real 1920s of our own world. By the futuristic-sounding year of 1958, the Tokyo skyline is dominated by giant Tesla coils, and dirigibles with German names take the imperial nobility to and from their lavish parties. Kitamura's 1958 cunningly mixes positive and negative effects of the shift in history – this Tokyo has never been firebombed, so still comprises miles of samurai-era wooden slum housing.

Kitamura's stories truly embraced the 'punk' element, leading them to the provocative conclusion that if pre-war Japan had been allowed to endure as a militarist aristocracy, anyone supporting such a society would be complicit in crimes against humanity. This entirely reversed the characters from the original inspirations, turning Akechi the loyal detective into a government stooge, and the 'evil' Fiend With Twenty Faces into a noble-hearted anarchist vigilante Batman figure. Although this element was reduced in the subsequent overlong live-action movie adaptation *K20: Legend of the Mask* (2008), it still demonstrated a powerful sense that while much Japanese Steampunk might be little more than superficial frills and cogs, a significant part of it retains the deeper considerations to be found in the best that the wider genre has to offer.

Earth is the alien planet: The Japanese John Carter novels

Disney's *John Carter* (2012, based on *John Carter of Mars*) isn't the only modern spin to be found on the works of Edgar Rice Burroughs. There's a whole world of as-yet untranslated Japanese novels that delve into the worlds of Victorian science fiction and adventure from the prolific author Hitoshi Yoshioka, best known in English as the creator of *Irresponsible Captain Tylor* (2003–present) and *Idol Defence Force Hummingbirds* (1993–94).

Yoshioka also seems to have been the first man to use the term 'Steampunk' in a Japanese context with his novel *Steampunk!* (1995), set in a world in which maverick engineers duel with sci-fi steam locomotives. But his serious, ongoing obsession with the Gilded Age began in 1995 with *Going with the Wind*, an epic spin-off from *Gone with the Wind* (1939) that asked the searching question of exactly how the original's Rhett Butler made money as a blockade runner. Yoshioka homed in on the simple fact that if Butler were a rich cad in the 1870s, he had probably made a lot of his fortune running guns to one of the world's military hotspots in the previous decade – revolutionary Japan. Yoshioka's novel was populated with fictional characters from *Gone with the Wind* and real names from Japanese history, retelling the story of the Meiji Restoration with an adventurous twist.

Yoshioka's researches also led him back to the works of Edgar Rice Burroughs, whose character John Carter was also a veteran of the American Civil War. This in turn inspired him to write another pastiche in which a young soldier is transported to another world instead of dying on Earth. *Toshizo Hijikata of Mars* (2004) is inspired by the tragic figure of one of the 'last samurai', who died fighting restorationist forces in a battle he knew he could never win. Yoshioka's version has Hijikata transported to Mars by astral projection at the moment of his apparent death. There, he enjoys a new career as a samurai mercenary, fighting in the realm of John Carter, Prince of Helium.

That was not enough for Yoshioka. He soon followed up with *Z-Signal on Venus* (2004), which transported the Japanese naval hero Saneyuki Akiyama to the oceans of Earth's sister planet, and his tour-de-force, *Southern Cavalry Captain John Carter* (2005), which imagines what kind of man Burroughs's hero would have been before he made his fateful journey to the Red Planet. In this latter book, Yoshioka imagines Civil War America itself as a fantasy realm, where scantily clad first-nation girls take the place of Martian slaves, and Victorian technology is regarded with awe and fear on the great and largely unexplored plains of the 'new world'. As in *Going with the Wind*, he drags in both factual and fictional characters, including the future US president William McKinley and a Reverend March who appears to be the future paterfamilias of Louisa May Alcott's *Little Women*!

8

OF COGS AND CORSETS

Exploring the burgeoning, diverse and creative subcultures of Steampunk fans and fandom.

Although it had its origins in literature and its most populist explorations have been in film and television, there is much more than that to Steampunk. There's a whole creative lifestyle and subculture modelled after the Steampunk aesthetic that has exploded from a cult into the mainstream. From costumers and role-players to gadget-builders and retro-fitters, through musicians and short filmmakers, as well as the burgeoning world of online communities, Steampunk has become a thriving creative force.

Clockwork couture

Ever since prominent twenty-two-year-old fan Forrest J. Ackerman attended the First World Science Fiction Convention ('Worldcon') in Los Angeles in 1939 in his 'futuristicostume' (modelled after *Things to Come*, 1936), fan costuming has been part of science fiction fandom. The following year saw around two dozen fans attend in costume, and it has grown unstoppably. From Ackerman through 'cosplay' to the

vogue for Steampunk costuming, funky fashion has become part of fans creatively expressing themselves.

Organized science fiction fandom developed in the 1930s, growing out of the regular correspondence between a few aficionados in the letter columns of prominent pulp magazines such as *Amazing Stories* (1926–2005) and *Wonder Stories* (1929–55). Local clubs developed in New York and Los Angeles, and among the first members were Frederick Pohl (later an SF author) and Ackerman. The first Worldcon (held as part of the 1939 New York World's Fair) launched the idea of science fiction conventions, making the genre the 'most social of all literary genres', according to writer and critic Cory Doctorow. 'Science fiction is driven by organized fandom, volunteers who put on hundreds of literary conventions in every corner of the globe, every weekend of the year.' Thousands of conventions followed, with the original Worldcon 'brand' still going strong; recent events have been held in such diverse cities as Glasgow (2005), Yokohama (2007), Montreal (2009), and Chicago (2012).

Costuming became a larger part of such conventions as they embraced media tie-ins and began featuring movies and television alongside literary science fiction, absorbing much of *Star Trek*, *Star Wars* and *Doctor Who* fandom. Costuming competitions were held regularly, while the halls of SF conventions often featured fans dressed as their favourite characters. Stewards dressed as armoured stormtroopers regularly police the *Star Wars* Celebration conventions (1999–present), while increasingly popular competitions have seen ever more outlandish costumes paraded.

Originating in Japan, 'cosplay' (a portmanteau of 'costume' and 'play', a term introduced in 1984) saw fans adopting the looks and personas of anime, manga and videogame characters, including the all-pervasive giant mecha robots. An entire area around Tokyo's Harajuku district became a centre for costumed fans to gather, while the Akihabara district developed several cosplay cafes.

Steampunk was a natural subject for costuming. Although it had originated in a literary form, it wasn't until the visual iconography became familiar (due to *Wild Wild West*, 1999) that Steampunk costuming became widespread. The Steampunk subculture has become increasingly divorced from novels or films and grown exponentially as an independent creative outlet focusing on costuming, events and the creation of Steampunk gadgets. This development coincided with the rise of the internet. Whereas science fiction fans prior to the mid 1990s had to rely on conventions, events, local gatherings, the telephone and the mail (to circulate small press fan

THE MUSEUM OF THE HISTORY OF SCIENCE

STEAMPUNK

THE FIRST MUSEUM EXHIBITION

CURATED BY ART DONOVAN

13 OCTOBER 2009 TO 21 FEBRUARY 2010

Oxford Steampunk Exhibition 2009–10

Curated by Art Donovan, the Oxford Steampunk Exhibition was held at the Museum of the History of Science between October 2009 and February 2010. It was billed as 'The world's first exhibition of Steampunk [featuring] devices and contraptions extraordinary'. Divided into the practical and the fanciful, the event showcased the work of eighteen Steampunk artists from around the world and welcomed over 70,000 visitors. Interactive, with many audience participation events for children and school groups, the exhibition included Steampunk in fashion, movies, performance and art. Videos and images of the event are maintained in an online exhibit at: www.mhs.ox.ac.uk/exhibits/steampunk.

Top, left: Cosplay pioneer Forrest J. Ackerman, pictured at the First World Science Fiction Convention in Los Angeles in 1939.

magazines known as 'fanzines'), Steampunk developed as a subculture when it was much easier for people to connect with each other and as groups, thanks to online social networks. This allowed a rapid expansion of the phenomenon, with like-minded groups coalescing around websites and forums as the ability to share photographs of their costumes (as well as hints on costuming techniques) online proved particularly useful.

The combination of historically sourced styles of dress (largely, though not exclusively, Victorian) with fantasy has given Steampunk costuming an extra edge. There had long been an interest in Victorian style among fashion practitioners, with New York designer Kit Stølen among the first to identify this fashion trend in connection with Steampunk. His expansion of Victoriana through the short-lived fad for Cyberpunk gave rise to more enduring Steampunk fashions. Photos of Stølen's style on the internet were an important factor in kickstarting the look.

Many early adopters of Steampunk fashion styles often had little or no knowledge of its literary origins, and were perhaps only sketchily aware of its uses in film and TV. A vague idea of Victorian fashion and a limited knowledge of the retro-science fiction of Wells or Verne was often enough. The explorations of the wider imaginative worlds of visual or literary Steampunk could follow. Others took the opposite

163

trajectory, coming to the fashion as an expression of their interest in the wider literature or films. This was a movement that evolved outside of organized science fiction conventions and costuming contests, although those events became the primary arena in which the styles could be displayed. While full-on Steampunk-inspired outfits can be elaborate, it has become possible to buy into the Steampunk style cheaply by subtly adapting existing clothing or making small additions to shop-bought items. This DIY punk approach was entirely appropriate to the movement, although retailers like Hot Topic and online providers like ParaNoire and Steampunk Couture were quick to offer off-the-shelf Steampunk looks.

While the subtle, casual 'daily wear' approach suited the needs of many, more serious practitioners developed elaborate bespoke outfits specifically to be seen as part of the growing Steampunk event scene. The movement began infiltrating general science fiction conventions before spinning off on its own, with California claiming the first dedicated Steampunk convention. Steam Powered took place over Halloween 2008 (an ideal time for costumes). This Sunnyvale event had 500 people in attendance and featured a panel that attempted to define the genre using a Venn diagram segmenting Steampunk into four main groups: Literature, Fashion, Makers and Music. In addition to the regular panels and a busy dealers room, the event featured Steampunk band Abney Park.

The rise of Steampunk events brought the vogue for costuming to a more

STEAMPUNK

public space. The performance and roleplaying aspects of these developments cannot be ignored, as a flood of airship captains, flamboyant pirates, madcap inventors, ladies of Victorian leisure, and gentlemen explorers began parading convention floors. An assortment of corsets, parasols, fancy hats and goggles with additional mechanical contrivances like cogs or pistons came to make up the most widely observed Steampunk style. Accessories often included ray-guns, ornate timepieces or Steampunk-modified modern items like mobile phones or iPods. The number of hand-made Steampunk items available via the craft website Etsy grew markedly from 2009, leading to debates within the community as to what did and what did not conform to Steampunk fashion.

While the definitions of Steampunk have always been loose, the magpie nature of fashion pushes these boundaries further. Influences can range as far back as medieval Europe and samurai Japan, via pirate style to Napoleonic military chic, high Victoriana and Weird Western gunslinger right up to 1920s Prohibition-era gangsters. That's well beyond the late-Victorian, pre-Great War boundaries generally accepted, and displays the subculture's tendency to sprawl.

As in many subcultures, Steampunk costuming has associations with public display and performance. In an academic paper entitled 'Negotiating the Punk in Steampunk: Subculture, Fashion and Performative Identities' (2011), Dr Brigid Cherry and Maria Mellins charted this new frontier, identifying those who create and parade Steampunk-influenced costumes as being participants in 'a performative style subculture associated with recognizable fashion and lifestyle accessories'. They went on to assert that the Steampunk lifestyle is 'a subcultural constructor of identity, articulating complex discourses concerning gender and class. The pleasures of [the] Steampunk lifestyle are associated with the rejection of contemporary lifestyles and social mores, and a return to ingenuity, craftsmanship and invention, and a real-world 'acting out' of imagined histories.'

There are levels of performance when fans adopt public Steampunk personas. For many it goes beyond embracing a clothing or fashion style. Many concoct role-playing character identities alongside their outlandish outfits. This often involves developing a suitable name for their Steampunk alter ego, complete with an imagined history and a current pursuit, whether exploration, invention or the quest for power or immortality (all themes in Steampunk fiction).

This takes the escapist nature of Steampunk costuming one step further. While most will only play out their alter ego identity during Steampunk events, some might extend their fictionalized selves by writing stories about their adventures or maintaining their imagined selves in online identities in Steampunk forums. Here Steampunk is extended beyond a visual aesthetic into a display of personal and community identity.

Cherry and Mellins posit the 'emergence of subcultural activities and identities' in

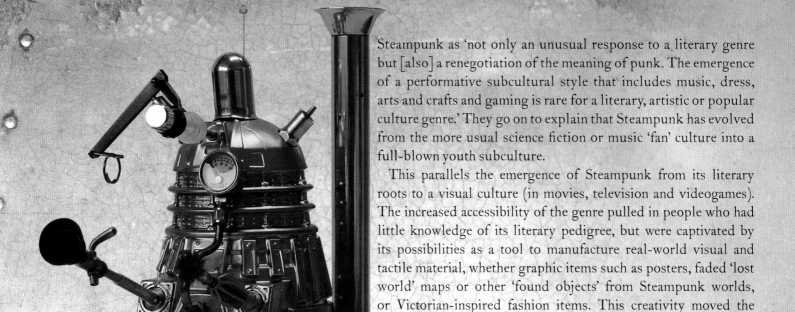

Steampunk as 'not only an unusual response to a literary genre but [also] a renegotiation of the meaning of punk. The emergence of a performative subcultural style that includes music, dress, arts and crafts and gaming is rare for a literary, artistic or popular culture genre.' They go on to explain that Steampunk has evolved from the more usual science fiction or music 'fan' culture into a full-blown youth subculture.

This parallels the emergence of Steampunk from its literary roots to a visual culture (in movies, television and videogames). The increased accessibility of the genre pulled in people who had little knowledge of its literary pedigree, but were captivated by its possibilities as a tool to manufacture real-world visual and tactile material, whether graphic items such as posters, faded 'lost world' maps or other 'found objects' from Steampunk worlds, or Victorian-inspired fashion items. This creativity moved the Steampunk lifestyle from one of consumption (watching films, reading novels) to one of production (making clothes, adapting or constructing objects) following the DIY aesthetic of mid-1970s punk. This productivity gave rise to a thriving Steampunk musical subculture that drew on original punk, Goth, industrial and metal musical styles. This, allied with the emergence of diverse online and real-world Steampunk communities, saw the fan base of the Steampunk lifestyle break out into mainstream youth culture.

Previous fan cultures (especially in science fiction) had fostered creativity in writing (fiction or journalism through fanzines) and filmmaking (through 'fan films'). While science fiction fandom had always featured a degree of costuming – a trend intensified with cosplay – it never overwhelmed the non-costuming appreciation of the genre. It can be argued that due to its overall visual aesthetic, modern Steampunk has become a lifestyle in which it is necessary to participate in the creative costuming or object-adapting that so dominates the field in order to fully 'belong'. The style subculture facilitated by social networking has come to define what Steampunk is in the mainstream consciousness.

In adopting a 'style' spread through group connections, many involved were actively rejecting other fashion and lifestyle choices more widely available (and approved of by the mainstream). Whether in costuming or technology design, Steampunk encompasses the rejection of the contemporary and the embrace of the past (albeit an imaginary or weirdly developed idea of that 'past'). Through online communities Steampunk as an aesthetic evolved separately from the fiction. By the middle of the first decade of the twenty-first century, Steampunk had developed into a bona fide separate 'scene' distinct from the science fiction fandom that had spawned it.

Artisans of a future past

Modding – meaning 'to modify' – began primarily with 'case modding' by early adopters within the Steampunk online communities, who customized their laptops, computers and iPods, adapting various Steampunk-influenced designs seen in comic books, in movies or TV shows by adding cogs, wheels, steam pipes, radio valves and typewriter keys. The aim is to disguise modern technology, making it appear as though it had emerged from a reimagined Victorian past.

The recreation of existing material in a Steampunk vein was first applied to other science fiction franchises, such as the creation of a Steampunk *Star Wars* lightsaber (discussed in depth on the stardestroyer.com forums in October 2006). By January the following year, the Steampunk aesthetic filter had been applied to the long-running British science fiction TV show *Doctor Who*, when art depicting a 'Steampunked' Dalek appeared on deviantart.com.

This creative combination of existing intellectual property and Steampunk was a natural outgrowth from film and television. An underground Steampunk style spread to a wider audience through the reinvention of these well-known science fiction icons.

Two real-world practitioners of Steampunk modding were largely responsible for the explosion of the style from the mid 2000s. Jake von Slatt's Steampunk Workshop and Datamancer's Technical Art and Steampunk Creations produced the first works that many fans saw in which the Steampunk style was applied to real-world objects.

Based in Boston, Jake von Slatt brought a retro-futuristic approach to real-world objects, using found materials to adapt their otherwise bland modern appearance into something suitably fantasy Victorian. The Steampunk Workshop website became an online art gallery displaying von Slatt's work, including an ornate personal computer dismantled and rebuilt with a Steampunk sheen, and a Stratocaster guitar created for the Steampunk band Abney Park. The modding culture is a variation on the American arts and crafts movement, mixed with the DIY aesthetic of punk and the fantasy fiction that created the notion of advanced Victorian technology. Von Slatt has had a bigger audience since he self-identified as a Steampunk artisan. The community from which he gets feedback on his work and commissions for bespoke items helps reinforce the growth of the movement as a genuine subculture.

Datamancer – real name Richard Nagy – gained a higher profile when his modded Steampunk keyboard was showcased by the TV show *Warehouse 13*. The series made a claim to genuine Steampunk credentials in its use of community-created

Forevertron Park, Wisconsin

One of the more extreme examples of 'Steampunk art' must be Forevertron Park in Wisconsin, the work of Dr. Evermor – the fictional Steampunk alter ego of sculptor Tom Every. This art installation repurposes obsolete or broken items (a prime aim of the DIY movement is to recycle, repurpose or remake found items) in the creation of fantasy technology that has never existed. A retired engineer, Every began his project in 1983 and the work now incorporates two original Thomas Edison dynamos from 1882 and a decontamination chamber from the Apollo space missions. In addition to building the exhibit, Every's fictional character and backstory give Forevertron Park a true Steampunk provenance, as if it had grown out of one of the novels or films.

STEAMPUNK

props. Dubbed 'Sojourner', the keyboard – featured prominently in many episodes – was initially designed and built by Nagy for his girlfriend. It was repurposed when the show commissioned the creation of a keyboard, as the producers were keen to plug into authentic Steampunk designs. Its television exposure inspired many viewers to create their own.

Nagy describes himself as 'a Steampunk contraptor, technical artist, and jackass-of-all trades'. He sees the combination of the classical Victoriana with modern technology as something to be celebrated. His and others' work in redressing otherwise functional equipment with cogs and gears (revealing the functionality that most technology purposefully hides) is a return to the lost art of manufacture and fabrication. Being able to see 'the workings' of a piece of equipment is central to Steampunk modding.

Much of the technology involved has been rescued from redundant and abandoned equipment. Nagy's source material comes from old typewriters long discarded following the arrival of the first wave of 'word processors' of the 1980s. The idea of community fostered through the internet was important, as it gave Nagy a chance to research ideas and discuss them with other like-minded individuals.

Much of the work of von Slatt and Nagy involves the creation of items that 'look right' aesthetically, rather than being practical. They each have a sense of what their own individual artistic Steampunk style is, while still adhering to a look and feel

Above: Richard Nagy – pseudonym Datamancer – at work. He has pioneered and popularised the Steampunk artform known as modding.

169

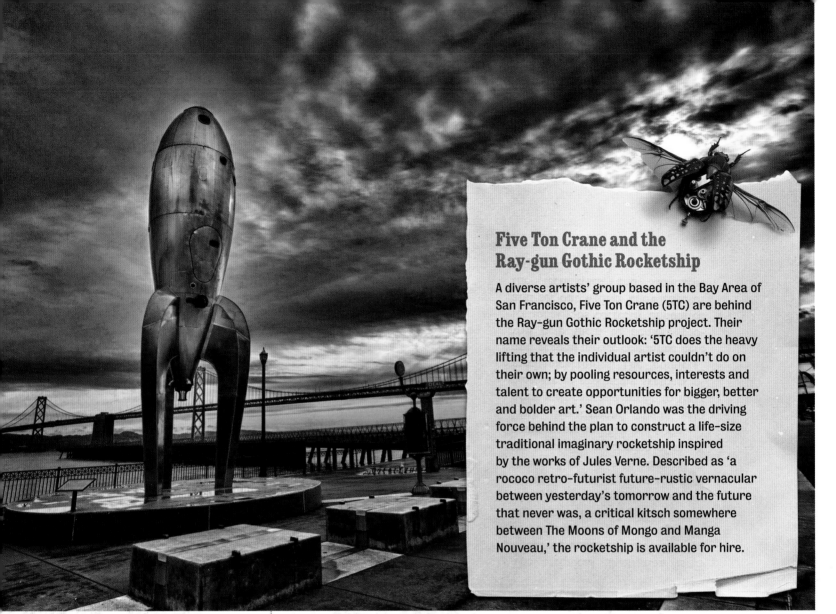

Five Ton Crane and the Ray-gun Gothic Rocketship

A diverse artists' group based in the Bay Area of San Francisco, Five Ton Crane (5TC) are behind the Ray-gun Gothic Rocketship project. Their name reveals their outlook: '5TC does the heavy lifting that the individual artist couldn't do on their own; by pooling resources, interests and talent to create opportunities for bigger, better and bolder art.' Sean Orlando was the driving force behind the plan to construct a life-size traditional imaginary rocketship inspired by the works of Jules Verne. Described as 'a rococo retro-futurist future-rustic vernacular between yesterday's tomorrow and the future that never was, a critical kitsch somewhere between The Moons of Mongo and Manga Nouveau,' the rocketship is available for hire.

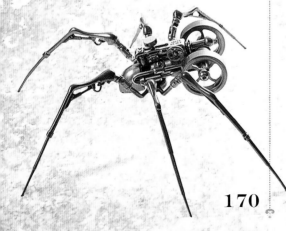

that would be easily recognized by the wider community. Nagy's theory is that much Victorian technology looked the way it did because the techniques were brand new and the craftsmen of the time were keen to show off their handiwork. There was also a wider appreciation of the aesthetics of industry that is lacking in the sleek world of Apple computers.

Beyond modding, there is a further world of Steampunk art in which the aesthetic is applied to smaller, sculptural works. Maine-based Mike Libby was inspired by Steampunk items in movies, including the vampire device in Guillermo del Toro's *Cronos* (1993) and the insect-like spy bugs from *The Golden Compass* (2007). He builds clockwork insects, remaking the organic in mechanical form. 'One day I found a dead intact beetle. I then located an old wristwatch, thinking of how the beetle looked like a little mechanical device. [I] decided to combine the two. After sometime dissecting the beetle and outfitting it with watch parts and gears, I had a nice little sculpture.' Libby's Insect Lab Studio website offers prints of his mechanical models for sale.

The impulse to reconstruct the organic in mechanical form reached its most impressive expression in the 2007 event Les Machines de L'ile, in Nantes – Jules

Verne's birthplace. French urban sculptors François Delacrozière and Pierre Orefice described their ongoing project as 'a blend of the invented worlds of Jules Verne, the mechanical universe of Leonardo da Vinci and the industrial history of Nantes'. Based on the site of a former shipyard, itself a relic of the Victorian Industrial Revolution, Delacrozière and Orefice, alongside a diverse group of 'machine builders', constructed a series of 'living machines' including the Great Elephant, the Marine Worlds and the Heron Tree. 'Like doors to the world of dreams and magical journeys, they give this island a mysterious feel,' notes their website.

The most famous of their creations is The Sultan's Elephant, an impressive mechanical construction displayed as part of street theatre events around Europe. The 12m-high, 8m-metre wide construction is described as 'a steel cathedral, architecture in motion', recalling Verne's mechanical pachyderm from *The Steam House* (1880). This most unusual vehicle can carry up to forty-nine passengers within the elephant shell, allowing them to view the moving gears. Riders within the device can control some of its movements, including making the elephant 'trumpet'. The pair noted of the elephant that it is like a 'voyage to the imaginary world of Jules Verne ...'

The imaginary worlds of Verne, Wells, Jeter and Blaylock and many others working

171

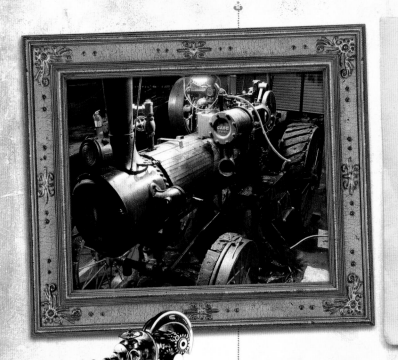

Above: A number of artists have applied the Steampunk aesthetic to the animal kingdom. Christopher Conte, whose biomechanical sculpture is featured here and on page 170, has taken a particular interest in insects. Right: The band members of Abney Park.

within the diverse field of Steampunk are brought into the real world by creative and inventive 'modders' who make their fantasies real.

The sounds of steam

One of the indicators that Steampunk has grown into a mainstream youth subculture, rather than simply an offshoot of a literary genre, is the growth of Steampunk music, dedicated bands and performers. There can be few literary genres that can boast their own soundtracks. Defining the sound of Steampunk is difficult. The bottom line tends to be that if a band claims itself to be Steampunk and if enough 'fans' agree, then it is. This plays into the already established DIY approach that the subculture embraces, and the fact that any Steampunk artefact can only lay claim to a certain degree of the essentials of the definition. It wasn't until the mid-2000s, in common with the explosion of Steampunk costuming and 'modding', that a certain type of musical output became associated with the lifestyle.

Perhaps the two best-known Steampunk bands are Abney Park (named after a graveyard in Stoke Newington, London) and Vernian Process, whose name harks back to Jules Verne and which is the personal musical project of Joshua Pfeiffer. Based in that most Steampunk of cities, Seattle, Abney Park, according to Captain Robert himself, mix a blend of musical styles, such as 'Gypsy Dance, Neo-Vaudeville, Rag Time, Electroswing, Modern Dance and Rock, all assembled in a way which sounds like an adventure movie soundtrack'.

Following the band's founding in 1997, it took several albums and changes in personnel line-ups before Abney Park developed a Steampunk sound. In 2006, in response to the sudden mainstream proliferation of the Steampunk aesthetic, band leader Robert Brown made the switch. As well as changing their musical identities,

STEAMPUNK

the band members were true to the trend within Steampunk of adopting fictional characters.

According to the new backstory created by the band, during an unexpected storm their tour aeroplane collided with a time-travelling dirigible called the Ophelia (created by Dr Leguminous Calgori). As a result, the band members took over the Zeppelin, becoming 'airship pirates'. This imaginary background formed the basis for the band's first Steampunk album, *Lost Horizons: The Continuing Adventures of Abney Park*, released in 2008. Opening track 'Airship Pirate' (beginning with the sound of propellers) outlined their new personas, while others – such as 'The Secret Life of Doctor Calgori' (packed with mentions of Tesla and airships), and hidden track 'The Ballad of Captain Robert' – further developed the fictional world the band now inhabited. In addition, band members adopted Steampunk costuming to further reinforce their identities as musical airship pirates. The band's new sound mixed a lighter 'industrial' feel with sea shanties (their next album was *Aether Shanties*, 2009), or folk ballads, amid the use of classical instruments. These musical developments reflected the niche practice of science fiction folk singing at conventions, known as 'filk'.

What Abney Park and Vernian Process realized was that rather than practising or developing an identifiable musical style, Steampunk was about adopting the rich visual design seen in movies and comic books as a connective thread upon which to hang a post-punk musical style. The unity in Steampunk music does not come from the sound, but from the look (band members' costumes and persona, their stage shows – complete with 'modded' instruments – and the design of their album covers).

For his part, Joshua Pfeiffer regarded Vernian Process as a way to create 'music that

'Just Glue Some Gears On It (And Call It Steampunk)'

Created by Sir Reginald Pikedevant, Esq., this amusing music video posted on YouTube in autumn 2011 neatly encapsulated the growing debate within the Steampunk community as a fresh wave of films, television shows and novels adopted the superficial aspects of the genre without fully engaging with it. The song was an example of the Chap Hop sound, mixing a hip hop musical approach with Chappist (named after *The Chap* magazine that calls for the return of the dandy way of life) or Steampunk subcultures while exploring stereotypical English obsessions like tea, cricket and the weather. Other examples include 'Steampunk Rap/Pass the Tea' by Poplock Holmes, 'The Victorian Rap' by Class Rhymes and the work of Professor Elemental, whose albums include *The Indifference Engine* and *More Tea?*

174

could accompany the Steampunk adventures in [my] own mind'. Pfeiffer was ahead of the mainstream, beginning his explorations of Steampunk music around 2003 in San Francisco, although it was only when he brought other musicians into the project around 2007 that he was able to fulfil his ambitions. Putting out his music through the aptly-named Gilded Age Records, Pfeiffer and Vernian Process are a prime exponent of the generic hybrid that is Steampunk music. *Behold the Machine* (2010) was the first widely available Vernian Process album (described by the band as 'an anthology rooted in the shadows of a fictional Victorian Age'). Tracks included 'The Alchemist's Vision', 'Unhallowed Metropolis', 'Into the Depths' and 'Vagues de Vapeur' (referencing the French term for Steampunk, *futur à vapeur*). The next album was entitled *The Consequences of Time Travel* (2012), while the group were said to be working on a Jules Verne concept album.

Influences on Steampunk bands such as Kozai Resonance, The Clockwork Dolls, Corset, Crimson Muddle and Unextraordinary Gentlemen include film soundtracks, classical music, cabaret and folk music, ragtime and swing, industrial and Goth, as well as 1970s-style prog rock and concept albums. Band names have been picked from Steampunk comic books (Unextraordinary Gentlemen) or prominent aspects of the Victorian era (The Men That Will Not Be Blamed For Nothing riffs on an infamous piece of Victorian graffiti attributed to Jack the Ripper). This magpie approach reflects the same system that operates in Steampunk costuming and in artefact creation: it is a style built up of bits and pieces co-opted from various time periods and design styles. Given this, Steampunk music can't be anything other than self-identifying. There is little generic consistency between bands (or between tracks from the same band) to indicate a coherent style, beyond some lyrical content and the tendency for album covers to feature airships and band members dressed as goggle-sporting sky-pirates. If anything, the music produced by Steampunk bands is an accessory to the lifestyle that helps validate it as a significant subculture.

In some ways the 'punk' suffix is more applicable to the music of Steampunk than anything else, as these are creators doing their own thing their own way, giving it a label (sometimes for convenience, sometimes for publicity or sales), but sticking to their own guns creatively. However, the narratives of the songs

Abney Park

On their website, *Abney Park: Aeronauts of Questionable Morals*, the band claim:

Abney Park comes from an era that never was, but one that we wish had been. An era where airships waged war in the skies, and corsets and cummerbunds were proper adventuring attire. They've picked up their bad musical habits, scoundrelous [sic] musicians, and anachronistically hybridized instruments from dozens of locations and eras that they have visited in their travels and thrown them into one riotous dervish of a performance. Expect clockwork guitars, belly dancers, flintlock bassists, middleastern [sic] percussion, violent violin, and Tesla-powered keyboards blazing in a post-apocalyptic, swashbuckling, Steampunk musical mayhem.

– particularly those of Abney Park – owe a huge debt to current Steampunk literature, and even ideas originated in the 1980s by Jeter, Blaylock and Powers.

Airship ambassadors of the Steampunk empire

The creation of Steampunk costumes, the curating of exhibitions, the building of modified artefacts and the realization of Steampunk music have all been facilitated by the rise of the internet. It is no coincidence that the sudden explosion of Steampunk into the mainstream almost directly parallels the widespread acceptance of the internet as a major communications medium.

It was in discussion forums that those who'd self-identified as 'Steampunks' found each other and formed communities. It was online that the DIY 'punk' ethos of Steampunk makers flourished. The spreading of Steampunk designs in fashion, clothing and costuming was largely achieved through the internet, reinforced by conventions, events and exhibitions in which like-minded people could meet each other away from the virtual world.

Communities, like those based around the Brass Goggles forums or Livejournal's Steamfashion site, supported one another in exploring their creative activities while also providing a space where the wider evolving culture could be discussed and shaped. Discussion of examples of Steampunk in film and television led to participants at Brass Goggles developing a list of visual media that

Brass Goggles

Brass Goggles is one of the most popular online Steampunk forums. It was started in 2006 by Tinkergirl because she felt there weren't many Steampunk websites around at the time (although Cory Gross was running Victorian Adventures in a Past That Wasn't, soon to morph into his Voyages Extraordinary blog). Tinkergirl decided to 'make the site I was desperate to find'. The site grew dramatically with the sudden popular explosion of Steampunk around the same time, and remains a thriving community to this day, with discussions arranged under the esoteric headings of Metaphysical, Tactile, Aural-Ocular, Textual, Anatomical and Geographical.

STEAMPUNK

Lady Clankington's Cabinet of Carnal Curiosities

Lady Clankington, heiress and adventuress, caused her Victorian industrialist husband to expire from exhaustion in an attempt to satisfy her desires before enlisting Dr Visbaun to create a variety of 'automata' (a range of Gothic ray-gun-shaped vibrators!). In the real world, Lady Clankington is Chicago-based fetish model and entrepreneur Sarah Herrick, whose Brute Force Studios (with her partner, Steampunk creator Thomas Willeford) offers a variety of Steampunk-infused items for sale at her littledeathray.com site (not all of them sex toys). She's at the forefront of the world of Steampunk erotica that has become widespread in art, artefacts, literature and burlesque performance.

Right: Described by movie director Guillermo del Toro as 'a post-industrial Rococo master', artist Kris Kuski produces astonishingly intricate sculptures that combine Steampunk-style mechanics with the aesthetic of the Baroque.

those who took part thought of as 'Steampunk'. There were other similarly detailed discussions of Steampunk in music, art and fiction (with the explosive growth in twenty-first century Steampunk fiction eclipsing the founding texts from the 1980s). Interestingly, the discussion of the literature was the smallest, least viewed section of Brass Goggles, with the developing lifestyle subculture prioritizing modding over reading or viewing. This bias highlights the newer, lifestyle-Steampunk fans who came to the aesthetic through a different route than the originators of the style.

Online Steampunk communities offered participants a social world where their shared perspectives could be explored with an understanding that the group would be speaking the same 'language' and operating within a distinctive set of shared assumptions and knowledge – what might be considered a 'tribal' identity. Individuals may have been attracted into such communities due to their appreciation of retro-futuristic or neo-Victorian style, but their participation would often lead to an exploration of the 'punk' side of Steampunk in which the creative DIY part of the movement came to the fore.

There is an interesting contradiction in this most modern of communication mediums being used to explore the partial rejection of modernity in favour of a retro-Victorian ethos – just one of the many inherent contradictions of Steampunk, in which an

alternative history is fused with a never-was future, blending nostalgia with a longing for a world that can't exist.

Embracing an imaginary past might seem like an odd use for cutting-edge contemporary technology, but there is no doubt that the supportive communities that the internet helped build around Steampunk have done much to propagate the aesthetic within and across mainstream culture – as well as prepare it for the future.

179

9

BACK TO THE FUTURE

Steampunk reimagines the Victorian past, but what is the future for this wide-ranging genre that has surpassed its literary origins to become a lifestyle subculture?

In its journey from minor literary subgenre to all-encompassing lifestyle and online phenomenon, Steampunk has evolved. In the opening episode of TV series *The Secret Adventures of Jules Verne*, Verne's visions of the future were forcibly ripped from his mind. Today's Steampunk practitioners have more gentle ways of realizing their visions of a retro-future – whether in novels, on film, in styles of dress or through creations of anachronistic technology. But where does Steampunk go from here? Can a genre based in a past that never was even have a future?

Extraordinary evolution

In May 2008, a leading feature article in the *New York Times* propelled the developing Steampunk subculture into the mainstream. Some participants felt this was the

moment that signalled the beginning of the end for Steampunk. Others took the view that this mainstream attention could only propel the genre in brilliant new directions.

That year saw the convergence of several other Steampunk-related projects. Especially notable were several collections of short stories exploring the new frontiers of Steampunk fiction. These 'taster' anthologies allowed those new to the genre to dip their toes in Steampunk waters without getting scalded. While Nick Gevers' *Extraordinary Engines: The Definitive Steampunk Anthology* (2008) oversold itself, it was one of the first chances for new readers to sample Steampunk. Included in the anthology was work by contemporary authors Ian R. MacLeod (author of the Steampunk duology *The Lights Ages*, 2004, and *The House of Storms*, 2006), James Lovegrove, Keith Brooke and Adam Roberts. What *Extraordinary Engines* lacked was any context-setting essays or older stories that showed where Steampunk had come from. That oversight was addressed by Ann and Jeff Vandermeer's anthology *Steampunk* (2008). An introductory essay by Jeff Nevins put the fiction in a larger context, while extracts from Moorcock's *The Warlord of the Air*, Di Filippo's *Victoria* (from his The Steampunk Trilogy) and Blaylock's *Lord Kelvin's Machine* explored its roots. The contemporary work fully explored Steampunk's diversity, including a Weird West tale by Joe R. Lansdale, a pseudo-sequel to Verne by Molly Brown, a 'planetary romance' by Michael Chabon, and non-fiction surveys of Steampunk in pop culture and comic books. Two further anthologies from the same editors – *Steampunk Reloaded* (2010) and *Steampunk Revolution* (2012) – proved the popularity of the format.

It wasn't only short stories that brought a new audience to Steampunk in 2008. From May to June, the Telectroscope project linked London with New York when giant, brass telescope-like art installations appeared on the banks of the Thames and

The Telectroscope project

This art installation connected New York and London via giant telescopes linked under the Atlantic by an imaginary cable. Peter Coleman, producer for the New York side of the project, told the BBC: 'It is a piece of art, and it's also a curiosity in a public space. London and New York are cities with millions of people. They can't believe that those are actually people in another city looking at them. That's what I find all these people are amazed at. It pulls you right into it.'

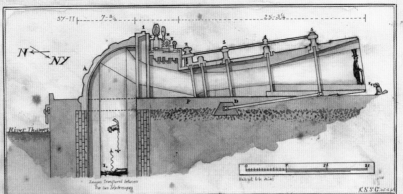

the East River. Artist Paul St George claimed that a trans-Atlantic tunnel allowed communication between the two devices, allowing viewers in London to see (but not talk with) those in New York. Using modern digital technology, the artist had presented an authentic Steampunk experience to the passing public creating what appeared to be a giant telescope protruding from the Earth. Future worldwide appearances of the Telectroscope were promised.

This explosion of Steampunk into the popular consciousness culminated with the Oxford Steampunk Exhibition at the Museum of the History of Science at the end of 2009. Art Donovan's display provided a new focus for the growing interest in the wider reaches of Steampunk culture, and drew a lot of mainstream media interest. Donovan noted that Steampunk was now being given 'an actual physical form by artists from around the world. It's a very broad-based discipline, from literature to sculpture.'

It was through the literature that Steampunk secured the cover of *Locus*, the magazine of the science fiction publishing industry, in September 2010. Among those who made contributions to this themed issue were Bruce Sterling, James Blaylock and the genre's 'grandfather' figure, Michael Moorcock. Contemporary Steampunk authors Cherie Priest, Gail Carriger and *Girl Genius* creators Phil and Kaja Foglio were interviewed. Priest noted, 'Steampunk is a style that's still searching for myths – the archetypes and icons and tropes by which it will be defined. There are these pop-culture shortcuts that we immediately recognize, [but] Steampunk doesn't have that shorthand yet. It seems to me that Steampunk needs a myth.' In his introduction to the issue, Steampunk anthology editor Gavin J. Grant noted of the genre: 'If Steampunk is only a design aesthetic, then surely any story can be Steampunk if enough brass goggles are added? Not quite. [The genre has an] openness to new interpretations and to new contributions from unexpected places. If every Steampunk story is set in nineteenth-century London, readers will soon start looking elsewhere.'

The impressive diversity of Steampunk music also continued. In a dramatic departure from the usual industrial Goth sound, British-American composer David Bruce was commissioned by Carnegie Hall to write an octet entitled 'Steampunk' in 2011; opera 'The Steampunk Opium Wars' premiered in February 2012 at the Royal National Maritime Museum in Greenwich (with music from Charles Shaar Murray); while 2012 saw Canadian band Rush release

183

their nineteenth studio album, a Steampunk-themed anthology entitled *Clockwork Angels*. In an interesting twist, science fiction writer Kevin J. Anderson was recruited to novelize the Rush album, describing the story as 'a young man's quest to follow his dreams … he is caught between the grandiose forces of order and chaos. He travels across a lavish and colorful world of Steampunk and alchemy, with lost cities, pirates, anarchists, exotic carnivals, and a rigid Watchmaker who imposes precision on every aspect of daily life.'

The Steampunk subculture also reached mainstream American television, with appearances in episodes of crime series *NCIS: LA* (2009) and *Castle* (2010), and a PBS mini-documentary on the subject. The *NCIS: LA* episode 'Random on Purpose' was promoted as depicting Steampunk culture in a mainstream show, but informed viewers were disappointed to discover that the producers seemingly viewed Steampunk as akin to Goth. Used as a backdrop for a couple of bar scenes (in a bar misleadingly named 'SteamPunk') and not integral to the other events in the episode, the Steampunk aesthetic was badly misappropriated.

More positive was the fun *Castle* episode 'Punked', starring *Firefly*'s Nathan Fillion (the show had form, having previously successfully tackled the vampire subculture in the episode 'Vampire Weekend'). Steampunk critic G.D. Falksen praised the episode as 'a love letter to the Steampunk community', comparing it in favourable terms to the poorly received *NCIS: LA* instalment. He credited the show with depicting the subculture with 'elegance, charm, respectfulness and accuracy', and noted that the show's depiction of clothing and characters was 'completely believable', concluding that the episode was 'the best first TV introduction to the mainstream world that the Steampunk community could have hoped for'.

The ongoing PBS web documentary series *Off Book* devoted a five-minute instalment to the Steampunk subculture in the summer of 2011, further reinforcing the idea that the genre was conquering the mainstream. Depicting the Steampunk lifestyle (with barely a mention of the literature), the short piece claimed the subculture had reached a 'tipping point' and was 'in the mainstream'. The craft (with creator Joey Marsocci,

The Steampunk Octet

David Bruce's 2011 'Steampunk' octet for Carnegie Hall prioritized brass wind instruments and clockwork rhythms. 'When Carnegie Hall offered me this commission, the horn and bassoon immediately stood out to me as defining the Steampunk world. Above all was the French horn with its crazy, complicated brass plumbing, making it about as iconic a Steampunk instrument as you could hope for; but similarly the bassoon, the bass clarinet and the cor anglais each have the distinct air of an eccentric Victorian gentleman, the product of a particular kind of obsession,' said Bruce. 'As a fan of home-made instruments it was a form of creativity that instantly appealed to me. The sound may not be steam-powered, but it is produced by muscles and breath alone.'

184

aka Dr Grymm), music (with composer David Bruce), and theatre (with Third Rail Projects alt-Alice production) of Steampunk were the focus, suggesting that a diverse Steampunk 'art movement' might be developing.

Vintage Tomorrows – a full-length independent documentary for Intel's The Tomorrow Project series of conversations about the future – took a wider view of the Steampunk subculture. Producer Brian David Johnson suggested that '…if Steampunk subculture is revising the past, in a way it is also making a request of the future by presenting a different model for it.' Taking the subject more seriously than previous showcase documentaries, *Vintage Tomorrows* had cultural historian James Carrott asking several subculture participants, 'How does Steampunk mediate the relationship between people and technology?' Among those contributing to this thoughtful production were Cherie Priest, Cory Doctorow and the Foglios. One conclusion reached is that Steampunk is a reaction against the modern rapid development of technology and social change. Steampunk is seen as a way of humanizing technology and making it understandable to the average person in the way that it used to be. The social aspects of Steampunk are not ignored, with personal stories from those whom the community has helped through difficult times.

Steampunk fiction continued to diversify, moving further away from the original works by Jeter-Blaylock-Powers. Steampunk novels delved into comic fiction in Gail Carriger's Parasol Protectorate series, and outright spoof in some of Robert Rankin's work (most fully in

Above: *Castle* star Nathan Fillion, here pictured as Captain Malcolm Reynolds from space western *Firefly* and the movie *Serenity*. *Firefly* itself betrayed a Steampunk sensibility.

The Japanese Devil Fish Girl and Other Unnatural Attractions, (2010) Steampunk began appearing in Young Adult fiction too, drawing in a new audience for the almost twenty-five-year-old genre. Philip Reeve was a prime exponent with his Mortal Engines series (The Hungry City Chronicles in the US, 2001–11). Other new authors came into the genre through the Young Adult field, such as Jay Lake who chronicled the adventures of a young clockmaker's apprentice in the Mainspring series (2007–10), while Scott Westerfeld's Leviathan series (2009–11) presented a muscular, mechanized form of Steampunk. Suzanne Lazear offered a young female take on the genre in her Aether Chronicles series, beginning with *Innocent Darkness* (2012). Younger audiences had also been exposed to elements of the Steampunk style in earlier animated Disney movies such as *Atlantis: The Lost Empire* (2001) and *Treasure Planet* (2002).

The new century saw the emergence of a group of new authors working almost exclusively in the Steampunk arena. Mark Hodder's trilogy – *The Strange Affair of Spring-Heeled Jack* (2010), *The Curious Case of the Clockwork Man* (2011), and *Expedition to the Mountains of the Moon* (2012) – followed George Mann with his chronicles of the investigations of Burton & Swinburne. Hodder admitted to being influenced by Michael Moorcock (especially his politically engaged take on the genre) in the same way that the originators of Steampunk had been influenced by Verne and Wells. S.M. Peters mixed Steampunk with horror in his debut novel *Whitechapel Gods* (2008) set in a walled-in Whitechapel that is essentially a fantasy secondary world, while Lavie Tidhar's Bookman Histories (*The Bookman*, 2010; *Camera Obscura*, 2011; *The Great Game*, 2012) focused on the fantasy side of the genre. Others who made a mark on modern fiction Steampunk included Felix Gilman (*The Half-Made World*, 2010), Arthur Slade (*Empire of Ruins*, 2011) and Tim Akers (*Heart of Veridon*, 2011). Even mainstream thrillers, such as *Angelmaker* (2012) by Nick Harkaway, adopted Steampunk styling in their storytelling.

These authors all produced their work when Steampunk was a widely accepted subculture that had made its mark on the mainstream. The literature that now laid claim to the label was not produced in a vacuum, like that of the 1980s and 1990s. It could draw on the wider aspects of the subculture that had evolved over the better part of a decade. Many non-fiction books appeared about the 'art' of Steampunk, or as guides on how to 'mod' your own items 'the Steampunk way'. Many of these works – fiction and non-fiction alike – did not engage with the political elements that had always been at the roots of Steampunk (from Jeter-Blaylock-Powers use of London Labour and the London Poor onwards), with several almost uncritically reviving and revering ideas of Empire. This was the almost inevitable mainstreaming of Steampunk as another form of innocent escapism. Perhaps the next batch of Steampunk novels will feature more punk and less steam?

Right: A mechanical Stormwalker and the great airbeast *Leviathan*, by illustrator Keith Thompson, from Scott Westerfeld's series of Young Adult Steampunk novels.

STEAMPUNK

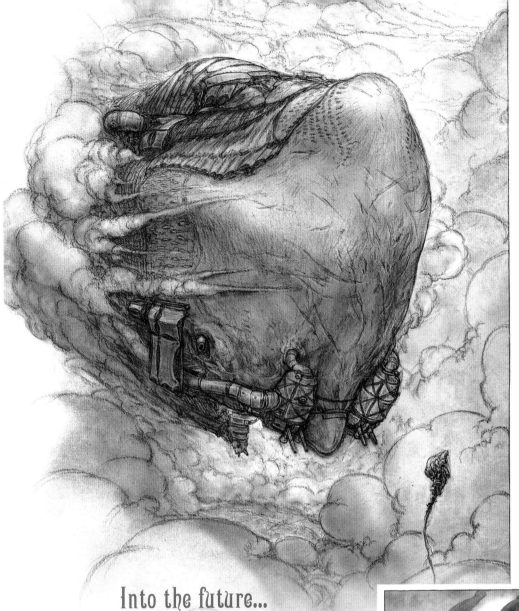

Into the future...

What's the future for Steampunk? Given that the genre consists of cultural products the majority of which only ever achieve degrees of fidelity to the original definitions of the term, it is remarkable how little those definitions have evolved. Jeter's letter to *Locus* in the late 1980s offered 'gonzo-historical Victorian fantasies' as a description of what he, Blaylock and Powers were up to. In the 1993 *Encyclopedia of Science Fiction*, Peter Nichols summed it up simply as a 'modern subgenre whose science fiction events take place against a nineteenth-century background' (thereby eliminating much of what we'd now regard as wider Steampunk). In *Science Fiction Studies* in late 2011, Jess Nevins wrote, 'As recently as 2005, F. Brett Cox's entry in the *Greenwood Encyclopedia of Science Fiction and Fantasy* defined Steampunk in essentially the same way as Peter Nicholls did... It's time we rethought the term, and

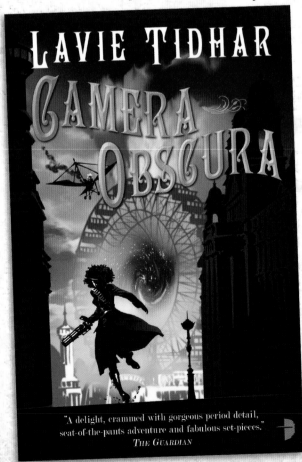

rethought how we define the genre, and how we formulate genre definitions.'

The Steampunk subculture has successfully breached the mainstream which means that the label (for the foreseeable future, anyway) can only be a 'catch-all term', as it will be abused, misapplied and misappropriated as it is discovered (and rediscovered) by new audiences and participants. The Brass Goggles forum collectively produced a definition of Steampunk in 2011 that hits enough bases for it to stand as a core description for a good while yet: 'Steampunk is a social, practical and creative movement which draws inspiration from Victorian and pre-war history in an anachronistic mix of science fiction and modern values (and is enjoyed by people who like gin, tea and cake!).'

One danger Steampunk faces is that the definition becomes so rigid ('it must be related to Victorian London') that it excludes much interesting and varied work, or so loose ('anything with cogs') that it becomes meaningless. Cyberpunk lost its edge through dilution and the failure of the surrounding subculture to catch on outside of science fiction fandom, so it was ultimately reabsorbed as just one more 'flavour'. Steampunk has at least escaped that fate by producing a thriving, ever-expanding subculture that is almost totally divorced from the literature that created it.

Asked about the future of their genre, a panel of authors naturally had a diverse range of opinions. One of the criticisms of Steampunk as a genre is that it is a form of fiction that looks backwards to a reimagined past, rather than forwards to an exciting future. Stephen Hunt, author of the Jackelian series, doesn't see that as a problem if the storytellers are imaginative enough: 'I know that much has been made of the fact that Steampunk is a form of fiction that spends too much time drawing upon the past (usually negative comments), but like all other genres, it's only really limited by the writer's imagination. That's one of the reasons why I set my Kingdom of Jackals in a far future Earth … as a fallen civilization rediscovering Victorian-level technology. It freed me from having to template my story against actual events. I might have lost the opportunity to have Captain Nemo and Sherlock Holmes as walk-on characters, but I gained the infinite world of the unknown.'

For Kevin J. Anderson, who turned Rush's album *Clockwork Angels* into a novel, 'Steampunk isn't about the "past" per se, but about the future as it was supposed to be, viewed from an optimistic past. To me the genre is technology and alchemy working hand-in-hand, not realistic in a scientific sense but all the more important in how it sparks the sense of wonder, the exciting faith in eccentric scientists and their crazy contraptions.'

Mark Hodder, author of the Burton & Swinburne series, sees revolutionary political engagement as central to the continued success of Steampunk: 'Although Steampunk seems to draw upon the past, it does so only to show that the attitudes and mores of Empire have become utterly divorced from reality. The entire world seems to have engaged in a struggle for greater equality in the distribution of wealth and power. As this transition continues, Steampunk will only become more relevant, as it continually reminds us that motives must be exposed, empire-builders are not heroes, and, though fights must be fought, good manners cost nothing!'

Lou Anders, editor at Pyr who has worked with many Steampunk authors (including Hodder), sees generic diversification as the way forward: 'I personally believe that in order for Steampunk to grow, survive and thrive, it must expand past its Victorian roots, and indeed it has. This is one of the reasons I've sought out works like Tim Elms's *The Horns of Ruin* (which mixes Steampunk with secondary world sword and sorcery), Andrew P. Mayer's The Society of Steam trilogy (which blends Steampunk with the superhero genre in nineteenth-century Manhattan), and Mark Hodder's Burton & Swinburne trilogy (which begins in Victorian England, but ends in Africa). I think works like this are the future of the subgenre. Steampunk is here to stay, but

in order to avoid descending into pastiche and remain a viable, active, relevant subgenre, its readers and writers need to be open to evolution and change.'

Writer of the comic book *Aetheric Mechanics* and the web comic *FreakAngels*, Warren Ellis has mused that Steampunk's resurgent popularity in the twenty-first century had come about as a response to a failure of vision with regard to the future. He suggests: 'There is something 'sticky' about Steampunk. The genre has not only persisted but has actually made it into the mainstream. Through films, comic books and increasingly videogames, there is a forthright and promiscuous inter-textuality that other genres would kill for. So what is it about our current socio-economic climate that fosters such things? Is this tantamount to a withdrawal from some of the complexities of cloning and genetic engineering that were so easy to attack from the 1950s onwards, but which are now part of everyday life and constant newspaper reports? Is there a speculative introspection going on here that happens to coincide with more prosaic science and biotech agendas in the twenty-first century? A wish to make it all 'magic' once again through an alternative timeline?'

Perhaps the last word should go to one of the genre's founding fathers, James P. Blaylock. 'I hope that Steampunk hangs around for a time. It produces art of great beauty and imagination, which I don't see happening with other literary subgenres. Hard to imagine vampire romances, for example, or zombie fiction, having that kind of multifarious effect on the arts.'

Once everything is covered in cogs, what then? Steampunk works well when it is constantly recombining the elements that go to make it up: no one work contains it all, yet all have degrees of 'Steampunkiness', whether that's airship pirates, mad scientists, steam, soot, time travel, or gaslamp fantasies, Martian invasions and Art Deco ray-guns.

Some think Steampunk's DIY ethos has equipped them to survive the 'inevitable forthcoming apocalypse' and accompanying collapse of civilization. While that thinking might be confined to a few fringe elements, there is a 'green' political side to Steampunk, and it is an area ripe for growth. Eco-Steampunk (or 'Greenpunk'?) might be a new iteration of the subculture, as the core DIY aesthetic is keenly concerned with reusing found objects.

And there is continued space for innovation in Steampunk from a more international perspective. The populist, widely available versions of Steampunk have been largely American and British, with healthy injections from France and Japan. Areas such as South America and China are sure to be new breeding grounds for a very different version, with unique perspectives on questions of Empire and the directions taken by technology. The Beyond Victoriana website explores just such multicultural and internationalist approaches.

Cherie Priest has noted that Steampunk is not a binary choice (suggesting that a work of art either 'is' or 'is not' Steampunk), but is instead a 'spectrum'. In one way this

means it can be 'all things to all people': Steampunk is inclusive, a creative playground, within which inspired individuals and their work can flourish.

As has been argued throughout this book, there are degrees of Steampunk, ranging from the severest, restrictive definition to the broadest use of the term as a 'catch-all' for any kind of retro-futurism. This all-encompassing approach – descriptive rather than prescriptive – encourages diverse and inclusive discussion. Wider definitions will allow Steampunk to live on, evolve, and be used in the way that suits each individual 'user', while still communicating a core notion of what Steampunk actually means.

It may reimagine the past, but the future belongs to Steampunk.

191

Picture credits

ABOUT THE AUTHOR

Brian J. Robb is the *New York Times* and *Sunday Times* bestselling biographer of Leonardo DiCaprio, Johnny Depp and Brad Pitt. He has also written books on silent cinema, the films of Philip K. Dick, Wes Craven and Laurel and Hardy, as well as television series *Doctor Who* and *Star Trek*. He is co-editor of the *Sci-Fi Bulletin* website and lives in Edinburgh.

ACKNOWLEDGEMENTS

I would like to thank my agent, Chelsey Fox of the Fox & Howard Literary Agency, and Jonathan Clements, without whom I would not have embarked upon this exploration of Steampunk. Indeed, Jonathan wrote chapter 7, *An Empire Strikes Back*, and chapter 4, *A Young Lady's Primer*, was written by Dr Brigid Cherry.

Thanks are also due to Steampunk's triumvirate of original creators: James P. Blaylock (for his foreword and more), K.W. Jeter and Tim Powers – without this trio the genre would simply not exist.

Following in their footsteps creatively, and of invaluable assistance in the writing of this book, were Lou Anders, Kevin J. Anderson, Gail Carriger, John Clute, Mark Hodder, Stephen Hunt, George Mann, Ekaterina Sedia and Lavie Tidhar.

My appreciation is also due to my editor at Aurum Press, Sam Harrison, the book's brilliant designer Tony Lyons, and indefatigable picture researcher Melissa Smith. Thanks once again to Paul Simpson for reading my efforts in the early stages and to Brigid Cherry for her on-going unconditional support.

Brian J. Robb, June 2012